EDWARD THE SECOND

broadview editions
series editor: L.W. Conolly

Putative portrait of Christopher Marlowe. Reproduced with the permission of the Master and Fellows of Corpus Christi College, Cambridge.

EDWARD THE SECOND

Christopher Marlowe

edited by Mathew R. Martin

broadview editions

Library and Archives Canada Cataloguing in Publication

Marlowe, Christopher, 1564-1593
    Edward the Second / Christopher Marlowe ; edited by Mathew R. Martin.

(Broadview editions)
Includes bibliographical references.
ISBN 978-1-55111-910-6

1. Edward II, King of England, 1284-1327—Drama.
I. Martin, Mathew R., 1970– II. Title. III. Series: Broadview editions

PR2665.A2M38 2010   822'.3   C2010-904266-2

Broadview Editions
The Broadview Editions series represents the ever-changing canon of literature in English by bringing together texts long regarded as classics with valuable lesser-known works.

Advisory editor for this volume: Juliet Sutcliffe

Broadview Press is an independent, international publishing house, incorporated in 1985.

We welcome comments and suggestions regarding any aspect of our publications—please feel free to contact us at the addresses below or at broadview@broadviewpress.com.

North America
Post Office Box 1243, Peterborough, Ontario, Canada K9J 7H5
2215 Kenmore Avenue, Buffalo, NY, USA 14207
Tel: (705) 743-8990; Fax: (705) 743-8353
email: customerservice@broadviewpress.com

UK, Europe, Central Asia, Middle East, Africa, India, and Southeast Asia
Eurospan Group, 3 Henrietta St., London WC2E 8LU, United Kingdom
Tel: 44 (0) 1767 604972; Fax: 44 (0) 1767 601640
email: eurospan@turpin-distribution.com

Australia and New Zealand
NewSouth Books
c/o TL Distribution, 15-23 Helles Ave., Moorebank, NSW, Australia 2170
Tel: (02) 8778 9999; Fax: (02) 8778 9944
email: orders@tldistribution.com.au

www.broadviewpress.com

Broadview Press acknowledges the financial support of the Government of Canada through the Canada Book Fund for our publishing activities.

This book is printed on paper containing 100% post-consumer fibre.

Typesetting and assembly: True to Type Inc., Claremont, Canada.

PRINTED IN CANADA

Contents

Acknowledgements

I would like to thank Brock University's Humanities Research Institute for a grant that enabled me to hire a research assistant, Erin Julian, for this project. I would like to thank Erin for the substantial aid she gave me in all aspects of the preparation of this edition. I would also like to thank my colleague Dr. Leah Knight for providing rigorous and insightful commentary on the introduction. The editors at Broadview Press have been marvellous to work with, and I would like to thank them for providing guidance when I needed it.

Introduction

Christopher Marlowe's Life

Christopher Marlowe was born on 23 February 1564 in Canterbury, a city of roughly 5,000 inhabitants approximately 55 miles southeast of London, in Kent. He was the second child and first son of John and Katherine Marlowe, both immigrants from surrounding towns. Early modern English society was highly conscious of social status, and Christopher Marlowe was born squarely into the artisanal class: his father was a shoemaker who, although he managed to run his own shop and hold municipal office, did not escape modest financial circumstances. We know little about Marlowe's early life with certainty, other than that his family lived in St. George's parish and then St. Andrew's parish, poorer parishes in Canterbury, and that he was gradually surrounded by siblings: his older sister Mary was born in 1562, and Christopher was followed by Margaret (1566), Joan (1569), Ann (1572), Dorothy (1573), and Thomas (1576). Although the family's circumstances were humble, life was not necessarily miserable for Christopher. As the oldest son and, when Mary died in 1568, oldest surviving child, Marlowe would have been the privileged child of his family.[1] Moreover, Canterbury itself would have provided him with many distractions. Although small, Canterbury was not an insignificant city. Until Henry VIII destroyed it in 1538, Canterbury's cathedral housed the immensely popular (and profitable) shrine to Thomas Beckett (Honan 12). In the "General Prologue" to the *Canterbury Tales*, Chaucer tells us that "from every shires ende / Of Engelond to Caunterbury they wende, / The hooly blissful martir for to seke" (15-17). Even after 1538 Canterbury remained the diocese of the English church's highest prelate, the Archbishop of Canterbury. The city was also full of immigrants from the Netherlands and France who had fled

---

1   There are many biographies of Marlowe, but the three on which this introduction mainly relies are Park Honan's *Christopher Marlowe: Poet and Spy*, Constance Brown Kuriyama's *Christopher Marlowe: A Renaissance Life*, and David Riggs's *The World of Christopher Marlowe*. The foregoing brief account of Marlowe's parents and childhood is heavily indebted to them, as is the rest of the biographical section of this introduction. Full bibliographical information for these works and subsequent citations can be found in the Works Cited.

religious persecution and warfare (Honan 32). From these religious refugees Marlowe may have first heard of the slaughter of French Protestants in Paris in 1572, an event he would later dramatize in his play *Massacre at Paris*. He would also have had his first experiences of theatre in Canterbury, which had a long tradition of civic and religious drama, along with performances by troupes of travelling actors. As Park Honan, one of Marlowe's most recent biographers, puts it, "The city itself was like a gigantic theatre, always changing—if not prosperous, then full of opportunities and spectacles for a sharp-eyed viewer" (30).

Marlowe would not remain in Canterbury. His mobility was driven by his education. Although sixteenth-century England was hierarchical, its education system gave poor but intellectually gifted males a chance to rise in the world. Most boys, even those from humble backgrounds, had the opportunity to acquire a rudimentary schooling. At six or seven, Marlowe would have entered "petty school" to learn his alphabet and the catechism (Riggs 26). After petty school Marlowe would have progressed to grammar school for six years. The grammar school curriculum reflected the agenda of Renaissance Europe's dominant intellectual movement, humanism. Humanism stressed the value of reading and imitating classical Greek and Latin literature, and Marlowe would have been instructed in Latin grammar, translation from Latin to English and English to Latin, and original Latin prose composition. Here Marlowe would have encountered for the first time such figures as Virgil and Ovid, classical Latin poets whose work exercised an enormous influence on Marlowe's poetry and on English Renaissance literature in general (Kuriyama 22-23). Marlowe translated a number of classical poets. His first play, *Dido, Queen of Carthage*, draws its story and even quotes directly from Virgil's *Aeneid*. Even more tellingly, *Edward the Second* is full of allusions to classical literature even though its subject is the reign of a medieval English monarch. (An excerpt from one significant piece of classical literature to which the play alludes, the Diana-Actæon narrative in Ovid's *Metamorphoses*, can be found in Appendix C.) Marlowe may also have acquired his first acting experiences at the grammar school, where student performances of classical plays or suitably moralized adaptations or imitations were considered pedagogically useful. Having completed his final two years of grammar-school education on a scholarship at King's School in Canterbury, in 1580 Marlowe won a scholarship to pursue university studies at Cambridge, where he completed his BA in 1584 and his MA in

1587. Marlowe's university education extended his immersion in the classics, as well as providing him a solid background in rhetoric, philosophy, and theology.[1] His course of studies would also have frequently required him to participate in formal debates (Riggs 78-97, 159-89). By demanding that he be able to argue on the weaker as well as the stronger side of the question, these debates would have introduced Marlowe to the role of "sophister" (4.255) that Mortimer Junior is accused of playing at the beginning of *Edward the Second*. The play itself can be considered "sophistical" in the tension it maintains between both sides of the political, social, and sexual issues on which Edward and his barons are divided. At Christmas, some of Cambridge's colleges offered other role-playing opportunities for their students in the form of school plays acted and often written by the students (Honan 72). Marlowe's university education also brought with it social as well as intellectual and creative advancement. After completing his BA, Marlowe was entitled to style himself "Sir Christopher Marlowe" (Kuriyama 57) and according to the title pages of all four of its early modern editions, *Edward the Second* was "Written by Chri. Marlow Gent."[2] Like the socially mobile Baldock in *Edward the Second*, Marlowe "fetched" his gentry from education and "not from heraldry" (6.241).

Marlowe's university education was designed to prepare him to be a clergyman in the Elizabethan church, a vocational direction further encouraged by the terms of his scholarship, which offered six years of support rather than the basic three to those recipients who intended to take holy orders after completing their studies (Kuriyama 38). The church was one of the main avenues of social mobility open to commoners like Marlowe. Unlike his character Doctor Faustus, however, who rises from "parents base of stock" (Prologue 11) to be "graced with doctor's name" (Prologue 17), Marlowe did not pursue this route, even though he drew on his scholarship for the full six years. Instead, after the completion of his MA he journeyed to London, part of the tide of domestic and foreign immigrants who were rapidly swelling the population of the metropolis throughout the sixteenth century. Even though mortality rates significantly exceeded birth

---

1 Unlike today, in Marlowe's day a Cambridge MA student earned his MA by following a set course of study.
2 Kuriyama asserts that "The title 'Sr' or 'Sir,' the English equivalent of the Latin 'Ds.' or 'Dominus,' was reserved for students who had fulfilled the requirements for the bachelor's degree" (57).

rates, London had expanded from approximately 50,000 inhabitants at the beginning of the century to around 200,000 by the time Marlowe arrived to join a growing group of university graduates who had chosen to live by the pen rather than the pulpit (Griffiths 1). London was the heart of the printing and publishing trade, as well as the home of a variety of theatrical venues— halls, inns, large open-air playhouses—on whose stages companies of both semi-professional boy actors and professional adult actors performed regularly. The title page of *Dido, Queen of Carthage*, a play that Marlowe may have written while still at Cambridge, indicates that it was first performed by boy actors from the Children of Her Majesty's Chapel. *Tamburlaine the Great*, which dramatizes the eponymous hero's rise from shepherd to ruler of a Persian empire through brutal warfare, was the first of Marlowe's plays to be performed by one of London's adult companies, the Lord Admiral's Men. The play is characterized as much by its hyperbolic, exotic language ("high astounding terms" [5] in the play's Prologue's phrase) as by its violence. Probably first performed in 1587, the play was successful enough to incite Marlowe to write a sequel, performed the following year. Marlowe wrote another four plays before his death in 1593: *Doctor Faustus* (c. 1589), *The Jew of Malta* (c. 1590), *Massacre at Paris* (c. 1591), and *Edward the Second* (c. 1592) (Kuriyama 80-81). Although this chronology is not exact, from *Tamburlaine* to *Edward the Second* a basic trajectory is still perceptible. Socially mobile outsiders, cynical or at least sceptical in their attitude and ruthless, transgressive, or daring in their actions, feature prominently in Marlowe's plays: Tamburlaine, Doctor Faustus, Barabas the Jew of Malta, the Duke of Guise in *The Massacre at Paris*, and Piers Gaveston (and, in a complicated way, Edward) in *Edward the Second*. Though seductive and temporarily triumphant, these figures are ultimately destroyed—by themselves as much as by the forces to which they are opposed. From *Tamburlaine* to *Edward the Second*, however, the balance of power seems to shift further against the transgressive tragic protagonist: Tamburlaine is a conqueror, Edward a vacillating, weak, and finally deposed monarch; Tamburlaine's field of action is the world, while Edward ends the play and his life in a dungeon; if *Tamburlaine* is characterized by hyperbolic language, *Edward the Second* employs a more restrained, ironic rhetoric.

Marlowe's dramatic career came to an abrupt end on 30 May 1593, when he was fatally stabbed in the eye by one Ingram Frizer at an inn in Deptford, just down the Thames from London proper. The authorities accepted Frizer's claim that he had acted in self-defence. According to Frizer, he, Marlowe, and two other men had gathered at the inn to dine together, and Marlowe attacked him after the two had fought over the bill. Many modern scholars and Marlowe biographers have been less willing to believe Frizer's story than the Elizabethan authorities were, however, and have proposed as alternatives a number of conspiracy theories. These theories reach back into Marlowe's Cambridge days, when he may have been recruited into one of the several intelligence networks run by powerful aristocrats competing for Queen Elizabeth's favour, and extend to the weeks before his death, when his former roommate and fellow dramatist Thomas Kyd was arrested and tortured because government officials discovered in Kyd's room part of an heretical treatise Kyd claimed was Marlowe's.[1] Indeed, by the time of his death Marlowe had acquired the dangerous reputation of an atheist. A number of documents indicate that this reputation had caught the Elizabethan government's attention. The most extensive of these documents, a report submitted to the government three days after Marlowe's death by Richard Baines (with whom Marlowe was caught attempting to counterfeit Dutch coins in Flushing in early 1592), attributes the following beliefs, among others, to Marlowe: "That the first beginning of religion was only to keep men in awe"; "That Christ was a bastard and his mother dishonest"; "That St. John the Evangelist was bedfellow to Christ and leaned always in his bosom, that he used him as the sinners of Sodoma"; "That all they that love not tobacco and boys were fools" (Kuriyama 221; spelling modernized). Baines concludes by stating that "I think all men in Christianity ought to endeavour that the mouth of so dangerous a member may be stopped" (Kuriyama 222; spelling modernized). Thus it has been argued that Marlowe was assassinated, because he was a rogue spy, an atheistic rebel, or a convenient scapegoat figure sacrificed as part of a larger plot. Nonetheless, as Kuriyama points out, until further, less circumstantial evidence appears, it is at least as plausible to believe that Frizer's account of the events is largely accurate and that Marlowe died simply because of a quarrel over lunch (140).

---

1 See Charles Nicholl's *The Reckoning: The Murder of Christopher Marlowe* for an extended conspiracy theory account of Marlowe's death. Honan and Riggs are also sceptical of the official Elizabethan account of Marlowe's death.

Marlowe was notorious enough that even in death he was the subject of gossip and moralizing. The account of Marlowe in Thomas Beard's *The Theatre of God's Judgement* (1597), included below in Appendix E4, fashions Marlowe's death into a negative moral example illustrating the divinely ordained fate of epicures and atheists. After providing numerous examples from ancient and modern history, Beard writes that "[n]ot inferior to any of the former in atheism and impiety, and equal to all in manner of punishment, was one of our own nation, of fresh and late memory, called Marlin, by profession a scholar, brought up from his youth in the University of Cambridge, but by practice a playmaker and a poet of scurrility." Beard then asserts that "[t]he manner of his death being so terrible (for he even cursed and blasphemed to his last gasp, and together with his breath an oath flew out of his mouth) that it was not only a manifest sign of God's judgement but also a horrible and fearful terror to all that beheld him." If his life and death attracted comments such as these, however, Marlowe's poetry received high praise from his contemporaries, praise that lasted well into the seventeenth century. In the prologue written for a performance of *The Jew of Malta* in the 1630s, Thomas Heywood calls Marlowe "the best of poets in that age" (2). By the middle of the seventeenth century Marlowe had dropped into obscurity as a poet and playwright, but in the nineteenth century his reputation revived. His complete works were edited, literary historians began to recognize his importance in the development of English drama, and poets such as Swinburne responded to Marlowe in their own poetry. Modern criticism has consolidated this revival. Scholars generally acknowledge Marlowe's innovative use of dramatic blank verse, his formative influence on early modern English tragedy and Shakespeare's history plays, and even his influence on the comedies of Ben Jonson through the bleak farce of a play such as *The Jew of Malta*.[1] It is important, though, not to let Marlowe's plays and poems be overshadowed either by his life or by his more famous contemporaries Shakespeare and Jonson. Marlowe's plays are not autobiographical in any straightforward sense, nor are they merely works that paved the way for Shakespeare's and Jonson's supposedly more developed art.

---

1   See Thomas Dabbs's *Reforming Marlowe: The Nineteenth-Century Canonization of a Renaissance Dramatist* for a full account of the shifts in Marlowe's literary critical reputation.

Christopher Marlowe's Theatre

The year 1576 was a turning point in the history of early modern English drama. There was no lack of theatre in London or the provinces before this point. Medieval and early sixteenth-century English drama came in many forms: extended dramatizations of Biblical narratives, known as mystery plays, performed over several days in multiple outdoor locations on religious holidays; shorter plays on religious themes and subjects, like saints' plays, miracle plays, and morality plays; secular but often no less didactic dramas designed for performance in such locations as banqueting halls, where they might serve as interludes between other forms of festivity; civic and court pageantry, staged to celebrate the inauguration of a new mayor or to entertain the monarch during such festive seasons as Christmas; educational drama, performed by schoolboys of all ages. Not all of this drama was amateur. Travelling actors performed interludes and other fare in expectation of some recompense for their acting, whether that be food and lodging or cash (preferably both). Professional actors seem occasionally to have been hired in the production of mystery plays and other forms of largely amateur drama, too (Harris 136). Nor was this drama necessarily inexpensive to produce. Organized and mounted by the guilds of a municipal corporation, for example, mystery plays were large affairs that involved considerable expense. Court entertainments spared no cost, their lavishness being a reflection of royal grandeur. On the whole, though, English drama before 1576 was occasional or irregular. Plays or pageants were performed to celebrate a special occasion or during a special season, or at irregular intervals in shifting venues (the performances of a travelling troupe, for example).[1] In 1576 that changed, at least in London. James Burbage, who managed a company of adult actors known as the Earl of Leicester's Men, built a freestanding open-air playhouse in the northern suburbs of London. Aptly named the Theatre, this playhouse had a neighbour, the Curtain, a year later. More freestanding open-air playhouses were built over the next forty years in the suburbs to the north and the south of London proper. These playhouses offered adult acting companies a permanent performance venue, where they could mount a regular performance schedule (six days a week) and generate stable

---

1 Glynne Wickham's *The Medieval Theatre* is an excellent introduction to English theatre before 1576.

revenue by attracting a large and regular audience. During this time companies of boy actors were also performing in hall theatres in London, but the London adult acting companies did not acquire the use of a hall theatre until 1608, when Shakespeare's company made a hall theatre in the liberties[1] of Blackfriars one of their regular performance venues.[2] *Dido, Queen of Carthage* was performed in one of these hall theatres by a company of boy actors, and *Edward the Second* may have had its first performance in a hall in Leicester (Forker 14), but all of Marlowe's other plays were likely first performed on a regular basis by adult companies in open-air playhouses.

The open-air playhouses were large, wooden, polygonal structures that could seat between two and three thousand spectators, who sat in the three tiers of galleries or stood in the yard area surrounding the stage. The price of admission was a penny to stand in the yard, another penny to sit in the first level of galleries, and an additional penny to ascend to the upper galleries. The galleries were thatched, and performances typically began mid-afternoon, while there was still daylight. The raised stage projected into the yard area from one of the inner walls and was roughly 30 feet by 40 feet. At the back of the stage was a house-front façade with (at least) two doors for entrances and exits and an upper balcony area that could also be used as an acting area. The dressing room area was behind the façade. A cover, the "heavens," sheltered the central acting area from rain and could also house the machinery necessary for lowering and raising props and actors to and from the stage. At the front of the stage was a large trapdoor, the "hell mouth," which allowed the actors to use the area below the raised stage as an acting area (Gurr 122-23). The actors might also use the yard as an acting area. The acting area, then, had three distinct vertical levels: the upper balcony, the middle main stage,

---

1 Liberties were mostly former monastic grounds in and around London that, even after the dissolution of the monasteries, retained some of their previous privileges, such as freedom from municipal by-laws (Griffiths 81-82). Theatre entrepreneurs exploited this freedom by building theatres in the liberties in the face of opposition from London's municipal government, which consistently sought to close the theatres down. See Gurr 155-60 for an account of Shakespeare's company's acquisition of the Blackfriars hall theatre. Gurr notes that "The Blackfriars precinct was officially made part of the City of London in 1608" (118).
2 For a history of amphitheatre and hall theatres from Marlowe's day to the closing of the theatres in 1642, see Andrew Gurr's *The Shakespearean Stage 1574-1642*.

and the area below the stage. Elizabethan playwrights used the obvious dramatic symbolism of these different levels to great effect (Gurr 182). The main stage also contained three different horizontal areas: if the main action of the play took place in the central area of the stage, a withdrawal to the back of the stage could suggest a retreat into privacy or secrecy and the advance toward the front of the stage could be used by an actor to engage the audience, either through an aside or through direct address. The different sides of the stage, each perhaps centred on one of the stage façade's doors, could also be used as distinct acting areas. By modern standards the amphitheatre stage might seem rather bare. There were relatively few props, which were over-shadowed in importance by the actors' costumes. There were no background scene paintings or special lighting effects: the façade remained largely the same throughout the play, the performances took place in natural light, and consequently in the drama written for this stage the scene is set and detailed mainly through the references and descriptions in the actors' lines (Gurr 187-200). Nonetheless, with its various levels and acting areas the amphitheatre stage could be a very complex space.

One of the most noticeable aspects of Marlowe's stagecraft in *Edward the Second* is the limited use the play makes of vertical theatrical space, specifically the upper level of the façade. Marlowe uses this space in other plays, and *Edward the Second* contains moments, such as the barons' assault on Edward's castle at Tynemouth, which present opportunities for the effective use of the space. Shakespeare's *Richard the Second*, a play about another weak late-medieval English monarch, features an analogous moment in which the vertical spatial relations between characters are highly significant. In act three, scene three of the play, the army of the rebellious Henry Bolingbroke, Duke of Lancaster, surrounds the walls of the castle of Flint, into which Richard has retreated. Richard appears on the walls—the upper level of the façade—to speak with Bolingbroke. If the initial positions of the two characters emphasize the proper hierarchical relationship between subject and sovereign, however, their positions at the end of the scene foreground the destruction of that relationship. Richard is forced to descend to Bolingbroke's level: "Down, down I come like glist'ring Phaethon" (177), he says as he exits the façade's upper level, re-entering on the main stage to be taken prisoner by Bolingbroke. The difference between king and subject has been eliminated. In *Edward the Second*, however, Marlowe avoids such highly charged vertical symbolism. David

Bevington and James Shapiro comment on the appropriateness of this: "Marlowe confines his theatrical vision in this play to the middle ground of human history represented by the main stage … in order that he can intensify the brutal personal conflicts, the dismaying juxtapositions and confrontations, and the savage ironies that characterize for him the violent transitions of the political process" (276).

The middle ground of the main stage is a complex space in the play, however. In scene two, for example, the entrances on the opposite sides of the stage are used to dramatize the barons' mounting opposition to Edward and Gaveston, as the Mortimers enter from one side of the stage and Warwick and Lancaster enter from the other, both groups already fuming against Edward and Gaveston before they meet in the middle of the stage to plot Gaveston's exile together. In scene twelve, entrances from opposite sides of the stage are used to dramatize conflict, as Edward's army enters from one side of the stage, to be confronted shortly by the entrance of the baronial forces from the other side. The scene's dialogue echoes the head-to-head collision of these two forces, concluding with the clash of identically phrased but opposite claims to political legitimacy. "Saint George for England and the Barons's right!" (34), Warwick shouts. "Saint George for England and king Edward's right!" (35), Edward shouts back. Marlowe also makes effective use of the stage's depth to dramatize the complex relationship between public and private spaces in the play. In scene four, for example, Isabella draws Mortimer Junior apart from the rest of the barons in order to persuade him to consent to Gaveston's recall from banishment. By withdrawing to the side and toward the back of the stage, Isabella and Mortimer create a private space that the onstage audience of the barons and the real audience observe but cannot penetrate. Although their effect becomes clear once the two rejoin the other barons, the words Isabella speaks to Mortimer Junior in that private space remain unknown. How did Isabella persuade the man with whom she will later have an affair to consent to something to which he was only moments ago adamantly opposed? The scene here makes visible the uncertainty of our knowledge of history and the desires that motivate its agents, while also suggesting that our desire to know history and its secrets is not dissimilar to voyeuristic curiosity. When in the play's penultimate scene Marlowe inverts the relationship between public and private spaces, dramatizing in full view of the audience Edward's highly sexualized anal execution in

Berkeley castle's dungeon, he might seem to be satisfying that curiosity.

Costuming and symbolic action are two other important elements of the play's staging. On the early modern English stage costuming signalled identity in a multiplicity of ways. In early modern England the clothes a person could wear—their fabric, colour, and style—were regulated by legislation. On the street or stage, then, a character's costume would signal her or his social class or, if inappropriate to the character's already established social rank, her or his transgression of social hierarchy (Bailey 11-13). Gaveston's transgression of social hierarchy is visually foregrounded through his clothing (Bailey 79-81). Although of relatively humble origins—Lancaster calls him "base and obscure" (1.99)—Gaveston dresses lavishly, well above his social station. "He wears a lord's revenue on his back" (4.406), Mortimer Junior complains, "and in his Tuscan cap / A jewel of more value than the crown" (4.413-14). Through his clothing Gaveston aggressively flaunts his rapid social rise, and "'tis this that makes me impatient" (418), Mortimer Junior tells his uncle. The use of clothing to transgress social class made many early modern English moralists impatient, too, and in their treatises they often connect the theatre to this type of socio-symbolic disorder. Appendix E3 contains a representative excerpt from one such treatise, Philip Stubbes's *The Anatomy of Abuses* (1583). Clothes also signalled gender, and the same moralists who warned against any confusion of the class symbolism of clothing vehemently denounced gender transvestism. Early modern English theatre was here also a major culprit, as professional adult acting companies were all-male, and female roles were played by the male youths of the company. Gaveston glances at the titillating potential of gender transvestism on the stage when he imagines entertaining Edward with a performance of the Diana-Actæon myth in which "a lovely boy in Dian's shape, / With hair that gilds the water as it glides, / Crowneto of pearl about his naked arms" (1.59-61) holds "in his sportful hands an olive tree / To hide those parts which men delight to see" (1.62-63).

The symbolism of the play's action is also important. The barons' refusal to kneel in scene one, Edward seating Gaveston on the throne beside him in scene four, and Edward's kneeling in scene eleven to swear revenge upon the barons for Gaveston's death are simple examples of symbolic action. More extended examples include the barons' display of shields in scene six, Edward's vacillation with his crown in scene twenty, and the champion's challenge in scene twenty-three. Edward's degradation, torture, and death also acquire symbolic resonance, echoing both the Diana-Actæon myth invoked in the play's opening scene and narratives of Christ's passion. Edward's murder, of course, is the play's major piece of symbolic action. The play contains no stage directions for Edward's murder, and the cues provided by the dialogue are somewhat ambiguous, but most modern editors of the play have followed Marlowe's historical sources (see Appendix A1[i]) in specifying in their stage directions that Edward is held down by his jailers and anally penetrated by the assassin Lightborn with the red-hot spit that he demanded be made ready earlier in the scene. Some critics have detected in the scene's symbolism a moralization of the manner of Edward's death: Edward's anal execution is the fitting punishment, they suggest, for a monarch whose homosexual desires led him to neglect his kingdom. The symbolism is more ambiguous than this, however. After all, the character who administers the punishment is the assassin Lightborn, whose name is an anglicization of Lucifer and whose employer, Mortimer Junior, is a usurper whose own sodomitical political desires are being realized in the scene. Indeed, Edward's dying words, which echo Christ's, position him as a martyr as much as a criminal.

Edward the Second was probably first performed in London in 1592-93 by a group of actors known as the Lord Pembroke's Men (all acting companies needed the patronage of an aristocrat in order to escape punishment as unemployed "rogues" or "masterless men"). According to the title page of a second printing of the fourth edition of the play (1622), it was revived by another company, the Queen Anne's Servants, in the second decade of the seventeenth century. There are no further recorded performances of the play, however, until the twentieth century, when William Poel directed the play at the New Theatre in Oxford in 1903. As in many subsequent early twentieth-century productions, Poel's production de-emphasized the explicitly homoerotic dimension of the play in favour of the political, and did not stage Edward's murder. With the Prospect Theatre's Edinburgh Festival production of the play in 1969, two years after Britain decriminalized homosexuality, the pendulum swung in the other direction. The production dramatized the relationship between Edward and Gaveston as explicitly homosexual, and in the murder scene Lightborn kissed and embraced Edward before killing him. The Royal Shakespeare Company's 1990 production took the homoerotic dimension even further, staging Edward's execution with full frontal nudity, and Derek Jarman's provocative 1991 film adaptation undertook to transform what Jarman called a "dusty old play" into "a film of a gay love affair" (qtd. in Forker 116).[1] Deborah Willis comments that "Marlowe's play has provided an important testing ground for contemporary views of such matters as the relative importance of sexuality and class, the relation of 'the personal' and 'the political,' and the tendency of liberation struggles to reinscribe pre-existing power relations" (600). The play continues to be performed regularly by amateur and professional companies in North America and Britain, the most recent major Canadian production taking place at the Stratford Festival in 2005 as part of the festival's "Saints and Sinners" theme.

Edward the Second and History

Edward of Caernarfon was born on 25 April 1284. He became Edward II of England when his father, Edward I, died on 7 July 1307. In January 1308, Edward married Isabella of France in Boulogne. Edward was 23 years old at the time; Isabella was 12. Edward I and Philip IV of France, Isabella's father, had negotiated the match in 1299 as part of their efforts to bring harmony to the relationship between the two countries. Edward II reigned for approximately twenty years. He abdicated in January 1327 and was murdered in September of the same year. Historian Michael Prestwich comments that "Edward II was one of the most unsuccessful kings ever to rule England" (79), and he had the double misfortune to be preceded and followed by two very successful kings: his father, an admired and feared crusader, soldier, and legal reformer, and his son, Edward III, who very nearly conquered France. Along with the crown, Edward inherited from his father several problems: baronial opposition, and conflict with Scotland and France. Baronial opposition to royal authority, the central political conflict of *Edward the Second*, was not a new problem in English history. In 1215 it had culminated in the barons compelling King John to sign the Great Charter or Magna Carta, a bill of baronial rights to property, due legal

---

1 For a full account of the play's stage history until the 1990s, see Forker 99-116. For a detailed examination of the relationship between modern criticism and performance, including an examination of David Bintley's 1995 ballet version of the play and the 2003 Globe Theatre production, see Fuller.

process, and power. Edward I reissued the Magna Carta in 1297, and Edward II was compelled early on in his reign, in 1310, to agree to a set of Ordinances that reaffirmed the Magna Carta and gave the barons the right to appoint the king's advisors. This latter part of the Ordinances was clearly directed against Edward's favourite, Piers Gaveston, whose conduct after being recalled from banishment upon Edward's accession the barons had found intolerable. Indeed, under duress from the barons Edward consented to Gaveston's exile several times. The barons were not satisfied on this score, however, until they had seized Gaveston from the king and executed him in June 1312. The conflict between the king and the barons continued until 1321, when it broke into civil war. Edward won, and in 1322 the leader of the baronial opposition, Thomas of Lancaster, was executed. Edward immediately annulled the Ordinances and reigned with a free hand with his two favourites, the Despensers, until 1326, when he was effectively dethroned after quickly losing a civil war against forces led by his disaffected queen, Isabella, and Mortimer. The Despensers's rapacity and consequent unpopularity contributed in no small measure to the ease with which Edward was defeated. Edward's 1322 triumph proved to have been temporary, and ultimately the conflict between Edward and his barons ended with Edward's deposition.[1]

Edward's deposition raised a number of political questions that were as pressing for Elizabethans as they were for Edward's rebellious subjects. If the monarch is appointed by God, as medieval and early modern political theory generally held to be the case, then in what circumstances, by whom, and with what means can a monarch be legitimately resisted and even removed? This question is on the barons' minds throughout *Edward the Second*, and it certainly was on many Elizabethans' minds after Elizabeth was excommunicated in 1570. By excommunicating her, the pope declared Elizabeth's authority to be illegitimate: in the vocabulary of early modern political theory, she was not a monarch but a tyrant, to whom her subjects no longer owed allegiance. Out of their experiences of savage persecution by

---

1 All the historical information in the introduction's outline of Edward II's reign has been taken from Michael Prestwich's *The Three Edwards: War and State in England 1272-1377* and Roy Martin Haines's *King Edward II*. For an extended and very readable account of the importance of Scotland in Edward's reign, see David Cornell's *Bannockburn: The Triumph of Robert the Bruce*.

Catholic authorities, European Protestants developed their own theories of legitimate resistance to tyranny. Naturally, the position of the monarch and his or her government was that any resistance to the monarch's authority was illegitimate. Appendix F of this edition presents the reader with arguments from all sides of the debate.

Edward's reign was also marked by conflict with Scotland and France. The conflict with Scotland began in the previous reign, when Edward I intervened in the 1290s in the dispute between two rival claimants to the Scottish throne, Robert Bruce and John Balliol. Edward established the latter as Scottish king, in the process asserting English overlordship over Scotland. The Scottish rebelled and continued to do so throughout Edward II's reign, regularly conducting extended and extremely destructive raids into northern England. Edward II did not meet the Scottish challenge well. One of his first acts as king was to cancel the campaign against the Scots that his father had left in progress at his death. In 1314 he led a large army against the Scots only to see his poorly organized forces crushed at the battle of Bannockburn. Subsequent forays were inconclusive, and in 1323 Edward concluded a thirteen-year truce with the Scots that merely deferred the issue of English sovereignty over Scotland. The truce was followed a year later by war with France. As Duke of Aquitaine, Edward owed homage to the new French king, Charles IV, who was also Isabella's brother. Because of Edward's reluctance to perform his homage, Charles in 1324 confiscated Edward's French territories in Gascony. In 1325 Isabella and Prince Edward sailed to France, ostensibly to negotiate peace between the English and French monarchs. They returned to England in 1326, however, at the head of an army. Edward and the Despensers were captured. Edward's deposition and murder and his son's installation as Edward III quickly followed. For three years Isabella and Mortimer, created Earl of March in 1328, controlled government under Edward III's seal. In 1330, perhaps in response to rumours that Mortimer intended to make himself king, Edward seized him at Nottingham castle and sent him to London to be hanged and drawn.

For the facts about Edward II's reign, Marlowe turned chiefly to the 1587 edition of Raphael Holinshed's *The Third Volume of Chronicles of England, Scotland, and Ireland*, which he supplemented with the accounts of Edward's reign found in John Stow's *The Annals of England* (1592) and the *Chronicle* (1559) of Robert Fabyan. Excerpts from Holinshed and Stow can be found in Appendix A of this edition, and if the reader compares the play and its historical sources she or he will discover that Marlowe reshaped the history of Edward's reign considerably as he transferred it from the history books to the public stage. Obviously, dramatic necessity compelled Marlowe to select from, rearrange, and compress the events recounted in his historical sources. For example, Holinshed relates that in 1318

> a naughty fellow called John Poindras, or (as some books have) Ponderham, a tanner's son of Exeter coming to Oxford, and there thrusting himself into the king's hall that stood without the walls, gave forth that he was son and right heir of king Edward the first, and that by means of a false nurse he was stolen out of his cradle, and this Edward the second being a carter's son was brought in and laid in his place. (324)

This incident has considerable dramatic potential, but Marlowe ignores it. He also plays quite freely with the sequence of historical events, for example by inverting the order of Edward's and Gaveston's marriages, giving Mortimer Junior a prominence in the early years of Edward's reign that he does not have in Holinshed's account, and having Kent executed before Edward's death rather than after, as in historical fact and Holinshed. Gaveston's banishment and the amount of time between the play's final two scenes are good examples of dramatic compression. As Holinshed records, Gaveston was banished several times from England before his death in 1312, but for the sake of dramatic economy Marlowe condenses them into one. Very little time seems to pass in the play between the scene of Edward's murder and the play's final scene, in which Edward III commands Mortimer Junior's execution, yet historically three years intervene between these moments, and Mortimer Junior's arrest and execution proceed very differently (see Appendix A2[c]). Moreover, the transfer from page to stage involves elaboration and a redirection of attention from action to character. Holinshed records, for instance, that Gaveston encouraged Edward to "spend both days and nights in jesting, playing, banqueting, and in such other filthy and dishonourable exercises" (Appendix A1[a]). Marlowe elaborates on this by providing Gaveston with a richly poetic soliloquy in which he imagines the kinds of entertainment that will "best please his majesty" (1.69). At the play's other end, in scene twenty Marlowe converts Holinshed's account of Edward's response to the demand that he abdicate (see Appendix A1[h]) into a powerful dramatization of Edward's conflicted self.

Marlowe's reshaping of his historical sources indicates more than just considerations of dramatic economy, coherence, and power, however. Every historical narrative tells its story in a particular way, with its own ideological bias or slant. Holinshed's account provides a running moral commentary on the people and events of Edward's reign, converting them into (mostly negative) moral examples that illustrate the destructiveness of various vices, especially in kings, and the fickleness of fortune. For Holinshed history has a moral order. That moral order is largely absent from Marlowe's play. Most critics concur with Irving Ribner's assessment that "Marlowe sees the events of history not as the working out in human affairs of a divine providence, but rather as the products of human strength and will which shape worldly events independently of any supernatural power" (246). Pointing to echoes of accounts of Christ's suffering in the play's dramatization of Edward's suffering and death (see also Stow's account in Appendix A2[b]), Patrick Ryan has argued contrariwise that "Marlowe invokes, as the widest frame of reference for witnessing this king's tragedy, the providential design of Anglican historiography, with *Christus crucifixus* its center" (189–90). One might reply, however, that echoes of Christ's suffering and death in Edward's only foreground the absence of providence and Edward's failure to be a Christ figure.

The slant Marlowe gives to Edward's reign differs from Holinshed's politically as well as theologically. According to Joan Parks, sixteenth-century chronicle histories such as Holinshed's "create a national history that will encompass not just king and court but also citizens and even the artisanal and labouring classes" (276) by including a wide range of documents and narrating events in which citizens and other commoners as well as aristocrats are active participants. These histories "tell the history of the enduring country at the expense of individual historical actors, and all create a nation centered not on the monarch but on the land and its continuing traditions and customs" (278). In contrast, in *Edward the Second*, "the public, political world is constituted and determined by private forces" (283). In Holinshed, for example, the common people play a role in the major events of Edward's reign. As Isabella's army advances on London in 1326, London's artisans revolt against the authorities established by Edward and deliver the city to her; after parliament legislates Edward's deposition in favour of his son, the Archbishop of Canterbury acknowledges the role of the people in these historic events by preaching a sermon on the theme of *Vox populi, vox dei*, the voice of the people is the voice of God. The role of commoners in *Edward the Second* is much more limited. Although the mayor and citizens of Bristol hand Spencer Senior over to Isabella's forces, the mayor does not have a speaking part. Similarly, the parliamentary representative, Trussel, speaks little in scene twenty, in which Edward resigns his crown, and Canterbury's sermon is not mentioned. In Shakespeare's *Richard the Second*, a history play that reflects Holinshed's concern with England as a nation, the dying John of Gaunt deplores the fact that "This blessèd plot, this earth, this realm, this England" (2.1.50) has been "leased out—I die pronouncing it— / Like to a tenement or pelting farm" (2.1.59-60). In Marlowe's play, Edward offers to let his barons "Make several kingdoms of this monarchy" (4.70) as long as he "may have some nook or corner left / To frolic with my dearest Gaveston" (4.72-73). In *Edward the Second*, the common people are largely excluded from history, entering it only as pawns or victims, and there is no nation that transcends the aristocratic historical agents.

Male Friendship and Sodomy

When Edward offers England to his barons in exchange for "some nook or corner" in which he can "frolic with my dearest Gaveston" (4.72-73), he is desperately seeking to separate the political from the personal or private. Edward's retreat with Gaveston into the castle at Tynemouth and his flight to the abbey at Neath with the Spencers can be seen as similar attempts to carve out a private space away from the political sphere, in which he can enjoy or at least protect the intense personal relationships he has established with his male favourites. "[W]e'll live in Tynemouth here," Edward asserts after retreating into Tynemouth castle, "And so I walk with him [Gaveston] about the walls, / What care I though the earls begirt us round?" (6.218-20). The barons, however, force Edward to care. They assault Tynemouth and capture and execute Gaveston, just as later in the play they will hunt Edward down in the abbey at Neath and capture and execute the Spencers. They will not allow Edward to separate the political and the private. Edward himself throughout the play fully politicizes his relationships with his male favourites. In the play's first scene Edward tells his barons that "I will have

Gaveston, and you shall know / What danger 'tis to stand against your king" (1.94-95). In scene four Edward provocatively places Gaveston next to him after ascending to his throne and tells the audience of incensed barons that "Were he [Gaveston] a peasant, being my minion, / I'll make the proudest of you stoop to him" (4.29-30). Edward's relationships with male favourites of relatively humble origins are as political as they are personal and provide the focal point for the conflict between the king and the barons over the limits of royal authority and the extent of baronial rights. For Edward, Gaveston's rapid social rise from son of a knight to Earl of Cornwall is an emphatic display of his power as king and an attempt to fill important government positions with men who are far more obliged to him than the well-established and independent barons. "The headstrong barons shall not limit me: / He that I list to favour shall be great" (259-60), Edward declares in scene six. For the barons, conversely, Edward's advancement of Gaveston and then the Spencers is an attack on their privileges and what they perceive to be their right to participate in the government of the realm. They would be willing to end their conflict with the king, their herald announces to Edward in scene eleven, were he to "cherish virtue and nobility, / And have old servitors in high esteem, / And shake off smooth dissembling flatterers" (167-69).

The sexual dimension of the relationship between Edward and Gaveston must be understood within this politicized context. The sexual *is* the political in *Edward the Second*, as Isabella's adulterous relationship with Mortimer Junior demonstrates as forcefully as Edward's homoerotic relationship with Gaveston. The play's representation of sexuality, however, like its representation of politics, has an early modern configuration. Bruce R. Smith observes that "No one in Shakespeare's day would have labelled himself a 'homosexual'" (11). Following the work of French theorist Michel Foucault, Smith emphasizes that the categories of homosexual and heterosexual, categories that divide sexuality into two opposed types that provide the basis for personal identity, are the inventions of nineteenth-century medical, legal, and moral discourses. In contrast, Smith observes, in the early modern period it was assumed that all men might desire other men as well as women (10-13). The assumption did not indicate approval. Alan Bray writes that "it is difficult to exaggerate the fear and loathing of homosexuality" (62) in the early modern period. Bray's assertion is supported by early modern English laws against sodomy, a category of sexual deviance that included but was not limited to male-male anal penetration and which took its name from the biblical city of Sodom destroyed by God because, in St. Paul's words, "the men left the natural use of the woman, and burned in their lust one toward another, and man with man wrought filthiness, and received in themselves such recompense of their error, as was meet" (Romans 1: 27). Smith comments that "The letter of the law, in England as in Renaissance Europe generally, was unambiguous: sodomy was an offense punishable by death" (41). The reader can examine the text of the first Tudor sodomy law in Appendix E1, followed in E2 by the eminent early modern English lawyer Edward Coke's commentary.

In the years spanning Elizabeth I's and James I's reign, 1558-1625, however, there are only six recorded cases of sodomy charges, all of which seem to have involved the anal rape of a boy (Smith 48). Moreover, during the early modern period intense male friendships were highly prized. Echoing classical writers on friendship, Sir Thomas Elyot describes friendship as God's greatest gift to mankind: "For in God and all thing that cometh of God, nothing is of more greater estimation than love, called in Latin *amor*, whereof *amicitia* cometh, named in English friendship or amity" (Appendix· D1), and according to Elyot true friendship can exist only between "good men." Conversely, in his essay on friendship Francis Bacon states that "it is a mere and miserable solitude to want true friends, without which the world is but a wilderness" (Appendix D2). Male friendships involved a physical as well as emotional closeness: sharing a bed and public kissing and embracing were outward signs of an emotional intimacy that rendered each friend an *alter ego* or "other I." Early modern English writers on friendship could draw on an extensive body of classical literature that included the philosophers Aristotle and Plato, the rhetorician Cicero, the historian Plutarch, and Virgil, the pre-eminent classical poet in the Renaissance. Richard Barnfield's *The Affectionate Shepherd* (1594), excerpts from which are included in Appendix D3, is modelled on Virgil's second eclogue, which features the shepherd Corydon bemoaning his frustrated love for the youth Alexis.

What distinguished male friendships from sodomitical male-male relationships, then? It was not, or not primarily, the presence or absence of sexual activity. More important was whether the relationship respected or transgressed social and political order. Mario DiGangi explains that "in the early modern period 'sodomy' was neither a neutral description of a sexual act nor a synonym for homoerotic relations generally, but a political category deployed to stigmatize and control a multitude of social disorders" (ix). Male friendships could be manipulated to acquire personal wealth, advanced social status, and political power otherwise out of reach. In male friendships between men of unequal social status, this might involve an inversion of the proper hierarchical relationship between social superior and social subordinate. Were this perceived to be the case, what in other contexts might be read as male friendship might instead be read as sodomy. Whether or not the relationship between the two men was sexual, the imputation of sodomy followed upon the perception of the transgression of social and political order and summed that transgression up in the stigma of criminalized sexual deviance. Male friendship could also come into conflict with the marriage relationships by which patriarchal order was maintained. Eve Kosofsky Sedgwick has argued that in patriarchal societies such as early modern England marriage relationships are homosocial: a man (the father) gives a woman (the bride) to another man (the bridegroom) in order to cement a relationship—personal, commercial, or political—between the two men (*Between Men* 1-5). This act of exchange could in itself be the product of and serve to strengthen an already existing male friendship. Nonetheless, the competing emotional demands of male friendship and heterosexual marriage could be mutually disruptive. In Shakespeare's *The Merchant of Venice*, we see a male friendship strained to breaking point by the formation of a heterosexual romantic relationship. We also see the disruptive pressure that male friendship could place on marriage, as Portia must work hard to ensure the subordination of her new husband Bassanio's love for his friend Antonio to the demands of his relationship with her.

Critics have struggled with the question of whether or not Edward's relationship with Gaveston should be considered transgressively sexual. Its emotional intensity is apparent throughout the first half of the play, most notably in scene four, in which Edward is forced to consent to Gaveston's exile. The two men are very close physically. "[A]rm in arm, the king and he doth march" (2.20), Lancaster remarks in the second scene, adding bitterly that "Thus leaning on the shoulder of the king, / He [Gaveston] nods, and scorns, and smiles at those that pass" (2.23-24). In the same scene we learn that Edward and Gaveston's emotional and physical intimacy disrupts not only

Edward's relationship with his peers but also his relationship with his wife. Isabella enters the scene having been repulsed from her husband's presence and tells the assembled peers that

> my lord the king regards me not
> But dotes upon the love of Gaveston.
> He claps his cheeks and hangs about his neck,
> Smiles in his face and whispers in his ears,
> And when I come he frowns, as who should say,
> "Go whither thou wilt seeing I have Gaveston." (49-54)

The play brings the conflict between Edward's relationship with Gaveston and his relationship with Isabella into dramatic focus in the fourth scene as Edward reacts to Gaveston's banishment by banishing Isabella from his presence. "Villain, 'tis thou that robb'st me of my lord" (160), Isabella accuses Gaveston, who replies with "Madam, 'tis you that rob me of my lord" (161). Tellingly, as the members of the royal court flee Tynemouth in scene eight, Edward is more concerned with Gaveston's safety than Isabella's.

The sexual suggestiveness of Edward and Gaveston's emotional and physical intimacy is reinforced by the classical allusions by which the play's characters describe their relationship. In the soliloquy that opens the play, for example, Gaveston reads Edward's letter recalling him from banishment and declaims

> Sweet prince, I come. These, these thy amorous lines
> Might have enforced me to have swum from France
> And like Leander gasped upon the sand,
> So thou wouldst smile and take me in thy arms. (6-9)

Gaveston compares himself and Edward here to the tragic protagonists of the classical Greek poet Musaeus's epyllion *Hero and Leander* (which Marlowe translated), significantly placing himself in the masculine position of the poem's romantic, heterosexual coupling. Elsewhere the two are compared to other sexually involved couples from classical myth: Jove and Ganymede, Jove and Danaë, and (less favourably) Helen and Paris. The homoerotic element in Edward and Gaveston's relationship does not necessarily render it sodomitical: it has not prevented Edward from producing a legitimate heir, and it does not prevent Edward from arranging a good marriage for Gaveston. Even the barons do not find it necessarily disruptive. At the end of scene four, after the king has been reconciled with his peers and Isabella, Mortimer Senior advises his nephew to "Leave now to oppose thyself against the king" (388), for "The mightiest kings have had their minions" (392) and "riper years will wean him from such toys" (402) as Gaveston. "[H]is wanton humour grieves not me" (403), Mortimer Junior replies. What grieves him is that

> one so basely born
> Should by his sovereign's favour grow so pert
> And riot it with the treasure of the realm
> While soldiers mutiny for want of pay. (404-07)

Mortimer Junior is accusing the "basely born" Gaveston of manipulating his relationship with the king for his own benefit and to the disadvantage of the kingdom. As far as Mortimer Junior is concerned, Edward and Gaveston's relationship is sodomitical, because of the domestic, social, and political disorder it creates.

It must not be forgotten, however, that Mortimer Junior is not a disinterested party. He among the barons most vociferously insists upon the disorder that Edward's relationship with Gaveston has created, yet he himself is a considerable source of disorder. As Gregory Bredbeck argues, Mortimer Junior insists on making Edward and Gaveston's sodomitical relationship a political cause, and by doing so he deflects attention away from his own treasonous, sodomitical desires and actions (*Sodomy and Interpretation* 70-71). Mortimer Junior is a subject in rebellion against his sovereign; through his adultery with Isabella he as much as Edward violates patriarchal order; he as much as Gaveston manipulates his sexual relationship with his royal partner for his own benefit. Bredbeck writes that "What Mortimer as a character embodies is the simple but central principle that once sodomy is constructed as an affront to order, it then can be used to affront order" (75). By insisting that Edward's desires are a threat to the nation's welfare, Mortimer Junior makes them seem, or "constructs" them as, disorderly. By claiming to oppose Edward's disorderliness, he can then pursue his own disorderly sexual and political ambitions. Indeed, the scene of Edward's murder can be seen as the most vivid example of Mortimer's sodomy as much as it can be read as punishment for Edward's, and the play concludes with Mortimer Junior's, not Edward's, execution for his sodomy. DiGangi argues that "no matter how disorderly, how scandalous, how improvident the homoerotic relations between Edward II and his favourites might be, it is Mortimer's access to the body of the king [in his confinement and murder] that the legitimate authority of Edward III finally constructs, and visibly punishes, as a sodomitical transgression against the body politic" (115). It is not easy to determine who the play's "real" sodomite is, and perhaps that is the play's point: sodomy, like its ostensible opposite male friendship, is a discursive construct, a rhetorical weapon as much a part of the power struggle between Edward and his barons as the combatants' naked swords.

The play's complex treatment of sodomy and, more generally, sexual politics has relevance not only to the history of a medieval monarch. Many early modern writers wrote their histories as indirect commentaries on contemporary politics. Dennis Kay and Mark Thornton Burnett have argued that *Edward the Second* obliquely comments on the sexual politics of Elizabeth I's court, especially the queen's treatment of favourites. Lawrence Normand, Mario DiGangi, and others have suggested that the play also glances at James VI of Scotland, later James I of England, who was known for his passionate relationships with male favourites such as Esmé Stuart. Marlowe was not the only writer to use the history of Edward II's reign as a vehicle for contemporary commentary. According to Joseph Cady, "the Edward II-Gaveston story functioned widely in informed European Renaissance culture as a symbol of male homosexual attraction" (141). In 1588 Jean Boucher published his *Histoire tragique et memorable de Pierre de Gaverston*, a condemnation of the French king Henri III's sodomitical addiction to his minions (Perry 1063). Later English narratives of Edward's reign, such as Michael Drayton's *Mortimeriados* (Appendix B), Francis Huebert's *The Deplorable Life and Death of Edward the Second* (1628), and Elizabeth Cary's *History of the Life, Reign, and Death of Edward II* (1680), are also inflected by Elizabethan and Jacobean concerns. For early modern writers, to write history was to engage the present as well as the past.

Christopher Marlowe: A Brief Chronology of His Life and Times

1558   The Protestant Elizabeth Tudor, daughter of Anne Boleyn and Henry VIII, accedes to the throne of England.

1562   Parliament re-establishes Henry VIII's law against sodomy.

1564   Christopher Marlowe is born in Canterbury, Kent.

1564   William Shakespeare is born in Stratford-upon Avon, Warwickshire.

1569   The Northern Rebellion. A group of northern earls rebels against Elizabeth I in support of establishing the Catholic Mary, Queen of Scots as Elizabeth's successor. The rebellion fails.

1570   Pope Pius V excommunicates Elizabeth I.

1572   The Act for the Punishment of Vagabonds criminalizes actors without aristocratic patrons.

1573   Ben Jonson is born in London.

1574   Elizabeth I issues the Statutes of Apparel regulating clothing.

1576   James Burbage builds the Theatre, a freestanding, open-air playhouse, in the northern suburbs of London.

1576-84   The Children of Her Majesty's Chapel perform regularly at a hall theatre in Blackfriars, London.

1584   Marlowe receives his BA from Cambridge.

1584-86   Composition of *Dido, Queen of Carthage*, first performed by the Children of Her Majesty's Chapel. Marlowe also likely produced his translations of Ovid's *Amores* during his time at Cambridge.

1587   The imprisoned Mary, Queen of Scots is executed by Elizabeth I's command.

1587   Marlowe receives his MA from Cambridge.

1587   First performance of *Tamburlaine the Great Part One*.

1587   Second edition of Raphael Holinshed's *Chronicles of England, Scotland, and Ireland*.

1588   The English repulse a massive Spanish naval invasion (the Spanish Armada).

1588   First performance of *Tamburlaine the Great Part Two*.

1589   First performance of *Doctor Faustus*.

1589	Marlowe is involved in a duel with one William Bradley; the poet Thomas Watson, Marlowe's friend, intervenes and kills Bradley in self-defence. The coroner's jury acquits both Marlowe and Watson.
1590	First performance of *The Jew of Malta*.
1590	*Tamburlaine the Great* (both parts in one volume) published.
1591-92	First performance of *The Massacre at Paris*.
1591-99	Shakespeare writes a series of history plays, including *Richard the Second* (1595), to which *Edward the Second* has often been compared.
1592	Marlowe and Richard Baines are arrested in Flushing for counterfeiting. Later this year in Canterbury Marlowe is sued for assault by William Corkine.
1592-93	First performance of *Edward the Second*.
1593	Marlowe translates the first book of Lucan's *Pharsalia* and Musaeus's *Hero and Leander*.
1593	Marlowe dies, stabbed in the eye by Ingram Frizer at an inn in Deptford on 30 May. On 12 May Marlowe's former roommate, the playwright Thomas Kyd, is arrested and interrogated for his possible connections to the circulation in London of threatening anti-immigrant libels. Kyd implicates Marlowe in the writing or copying of part of a heretical treatise found in Kyd's quarters. On 18 May Marlowe is summoned to meet the Privy Council; after obeying the summons on 20 May, Marlowe is released but required to remain available should the Privy Council have further need of him. The connection between these events and Marlowe's death on 30 May is unclear.
1594	*Edward the Second* and *Dido, Queen of Carthage* published.
c. 1595	Marlowe's translations of ten of Ovid's *Amores* are published in the same volume as John Davies's *Epigrams*. The volume is banned and publicly burned in 1599.
1598	*Hero and Leander* published.
1599	The Globe is built on the southern banks of the Thames from the timbers of the Theatre.
c. 1600	*The Massacre at Paris* published.
1600	*Lucan's First Book* published.

1603	Elizabeth I dies; James VI of Scotland accedes to the English throne as James I of England.
1604	*Doctor Faustus* (A text) published.
1616	*Doctor Faustus* (B text) published.
1633	*The Jew of Malta* published.

A Note on the Text

Edward the Second was first printed in 1594, a year after Marlowe's death, in quarto (Q) format. To make a quarto the printer printed four pages on each side of a series of large sheets of paper that were then folded twice and bound together. The play was reprinted three times in the sixteenth and early-seventeenth centuries: 1598 (Q2), 1612 (Q3), and 1622 (Q4). These reprintings are based on the 1594 quarto (Q) and do not possess any independent textual authority. This Broadview edition is based on the 1594 quarto or, in editorial terminology, takes Q as its copy text, although the later quartos have been consulted. Substantive emendations to the text have been indicated in the footnotes; where possible, the spelling and punctuation have been silently standardized and modernized. Archaic but readily intelligible verb forms have been retained, primarily in order to preserve the meter of the play's verse. Q provides neither act nor scene divisions. This edition indicates scene divisions in square brackets when the stage is cleared of actors, although an exception to this rule has been made in scene eighteen, in which Kent enters so quickly after the royal party has fled the battlefield that the scene seems to the editor to retain its integrity. This edition also supplements Q's sparse stage directions with its own (again in square brackets), mainly to mark entrances and exits. The only existing copy of Q is housed in the Zentralbibliothek in Zürich, Switzerland. This edition is based on the Early English Books Online digital facsimiles of this and the later quartos.

In keeping with the goal of producing a modernized edition, the titles of early modern texts have been given in abbreviated form and their spelling has been modernised throughout, except in Works Cited and Further Reading. In this section the titles of early modern texts quoted or edited from early modern editions have been given in their original spelling and in their extended form, followed by their publication information and their Short Title Catalogue (STC) or Wing number,[1] in order to give full and

---

1 The full title of the STC, compiled by A.W. Pollard and G.R. Redgrave and revised subsequently by several others, is *A Short-Title Catalogue of Books Printed in England, Scotland, and Ireland, and of English Books Printed Abroad, 1475-1640*. A standard library reference *(continued)*

precise bibliographic information to the reader interested in locating the original texts.

---

work, this bibliography assigns a reference number to each of its entries. Similarly, Wing numbers refer to the entries in Donald Wing's extension of Pollard and Redgrave's project in his *Short-Title Catalogue of Books Printed in England, Scotland, Ireland, Wales, and British America and of English Books Printed in Other Countries, 1641-1700.*

EDWARD THE SECOND

The troublesome

raigne and lamentable death of
Edward *the second, King of*
England: with the tragicall
fall of proud Mortimer:

As it was sundrie times publiquely acted
in the honourable citie of London, by the
right honourable the Earle of Pem-
brooke his seruants.

Written by Chri. Marlow *Gent.*

Imprinted at London for *William Iones*
dwelling neere Holbourne conduit, at the
figne of the Gunne. 1594.

Title page of the 1594 quarto of *Edward the Second*. Reproduced with
the permission of the Zentralbibliothek in Zurich, Switzerland.

Dramatis Personae

Edward II, King of England
Isabella, Queen of England and the King of France's sister
Prince Edward, later Edward III, son of Edward and Isabella
Edmund, Earl of Kent, Edward II's half-brother

Gaveston, Edward II's childhood friend and favourite, created
    Earl of Cornwall
Spencer Junior, Lady Margaret's servant, later created Earl of
    Wiltshire and Gloucester
Spencer Senior, his father, later created Earl of Winchester
Baldock, Lady Margaret's tutor, later Lord Chancellor

Mortimer Junior of Wigmore
Mortimer Senior of Chirke, his uncle
Earl of Lancaster
Earl of Pembroke
Earl of Warwick
Earl of Leicester
Earl of Arundel
Lord Berkeley
Sir John of Hainault
Lord Beaumont
Lady Margaret de Clare, the deceased Earl of Gloucester's
    daughter, Edward II's niece and ward

Mayor of Bristol
Rhys ap Howell
Matrevis
Gurney
Lightborn
Pembroke's Men
James, one of Pembroke's Men
Horse-Boy, one of Pembroke's Men
Three Poor Men
Clerk of the Crown
Trussel
The King's Champion
Mower
Herald
Levune, Edward's ambassador to France

Bishop of Coventry
Bishop of Canterbury
Bishop of Winchester
Abbot of Neath
Monks

Messengers, Guards, Soldiers, Lords, Ladies-in-Waiting,
    Attendants
[Scene 1]

Enter Gaveston reading on a letter that was brought him from
the king

Gaveston
    "My father is deceased; come, Gaveston,
    And share the kingdom with thy dearest friend."[1]
    Ah, words that make me surfeit with delight!
    What greater bliss can hap[2] to Gaveston
    Than live and be the favourite of a king?   5
    Sweet prince, I come. These, these thy amorous lines
    Might have enforced me to have swum from France
    And like Leander[3] gasped upon the sand,
    So thou wouldst smile and take me in thy arms.
    The sight of London to my exiled eyes   10
    Is as Elysium[4] to a new come soul,
    Not that I love the city or the men,
    But that it harbours him I hold so dear,
    The king, upon whose bosom let me die[5]
    And with the world be still at enmity.   15
    What need the arctic people love starlight,
    To whom the sun shines both by day and night?
    Farewell base stooping to the lordly peers,
    My knee shall bow to none but to the king.

---

1 Edward I exiled Gaveston to Gascony on 25 February 1307; Edward II
   recalled Gaveston immediately after his father's death on 7 July 1307
   (Haines 21, 50).
2 Happen, chance.
3 Tragic male lover of the fifth-century CE Greek poet Musaeus's minor
   epic, *Hero and Leander*. Leander drowns while attempting to swim the
   Hellespont to reach his beloved, Hero. Marlowe wrote his own free
   translation of the first portion of the poem.
4 Place of the departed souls of the blessed in classical mythology.
5 In early modern English, "die" had the additional meaning of "orgasm."

As for the multitude, that are but sparks   20
Raked up in embers of their poverty,
Tanti![1] I'll fan first on the wind
That glanceth at my lips and flieth away.
But how now, what are these?

Enter three poor men

Poor Men
Such as desire your worship's service.   25

Gaveston
What canst thou do?

First Poor Man
I can ride.

Gaveston
But I have no horses. What art thou?

Second Poor Man
A traveller.

Gaveston
Let me see, thou wouldst do well to wait at my trencher[2]
and tell me lies at dinner time; and as I like your discours-
ing, I'll have you. And what art thou?[3]

Third Poor Man
A soldier, that hath served against the Scot.[4]

Gaveston
Why, there are hospitals[5] for such as you.
I have no war, and therefore, sir, be gone.

Third Poor Man
Farewell, and perish by a soldier's hand,   35
That wouldst reward them with a hospital.

---

1 "So much for them!" (Italian).
2 Platter.
3 Q prints lines 30 to 31 as verse.
4 During the last decade of Edward I's reign and throughout Edward II's,
   England and Scotland fought a series of wars over English claims to
   sovereignty over Scotland.
5 Hospices.

Gaveston

[Aside] Ay, ay, these words of his move me as much
As if a goose should play the porcupine
And dart her plumes, thinking to pierce my breast.
But yet it is no pain to speak men fair;   40
I'll flatter these and make them live in hope.
[To the three men] You know that I came lately out of
    France,
And yet I have not viewed my Lord the king.
If I speed well, I'll entertain you all.

Three Poor Men

We thank your worship.   45

Gaveston

I have some business, leave me to myself.

Three Poor Men

We will wait here about the court.

Exit[1] [the three poor men]

Gaveston

Do. These are not men for me.
I must have wanton[2] poets, pleasant wits,
Musicians that with touching of a string   50
May draw the pliant king which way I please.
Music and poetry is his delight,
Therefore I'll have Italian masques[3] by night,
Sweet speeches, comedies, and pleasing shows;
And in the day when he shall walk abroad,   55
Like sylvan nymphs[4] my pages shall be clad;
My men like satyrs[5] grazing on the lawns,
Shall with their goat feet dance an antic[6] hay.[7]

---

1 Exeunt in Q. This Latin stage direction, which means "they exit," has
   been replaced throughout with the English "Exit" or "Exit all."
2 Playful, unrestrained, sexually promiscuous.
3 Court entertainments combining acting, dancing, and music.
4 Minor female forest deities in classical mythology.
5 In classical mythology, male forest creatures who were part human and
   part horse or goat.
6 Grotesque, fantastic.
7 Country dance.

Sometime a lovely boy in Dian's[1] shape,
With hair that gilds the water as it glides,   60
Crownets[2] of pearl about his naked arms,
And in his sportful hands an olive tree
To hide those parts which men delight to see,
Shall bathe him in a spring; and there hard by,
One like Actæon[3] peeping through the grove   65
Shall by the angry goddess be transformed,
And running in the likeness of an hart,[4]
By yelping hounds pulled down, and seem to die.
Such things as these best please his majesty.[5]
My lord! Here comes the king and the nobles   70
From the parliament. I'll stand aside.

Enter the King [Edward II], Lancaster, Mortimer Senior, Mortimer Junior, Edmund Earl of Kent, Guy Earl of Warwick, etc.

Edward
Lancaster.

Lancaster
My Lord.

Gaveston
[Aside] That Earl of Lancaster do I abhor.

---

1 Classical goddess of chastity.
2 Bracelets.
3 A young hunter whom Diana transforms into a stag because he enters her sacred grove and sees her bathing nude. See the excerpt from Ovid's *Metamorphoses* in Appendix C1.
4 Stag.
5 Marlowe here is elaborating upon Holinshed's account of Gaveston's influence on Edward at the beginning of his reign. According to Holinshed, Edward "began to have his nobles in no regard, to set nothing by their instructions, and to take small heed unto the good government of the commonwealth, so that within a while, he gave himself to wantonness, passing his time in voluptuous pleasure, and riotous excess: and to help them forward in that kind of life, the foresaid Piers, who (as it may be thought, he had sworn to make the king forget himself, and the state, to which he was called) furnished his court with companies of jesters, ruffians, flattering parasites, musicians, and other vile and naughty ribalds, that the king might spend both days and nights in jesting, playing, banqueting, and in other such filthy and dishonourable exercises." See Appendix A1(a).

Edward

Will you not grant me this? [Aside] In spite of them   75
I'll have my will, and these two Mortimers
That cross me thus shall know I am displeased.

Mortimer Senior

If you love us, my lord, hate Gaveston.

Gaveston

[Aside] That villain[1] Mortimer, I'll be his death.

Mortimer Junior

Mine uncle here, this Earl, and I myself   80
Were sworn to your father at his death
That he should ne'er return into the realm;[2]
And know, my lord, ere I will break my oath,
This sword of mine that should offend your foes
Shall sleep within the scabbard at thy need,   85
And underneath thy banners march who will,
For Mortimer will hang his armour up.

Gaveston

[Aside] *Mort Dieu!*[3]

Edward

Well, Mortimer, I'll make thee rue[4] these words.
Beseems it thee[5] to contradict thy king?   90
Frownst thou thereat, aspiring Lancaster?
The sword shall plane[6] the furrows of thy brows
And hew these knees that now are grown so stiff.
I will have Gaveston, and you shall know
What danger 'tis to stand against your king.   95

Gaveston

[Aside] Well done, Ned.

---

1   Peasant.
2   None of Marlowe's historical sources place either Mortimer among the
    earls who purportedly swore to Edward I not to permit Gaveston to
    return to England. Stow suggests that Edward II himself swore to his
    father not to permit Gaveston's return. See Appendix A2(a).
3   "Death of God!" (French).
4   Regret.
5   Is it appropriate for you?
6   Level, make smooth.

Lancaster

My lord, why do you thus incense your peers,
That naturally would love and honour you
But for that base and obscure Gaveston?[1]
Four Earldoms have I besides Lancaster: 100
Derby, Salisbury, Lincoln, Leicester.
These will I sell to give my soldiers pay
Ere Gaveston shall stay within the realm.
Therefore if he be come, expel him straight.

Kent

Barons and Earls, your pride hath made me mute,   105
But now I'll speak—and to the proof, I hope.
I do remember in my father's days,
Lord Percy of the North, being highly moved,
Braved[2] Mowbry in presence of the king,
For which, had not his highness loved him well,   110
He should have lost his head; but with his look
The undaunted spirit of Percy was appeased,
And Mowbry and he were reconciled.[3]
Yet dare you brave the king unto his face?
Brother, revenge it and let these their heads   115
Preach upon poles[4] for trespass of their tongues.

Warwick

O, our heads!

Edward

Ay, yours, and therefore I would wish you grant.

Warwick

Bridle thy anger, gentle Mortimer.

Mortimer Junior

I cannot, nor I will not; I must speak.   120
Cousin, our hands, I hope, shall fence our heads
And strike off his that makes you threaten us.

---

1 In fact, Gaveston was the son of a Bearnese knight, Arnold de Gaveston,
   who fled to England in 1296 after escaping imprisonment in France
   (Haines 20-21).
2 Defied, insulted.
3 No historical record exists of the incident Kent recounts here.
4 The severed heads of traitors and other criminals were mounted on
   poles for public display.

Come, uncle, let us leave the brainsick king
And henceforth parley[1] with our naked swords.

Mortimer Senior
Welshry[2] hath men enough to save our heads.   125

Warwick
All Warwickshire will love him for my sake.

Lancaster
And northward Gaveston hath many friends.
Adieu, my lord, and either change your mind
Or look to see the throne where you should sit
To float in blood, and at thy wanton head   130
The glozing[3] head of thy base minion[4] thrown.

Exit the Barons

Edward
I cannot brook[5] these haughty menaces.
Am I a king and must be overruled?
Brother, display my ensigns[6] in the field;
I'll bandy[7] with the Barons and the Earls   135
And either die or live with Gaveston.

Gaveston
I can no longer keep me from my lord.

[Gaveston steps forward]

Edward
What, Gaveston? Welcome! Kiss not my hand;
Embrace me, Gaveston, as I do thee.
Why shouldst thou kneel? Knowest thou not who
    I am?[8]   140

---

1 Debate, negotiate.
2 Wilshire in Q. Gill (1980) notes that the Mortimers had no connections
   to Wiltshire and suggests that Q may be a compositorial misreading of
   "Welshry." I have followed Forker (1994) and other editors in emending
   Q.
3 Deceitful, flattering.
4 Favourite.
5 Endure.
6 Military banners.
7 Literally, to return a ball in a racquet sport such as tennis.
8 "Why shouldst thou kneel? / Knowest thou not who I am?" in Q.

Thy friend, thy self, another Gaveston.[1]
Not Hylas was more mourned of Hercules[2]
Than thou hast been of me since thy exile.

Gaveston

And since I went from hence, no soul in hell
Hath felt more torment than poor Gaveston.   145

Edward

I know it. Brother, welcome home my friend.
Now let the treacherous Mortimers conspire,
And that high-minded earl of Lancaster.
[To Gaveston] I have my wish in that I joy thy sight,
And sooner shall the sea o'erwhelm my land   150
Than bear the ship that shall transport thee hence.
I here create thee Lord high Chamberlain,[3]
Chief Secretary to the state[4] and me,
Earl of Cornwall, king and lord of Man.[5]

Gaveston

My lord, these titles far exceed my worth.   155

Kent

Brother, the least of these may well suffice
For one of greater birth than Gaveston.

---

1 In *De amicitia* (*Of Friendship*), Cicero defines a friend as an "alter idem"
   or "another self" (XXI.80). In "The True Description of Amity or
   Friendship" (Appendix D1), Thomas Elyot states that "a friend is properly named of philosophers 'the other I,' for that in them is but one
   mind and one possession and that, which more is, a man more rejoiceth
   at his friend's good fortune than at his own." See also the note to 4.395.
2 In classical mythology Hylas is a young man who accompanies Hercules
   on the voyage of the Argonauts. Water nymphs fall in love with and
   drown him while he is looking for water on the coast of Mysia. While
   Hercules is grieving and looking for Hylas, the Argonauts leave.
3 Although the Lord High Chamberlain was an officer of state, the position was largely ceremonial and, historically, was held by the earls of
   Oxford. The Lord Chamberlain was manager of the royal household.
4 The secretary to the state, who was entrusted with the monarch's privy
   seal, was one of the three chief officers of state. The other two were the
   chancellor, who kept the great seal, and the treasurer.
5 The Isle of Man is located off the north-west coast of England. Its possession was contested by the English and the Scottish during the reigns of
   Edward I and Edward II. Although its governor enjoyed the titles of king
   and lord, it was a dependency of either the English or the Scottish crown.

Edward
    Cease, brother, for I cannot brook these words.
    Thy worth, sweet friend, is far above my gifts;
    Therefore to equal it receive my heart.   160
    If for these dignities thou be envied,
    I'll give thee more, for but to honour thee
    Is Edward pleased with kingly regiment.[1]
    Fear'st thou thy person? Thou shalt have a guard.
    Wants thou gold? Go to my treasury.   165
    Wouldst thou be loved and feared? Receive my seal,
    Save or condemn, and in our name command
    What so thy mind affects or fancy likes.

Gaveston
    It shall suffice me to enjoy your love,
    Which whiles I have, I think myself as great   170
    As Caesar riding in the Roman street
    With captive kings at his triumphant car.[2]

Enter the Bishop of Coventry

Edward
    Whither goes my Lord of Coventry so fast?

Bishop of Coventry
    To celebrate your father's exequies.[3]
    But is that wicked Gaveston returned?   175

Edward
    Ay, priest, and lives to be revenged on thee
    That wert the only cause of his exile.

Gaveston
    'Tis true, and but for reverence of these robes,
    Thou shouldst not plod one foot beyond this place.

Bishop of Coventry
    I did no more than I was bound to do,   180
    And, Gaveston, unless thou be reclaimed,
    As then I did incense the parliament,
    So will I now, and thou shalt back to France.

---

1 Rule, office.
2 Chariot.
3 Funeral rites.

Gaveston
Saving your reverence,[1] you must pardon me.

[Gaveston assaults the bishop]

Edward
Throw off his golden mitre,[2] rend his stole,[3]   185
And in the channel[4] christen him anew.

Kent
Ah, brother, lay not violent hands on him,
For he'll complain unto the see of Rome.[5]

Gaveston
Let him complain unto the see of hell!
I'll be revenged on him for my exile.   190

Edward
No, spare his life, but seize upon his goods;
Be thou lord bishop and receive his rents,[6]
And make him serve thee as thy chaplain.
I give him thee; here, use him as thou wilt.

Gaveston
He shall to prison and there die in bolts.[7]   195

Edward
Ay, to the Tower, the Fleet, or where thou wilt.[8]

Bishop of Coventry
For this offence be thou accursed[9] of God.

Edward
Who's there?

---

1 "Saving your reverence" is an apologetic phrase that introduces a criticism, contradiction, or other remark that the hearer might find offensive.
2 Ceremonial hat.
3 Strip of cloth worn by clergy over the shoulder and hanging down to the knees.
4 Open sewer.
5 The pope, whose diocese or "see" is Rome.
6 By claiming the right to make ecclesiastical appointments, Edward is encroaching on papal prerogatives.
7 Chains.
8 The Tower of London and the Fleet, also in London, were prisons.
9 Excommunicated, formally expelled from the Church.

[Enter guards]

Convey this priest to the Tower.

Bishop of Coventry
True, true.

[Exit bishop and guards]

Edward
But in the meantime, Gaveston, away   200
And take possession of his house and goods.
Come, follow me, and thou shalt have my guard
To see it done and bring thee safe again.

Gaveston
What should a priest do with so fair a house?
A prison may beseem his holiness.[1]   205

[Exit Edward, Gaveston, and Kent]

[Scene 2]

Enter both the Mortimers [from one side], Warwick and Lancaster [from the other side]

Warwick
'Tis true, the Bishop is in the Tower,
And goods and body given to Gaveston.

Lancaster
What, will they tyrannize upon the Church?
Ah, wicked king, accursèd Gaveston,
This ground which is corrupted with their steps   5
Shall be their timeless[2] sepulchre or mine.

Mortimer Junior
Well, let that peevish Frenchman guard him sure;
Unless his breast be sword-proof, he shall die.

Mortimer Senior
How now, why droops the earl of Lancaster?

---

1 See Appendix A1(a) for Holinshed's account of this incident.
2 Eternal; untimely.

Mortimer Junior
    Whereforc[1] is Guy of Warwick discontent?   10

Lancaster
    That villain Gaveston is made an Earl.

Mortimer Senior
    An Earl!

Warwick
    Ay, and besides, lord Chamberlain of the realm,
    And secretary too, and lord of man.

Mortimer Senior
    We may not, nor we will not suffer this.   15

Mortimer Junior
    Why post[2] we not from hence to levy men?

Lancaster
    "My lord of Cornwall" now at every word,
    And happy is the man whom he vouchsafes
    For vailing[3] of his bonnet[4] one good look.
    Thus, arm in arm, the king and he doth march;   20
    Nay more, the guard upon his lordship waits,
    And all the court begins to flatter him.

Warwick
    Thus leaning on the shoulder of the king,
    He nods, and scorns, and smiles at those that pass.

Mortimer Senior
    Doth no man take exceptions at the slave?   25

Lancaster
    All stomach[5] him, but none dare speak a word.

---

1 Why.
2 Ride, go quickly.
3 Lowering.
4 Hat.
5 Resent. That Marlowe is using the word in this sense, contrary to its modern usage, is confirmed by the word's use in 6.257: "I know, my lord, many will stomach me, / But I respect neither their love nor hate" (6.257-58), Gaveston states after Edward announces that he has arranged Gaveston's highly favourable marriage to the deceased Earl of Gloucester's daughter.

Mortimer Junior
Ah, that bewrays[1] their baseness, Lancaster.
Were all the Earls and Barons of my mind,
We'll hale[2] him from the bosom of the king
And at the court gate hang the peasant up,   30
Who, swollen with venom of ambitious pride
Will be the ruin of the realm and us.[3]

Enter the Bishop of Canterbury[4] [with messenger]

Warwick
Here comes my lord of Canterbury's grace.

Lancaster
His countenance bewrays he is displeased.

Bishop of Canterbury
First were his sacred garments rent and torn,   35
Then laid they violent hands upon him next,
Himself imprisoned and his goods asseized:[5]
This certify the Pope.[6] Away, take horse.

[Exit messenger]

Lancaster
My lord, will you take arms against the king?

Bishop of Canterbury
What need I? God Himself is up in arms   40
When violence is offered to the Church.

Mortimer Junior
Then will you join with us that be his peers
To banish or behead that Gaveston?

---

1 Betrays, reveals.
2 Drag.
3 See Appendix A1(b) for Holinshed's account of the barons's reaction to
   Gaveston's pride.
4 The Archbishop of Canterbury was the highest-ranking clergyman in
   the English church.
5 Confiscated.
6 Inform the pope of this.

Bishop of Canterbury
What else, my lords, for it concerns me near:
The Bishopric of Coventry is his.   45

Enter the Queen [Isabella]

Mortimer Junior
Madam, whither walks your majesty so fast?

Isabella
Unto the forest, gentle Mortimer,
To live in grief and baleful¹ discontent,
For now my lord the king regards me not
But dotes upon the love of Gaveston.   50
He claps his cheeks and hangs about his neck,
Smiles in his face and whispers in his ears,
And when I come he frowns, as who should say,
"Go whither thou wilt seeing I have Gaveston."

Mortimer Senior
Is it not strange that he is thus bewitched?   55

Mortimer Junior
Madam, return unto the court again.
That sly inveigling² Frenchman we'll exile
Or lose our lives; and yet, ere that day come,
The king shall lose his crown, for we have power,
And courage too, to be revenged at full.   60

Bishop of Canterbury
But yet lift not your swords against the king.

Lancaster
No, but we'll lift Gaveston from hence.

Warwick
And war must be the means, or he'll stay still.

Isabella
Then let him stay, for rather than my lord
Shall be oppressed by civil mutinies,   65
I will endure a melancholy life
And let him frolic with his minion.

---

1 Miserable, sorrowful.
2 Seducing.

Bishop of Canterbury
    My lords, to ease all this, but hear me speak:
    We and the rest that are his counsellors
    Will meet and with a general consent   70
    Confirm his banishment with our hands and seals.

Lancaster
    What we confirm the king will frustrate.

Mortimer Junior
    Then may we lawfully revolt from him.

Warwick
    But say, my lord, where shall this meeting be?

Bishop of Canterbury
    At the New Temple.[1]   75

Mortimer Junior
    Content.

[Bishop of Canterbury][2]
    And in the meantime I'll entreat[3] you all
    To cross to Lambeth[4] and there stay with me.

Lancaster
    Come then, let's away.

Mortimer Junior
    Madam, farewell.   80

Isabella
    Farewell, sweet Mortimer, and for my sake
    Forbear[5] to levy arms against the king.

Mortimer Junior
    Ay, if words will serve; if not, I must.

[Exit all]

---

1   Quarters of the Knights Templar before Edward arrested them at the
    pope's urging in 1308. The Knights Templar were an international
    military organization affiliated with the Church and dedicated to the
    Crusades.
2   Speech prefix omitted in Q.
3   Ask, request, plead.
4   Lambeth Palace is the Archbishop of Canterbury's residence.
5   Abstain, refrain.

[Scene 3]

Enter Gaveston and the earl of Kent

Gaveston
    Edmund, the mighty prince of Lancaster,
    That hath more earldoms than an ass can bear,
    And both the Mortimers, two goodly men,
    With Guy of Warwick, that redoubted[1] knight,
    Are gone towards Lambeth; there let them remain.   5

Exit Gaveston and Kent

[Scene 4]

Enter Barons [Lancaster, Bishop of Canterbury, Warwick, Mortimer Junior, Mortimer Senior, and Pembroke]

Lancaster
    Here is the form of Gaveston's exile.
    May it please your lordship to subscribe[2] your name.

Bishop
    Give me the paper.

Lancaster
    Quick, quick, my lord! I long to write my name.[3]

Warwick
    But I long more to see him banished hence.   5

Mortimer Junior
    The name of Mortimer shall fright the king,
    Unless he be declined[4] from that base peasant.

Enter the King and Gaveston [and Kent]. Edward ascends the throne and seats Gaveston beside him.[5]

---

1 Respected, feared.
2 Write, sign.
3 "Quick, quick, my lord! / I long to write my name" in Q.
4 Separated, turned away.
5 Marlowe may have drawn his inspiration from accounts of the banquet following Edward and Isabella's coronation (25 February 1308), in which Edward is said to have preferred Gaveston's to Isabella's couch and consequently enraged Isabella's royal French relations (Haines 55).

Edward
What, are you moved that Gaveston sits here?
It is our pleasure, we will have it so.

Lancaster
Your grace doth well to place him by your side,   10
For nowhere else the new earl is so safe.

Mortimer Senior
What man of noble birth can brook this sight?
Quam male conveniunt![1]
See what a scornful look the peasant casts.

Pembroke
Can kingly lions fawn on creeping ants?

Warwick
Ignoble vassal,[2] that like Phaëthon[3]   15
Aspir'st unto the guidance of the sun.

Mortimer Junior
Their downfall is at hand, their forces down;
We will not thus be faced[4] and overpeered.

Edward
Lay hands on that traitor Mortimer!

Mortimer Senior
Lay hands on that traitor Gaveston!   20

Kent
Is this the duty that you owe your king?

Warwick
We know our duties, let him know his peers.

Edward
Whither will you bear him? Stay or ye shall die.

Mortimer Senior
We are no traitors, therefore threaten not.

---

1 "How badly they agree!" (Latin).
2 Servant, subordinate, slave.
3 When the sun god Apollo granted his son Phaëton his wish to drive the
   god's chariot through the heavens, Phaëton lost control of the horses
   and would have engulfed the earth in flames had Zeus not killed him
   with a lightning bolt.
4 Openly or impudently confronted.

Gaveston
    No, threaten not, my lord, but pay them home.   25
    Were I a king—

Mortimer Junior
    Thou villain, wherefore talks thou of a king,
    That hardly art a gentleman by birth?

Edward
    Were he a peasant, being my minion,
    I'll make the proudest of you stoop to him.   30

Lancaster
    My lord, you may not thus disparage[1] us.
    Away, I say, with hateful Gaveston.

Mortimer Senior
    And with the earl of Kent that favours him.

[Gaveston and Kent exit under guard]

Edward
    Nay, then lay violent hands upon your king.
    Here, Mortimer, sit thou in Edward's throne;   35
    Warwick and Lancaster, wear you my crown.
    Was ever king thus overruled as I?

Lancaster
    Learn then to rule us better and the realm.

Mortimer Junior
    What we have done, our heart-blood shall maintain.

Warwick
    Think you that we can brook this upstart pride?   40

Edward
    Anger and wrathful fury stops my speech.

Bishop of Canterbury
    Why are you moved? Be patient, my lord,
    And see what we your counsellors have done.

Mortimer Junior
    My lords, now let us all be resolute
    And either have our wills or lose our lives.   45

---

1 Dishonour.

Edward
Meet you for this, proud overdaring peers?
Ere my sweet Gaveston shall part from me,
This isle shall fleet[1] upon the ocean
And wander to the unfrequented Inde.[2]   50

Bishop of Canterbury
You know that I am legate[3] to the Pope.
On your allegiance to the see of Rome,
Subscribe as we have done to his exile.[4]

Mortimer Junior
Curse[5] him if he refuse, and then may we
Depose him and elect another king.[6]   55

Edward
Ay, there it goes, but yet I will not yield.
Curse me, depose me, do the worst you can.

Lancaster
Then linger not, my lord, but do it straight.

Bishop of Canterbury
Remember how the Bishop was abused.
Either banish him that was the cause thereof,   60
Or I will presently discharge these lords
Of duty and allegiance due to thee.

Edward
[Aside] It boots[7] me not to threat, I must speak fair.
[To the barons] The Legate of the Pope will be obeyed.

---

1 Float.
2 India.
3 Representative, deputy.
4 According to the Church, the English and other monarchs received their
crowns from the pope and owed him their allegiance.
5 Excommunicate.
6 By excommunicating a monarch, the Pope freed the monarch's subjects
from their allegiance to him or her. The monarch's authority was thus
rendered illegitimate or tyrannous, and the monarch's subjects were
within their rights to assassinate or otherwise depose him or her. Queen
Elizabeth, whom the Pope considered to be heretic and whose position
as governor of the English Church he did not recognize as legitimate,
was excommunicated in 1570.
7 Benefits.

[To Canterbury] My lord, you shall be Chancellor of
   the realm,   65
Thou, Lancaster, high admiral of our fleet,
Young Mortimer and his uncle shall be earls,
And you, Lord Warwick, president of the North,
[To Pembroke] And thou of Wales. If this content you
   not,
Make several kingdoms of this monarchy   70
And share it equally amongst you all,
So I may have some nook or corner left
To frolic with my dearest Gaveston.

Bishop of Canterbury
Nothing shall alter us, we are resolved.

Lancaster
Come, come, subscribe.   75

Mortimer Junior
Why should you love him, whom the world hates so?

Edward
Because he loves me more than all the world.
Ah, none but rude and savage-minded men
Would seek the ruin of my Gaveston;
You that be noble born should pity him.   80

Warwick
You that are princely born should shake him off.
For shame subscribe and let the lown[1] depart.

Mortimer Senior
Urge him, my lord.

Bishop of Canterbury
Are you content to banish him the realm?

Edward
I see I must and therefore am content;   85
Instead of ink, I'll write it with my tears.

Mortimer Junior
The king is lovesick for his minion.

Edward
'Tis done, and now accursèd hand fall off.

---

1 Peasant.

Lancaster
Give it me, I'll have it published in the streets.

Mortimer Junior
I'll see him presently dispatched away.   90

Bishop of Canterbury
Now is my heart at ease.

Warwick
                            And so is mine.

Pembroke
This will be good news to the common sort.

Mortimer Senior
Be it or no, he shall not linger here.

Exit the Barons and Canterbury

Edward
How fast they run to banish him I love;
·   They would not stir were it to do me good.   95
Why should a king be subject to a priest?
Proud Rome, that hatchest such imperial grooms,
For these thy superstitious taper-lights,[1]
Wherewith thy antichristian churches blaze,
I'll fire thy crazèd[2] buildings and enforce   100
The papal towers to kiss the lowly ground,
With slaughtered priests make[3] Tiber's[4] channel swell,
And banks raised higher with their sepulchres.
As for the peers that back the clergy thus,
If I be king not one of them shall live.   105

Enter Gaveston

Gaveston
My lord, I hear it whispered everywhere
That I am banished and must fly the land.

---

1   Candles.
2   Cracked, flawed.
3   May in Q.
4   River flowing through Rome.

Edward
'Tis true, sweet Gaveston—O, were it false!
The Legate of the Pope will have it so,
And thou must hence, or I shall be deposed.　　　110
But I will reign to be revenged of them,
And therefore, sweet friend, take it patiently.
Live where thou wilt, I'll send thee gold enough,
And long thou shalt not stay, or if thou dost,
I'll come to thee; my love shall ne'er decline.　　　115

Gaveston
Is all my hope turned to this hell of grief?

Edward
Rend not my heart with thy too-piercing words.
Thou from this land, I from myself am banished.

Gaveston
To go from hence grieves not poor Gaveston,
But to forsake you, in whose gracious looks　　　120
The blessedness of Gaveston remains,
For nowhere else seeks he felicity.

Edward
And only this torments my wretched soul,
That whether I will or no thou must depart.
Be governor of Ireland[1] in my stead　　　125
And there abide till fortune call thee home.
Here, take my picture, and let me wear thine.
O, might I keep thee here as I do this,
Happy were I, but now most miserable.

Gaveston
'Tis something to be pitied of a king.　　　130

Edward
Thou shalt not hence. I'll hide thee, Gaveston.

Gaveston
I shall be found, and then 'twill grieve me more.

Edward
Kind words and mutual talk makes our grief greater.
Therefore with dumb[2] embracement let us part—
Stay, Gaveston, I cannot leave thee thus.　　　135

1　Gaveston was Governor of Ireland from 1308 to 1309.
2　Silent.

Gaveston
> For every look, my lord, drops down a tear;
> Seeing I must go, do not renew my sorrow.

Edward
> The time is little that thou hast to stay,
> And therefore give me leave to look my fill.
> But come, sweet friend, I'll bear thee on thy way.   140

Gaveston
> The peers will frown.

Edward
> I pass[1] not for their anger. Come, let's go.
> O, that we might as well return as go.

Enter Kent and Queen Isabella

Isabella
> Whither goes my lord?

Edward
> Fawn not on me, French strumpet;[2] get thee gone.   145

Isabella
> On whom but on my husband should I fawn?

Gaveston
> On Mortimer, with whom, ungentle Queen—
> I say no more; judge you the rest, my lord.

Isabella
> In saying this, thou wrongst me, Gaveston.
> Is't not enough that thou corrupts my lord   150
> And art a bawd[3] to his affections,
> But thou must call mine honour thus in question?

Gaveston
> I mean not so; your grace must pardon me.

Edward
> Thou art too familiar with that Mortimer,
> And by thy means is Gaveston exiled;   155

---

1 Care.
2 Whore.
3 Pimp, procurer.

But I would wish thee reconcile the lords,
Or thou shalt ne'er be reconciled to me.

Isabella
Your highness knows it lies not in my power.

Edward
Away then, touch me not. Come, Gaveston.

Isabella
Villain, 'tis thou that robb'st me of my lord.   160

Gaveston
Madam, 'tis you that rob me of my lord.

Edward
Speak not unto her, let her droop and pine.[1]

Isabella
Wherein, my lord, have I deserved these words?
Witness the tears that Isabella sheds,
Witness this heart, that sighing for thee breaks,   165
How dear my lord is to poor Isabel.

Edward
And witness heaven how dear thou art to me.
There weep, for till my Gaveston be repealed,
Assure thyself thou com'st not in my sight.

Exit Edward, Gaveston, [and Kent]

Isabella
O miserable and distressèd Queen!   170
Would when I left sweet France and was embarked,
That charming Circe,[2] walking on the waves,
Had changed my shape, or at the marriage day[3]
The cup of Hymen[4] had been full of poison,
Or with those arms that twined about my neck   175
I had been stifled and not lived to see

---

1 Waste away, languish.
2 Sorceress, a drink from whose magic cup transformed its drinker into a
   swine. Odysseus and his men land on her island and encounter her in
   Homer's *Odyssey*.
3 Edward and Isabella were married in Boulogne on 25 January 1308.
   Edward was 23, Isabella 12.
4 God of marriage in classical mythology.

The king my lord thus to abandon me.
Like frantic Juno[1] will I fill the earth
With ghastly murmur of my sighs and cries,
For never doted Jove on Ganymede[2]   180
So much as he on cursèd Gaveston.
But that will more exasperate his wrath.
I must entreat him, I must speak him fair
And be a means to call home Gaveston;
And yet he'll ever dote on Gaveston,   185
And so am I forever miserable.

Enter the Barons [Lancaster, Warwick, Pembroke, Mortimer
Junior, and Mortimer Senior] to the Queen [Isabella]

Lancaster
Look where the sister of the king of France[3]
Sits wringing of her hands and beats her breast.

Warwick
The king, I fear, hath ill entreated her.

Pembroke
Hard is the heart that injures such a saint.   190

Mortimer Junior
I know 'tis long of[4] Gaveston she weeps.

Mortimer Senior
Why? He is gone.

Mortimer Junior
              Madam, how fares your grace?

---

1 Wife and sister of Jove in classical mythology.
2 Jove in the form of an eagle snatched the beautiful Trojan young man
   Ganymede and made him his cup-bearer, displacing Jove and Juno's
   daughter Hebe from this office. Juno resented the displacement and the
   attention Jove paid to Ganymede; this resentment fuelled her animus
   against the Trojans during the Trojan War. Marlowe provides a brilliantly
   parodic dramatization of Jove's doting on Ganymede at the opening of
   Dido, Queen of Carthage. In the early modern period, the name Ganymede
   was often used generically to denote male youths who were the objects of
   male sexual attention. See Barnfield's poem (Appendix D3), line 85.
3 Isabella (1295-1358) was the daughter of Philip IV (r. 1285-1314) and
   sister of the succeeding four French kings.
4 Because of.

Isabella

Ah, Mortimer! Now breaks the king's hate forth,
And he confesseth that he loves me not.

Mortimer Junior

Cry quittance, Madam, then, and love not him.   195

Isabella

No, rather will I die a thousand deaths.
And yet I love in vain: he'll ne'er love me.

Lancaster

Fear ye not, Madam. Now his minion's gone,
His wanton humour¹ will be quickly left.

Isabella

O never, Lancaster! I am enjoined   200
To sue unto you all for his repeal.
This wills my lord, and this must I perform
Or else be banished from his highness's presence.

Lancaster

For his repeal? Madam, he comes not back
Unless the sea cast up his shipwrack² body.   205

Warwick

And to behold so sweet a sight as that,
There's none here but would run his horse to death.

Mortimer Junior

But, madam, would you have us call him home?

Isabella

Ay, Mortimer, for till he be restored
The angry king hath banished me the court.   210
And therefore as thou lovest and tend'rest³ me,
Be thou my advocate unto these peers.

Mortimer Junior

What, would ye have me plead for Gaveston?

---

1 Temperament, mood. Based on classical authorities such as Galen, early
   modern medical theory held that an individual's temperament was
   largely determined by the balance or imbalance of four body fluids or
   "humours": blood, phlegm, black bile, and yellow bile.
2 Shipwrecked.
3 Care for, hold dear.

Mortimer Senior
   Plead for him he that will, I am resolved.

Lancaster
   And so am I, my lord; dissuade the Queen.   215

Isabella
   O Lancaster, let him dissuade the king,
   For 'tis against my will he should return.

Warwick
   Then speak not for him, let the peasant go.

Isabella
   'Tis for myself I speak and not for him.

Pembroke
   No speaking will prevail, and therefore cease.   220

Mortimer Junior
   Fair Queen, forbear to angle for the fish
   Which, being caught, strikes him that takes it dead,
   I mean that vile torpedo,[1] Gaveston,
   That now, I hope, floats on the Irish seas.

Isabella
   Sweet Mortimer, sit down by me a while,   225
   And I will tell thee reasons of such weight
   As thou wilt soon subscribe to his repeal.

Mortimer Junior
   It is impossible, but speak your mind.

Isabella
   Then thus, but none shall hear it but ourselves.

[Isabella and Mortimer Junior withdraw to talk]

Lancaster
   My Lords, albeit the Queen win Mortimer,   230
   Will you be resolute and hold with me?

Mortimer Senior
   Not I against my nephew.

Pembroke
   Fear not, the queen's words cannot alter him.

---

1 Electric ray.

Warwick
No? Do but mark how earnestly she pleads.

Lancaster
And see how coldly his looks make denial.   235

Warwick
She smiles. Now, for my life, his mind is changed.

Lancaster
I'll rather lose his friendship, I, than grant.

[Isabella and Mortimer Junior rejoin the rest]

Mortimer Junior
Well, of necessity it must be so.
My Lords, that I abhor base Gaveston
I hope your honours make no question,   240
And therefore, though I plead for his repeal,
'Tis not for his sake but for our avail[1]—
Nay, for the realm's behoof[2] and for the king's.

Lancaster
Fie, Mortimer, dishonour not thyself!
Can this be true 'twas good to banish him,   245
And is this true to call him home again?
Such reasons make white black and dark night day.

Mortimer Junior
My Lord of Lancaster, mark the respect.

Lancaster
In no respect can contraries be true.

Isabella
Yet, good my lord, hear what he can allege.   250

Warwick
All that he speaks is nothing. We are resolved.

Mortimer Junior
Do you not wish that Gaveston were dead?

Pembroke
I would he were.

Mortimer Junior
Why then, my lord, give me but leave to speak.

---

1 Aid, benefit.
2 Benefit, advantage.

Mortimer Senior
But, nephew, do not play the sophister.[1]   255

Mortimer Junior
This which I urge is of a burning zeal
To mend the king and do our country good.
Know you not Gaveston hath store of gold,
Which may in Ireland purchase him such friends
As he will front[2] the mightiest of us all?   260
And whereas[3] he shall live and be beloved,
'Tis hard for us to work his overthrow.

Warwick
Mark you but that, my lord of Lancaster.

Mortimer Junior
But were he here, detested as he is,
How easily might some base slave be suborned[4]   265
To greet his lordship with a poniard,[5]
And none so much as blame the murderer
But rather praise him for that brave attempt,
And in the chronicle[6] enrol his name
For purging of the realm of such a plague.   270

Pembroke
He saith true.

Lancaster
Ay, but how chance this was not done before?

Mortimer Junior
Because, my lords, it was not thought upon.
Nay more, when he shall know it lies in us
To banish him and then to call him home,   275
'Twill make him vail the topflag[7] of his pride
And fear to offend the meanest nobleman.

---

1 Sophist, one who employs clever but false reasoning for dubious purposes.
2 Face, oppose.
3 While.
4 Bribed, corrupted.
5 Dagger.
6 Historical record.
7 Flag at the top of a ship's mast, flying the ship's colours and lowered in a sign of deference.

Mortimer Senior
But how if he do not, nephew?

Mortimer Junior
Then may we with some colour[1] rise in arms,
For howsoever we have borne it out,   280
'Tis treason to be up against the king.
So shall we have the people of our side,
Which for his father's sake lean to the king
But cannot brook a night-grown mushrump,[2]
Such a one as my Lord of Cornwall is,   285
Should bear us down of the nobility.
And when the commons[3] and the nobles join,
'Tis not the king can buckler[4] Gaveston;
We'll pull him from the strongest hold[5] he hath.
My lords, if to perform this I be slack,   290
Think me as base a groom as Gaveston.

Lancaster
On that condition Lancaster will grant.

Pembroke
And so will Pembroke.[6]

Warwick
                              And I.

Mortimer Senior
                              And I.

Mortimer Junior
In this I count me highly gratified,
And Mortimer will rest at your command.   295

Isabella
And when this favour Isabel forgets,
Then let her live abandoned and forlorn.
But see, in happy time my lord the king,
Having brought the Earl of Cornwall on his way,
Is new returned. This news will glad him much,   300

---

1 Reason, semblance of legitimacy.
2 Mushroom.
3 Common people.
4 Shield.
5 Castle, fortification.
6 The line is attributed to Warwick in Q.

Yet not so much as me. I love him more
Than he can Gaveston; would he loved me
But half so much, then were I treble blessed.

Enter King Edward mourning [with Beaumont, the Clerk of the
Crown, and attendants]

Edward

He's gone, and for his absence thus I mourn.
Did never sorrow go so near my heart   305
As doth the want[1] of my sweet Gaveston;
And could my crown's revenue bring him back,
I would freely give it to his enemies
And think I gained, having bought so dear a friend.

Isabella

Hark how he harps upon his minion.   310

Edward

My heart is as an anvil unto sorrow,
Which beats upon it like the Cyclops's[2] hammers,
And with the noise turns up my giddy brain,
And makes me frantic for my Gaveston.
Ah, had some bloodless Fury[3] rose from hell   315
And with my kingly sceptre struck me dead,
When I was forced to leave my Gaveston!

Lancaster

Diablo![4] What passions call you these?

Isabella

My gracious lord, I come to bring you news.

Edward

That you have parlied with your Mortimer.   320

Isabella

That Gaveston, my Lord, shall be repealed.

---

1   Lack, absence.
2   In classical mythology, the Cyclops were one-eyed creatures who made
    armour for heroes as the assistants of Vulcan, the god of fire and metal-
    working.
3   A goddess of vengeance in classical mythology, which names three
    Furies: Tisiphone, Megæra, and Alecto.
4   "The Devil!" (Spanish).

Edward
Repealed? The news is too sweet to be true.

Isabella
But will you love me if you find it so?

Edward
If it be so, what will not Edward do?

Isabella
For Gaveston, but not for Isabel.   325

Edward
For thee, fair Queen, if thou lov'st Gaveston.
I'll hang a golden tongue about thy neck,
Seeing thou hast pleaded with so good success.

[Edward embraces Isabella]

Isabella
No other jewels hang about my neck
Than these, my lord, nor let me have more wealth   330
Than I may fetch from this rich treasury.

[Edward kisses Isabella]

O, how a kiss revives poor Isabel!

Edward
Once more receive my hand, and let this be
A second marriage 'twixt thyself and me.

Isabella
And may it prove more happy than the first.   335
My gentle lord, bespeak these nobles fair
That wait attendance for a gracious look
And on their knees salute your majesty.

[The barons kneel]

Edward
Courageous Lancaster, embrace thy king,
And as gross[1] vapours perish by the sun,   340

---

1 Thick, heavy.

Even so let hatred with thy sovereign's smile.
Live thou with me as my companion.

Lancaster
This salutation overjoys my heart.

Edward
Warwick shall be my chiefest counsellor;
These silver hairs will more adorn my court   345
Than gaudy[1] silks or rich embroidery.
Chide me, sweet Warwick, if I go astray.

Warwick
Slay me, my lord, when I offend your grace.

Edward
In solemn triumphs[2] and in public shows
Pembroke shall bear the sword before the king.   350

Pembroke
And with this sword Pembroke will fight for you.

Edward
But wherefore walks young Mortimer aside?
Be thou commander of our royal fleet,
Or if that lofty office like thee not,
I make thee here lord Marshal[3] of the realm.   355

Mortimer Junior
My lord, I'll marshal so your enemies
As England shall be quiet and you safe.

Edward
And as for you, lord Mortimer of Chirke,
Whose great achievements in our foreign war[4]
Deserves no common place nor mean reward,   360
Be you the general of the levied troops
That now are ready to assail the Scots.

Mortimer Senior
In this your grace hath highly honoured me,
For with my nature war doth best agree.

---

1 Ornate, bright, colourful.
2 Tournaments, pageants.
3 Chief military officer, in charge of military justice and heraldry.
4 Against the Scots.

Isabella

Now is the king of England rich and strong,   365
Having the love of his renownèd[1] peers.

Edward

Ay, Isabel, ne'er was my heart so light.
Clerk of the Crown, direct our warrant forth
For Gaveston to Ireland. Beaumont, fly
As fast as Iris or Jove's Mercury.[2]   370

Beaumont

It shall be done, my gracious Lord.

[Exit the Clerk of the Crown and Beaumont]

Edward

Lord Mortimer, we leave you to your charge.[3]
Now let us in and feast it royally.
Against our friend the earl of Cornwall comes,
We'll have a general tilt[4] and tournament,   375
And then his marriage shall be solemnized,
For wot[5] you not that I have made him sure
Unto our cousin, the earl of Gloucester's heir?[6]

Lancaster

Such news we hear, my lord.

Edward

That day, if not for him yet for my sake,   380
Who in the triumph will be challenger,[7]
Spare for no cost; we will requite[8] your love.

---

1 Illustrious, famous.
2 Messenger gods of Juno and Jove respectively.
3 Commission, orders, assignment.
4 Joust, tournament.
5 Know.
6 Margaret de Clare, daughter of Gilbert de Clare, third Earl of Gloucester, and Joan of Acre, Edward II's sister. Gaveston and Margaret were
   married 1 November 1307 (Haines 52), before Edward and Isabella, but
   Marlowe here seems to have followed Stow, who places the marriage
   immediately after Gaveston's return from Ireland.
7 The knight who issued a general challenge to all the other knights competing in the tournament.
8 Repay.

Warwick
In this, or aught,[1] your highness shall command us.

Edward
Thanks, gentle Warwick. Come, let's in and revel.

Exit all but the Mortimers

Mortimer Senior
Nephew, I must to Scotland; thou stayest here.   385
Leave now to oppose thyself against the king.
Thou seest by nature he is mild and calm,
And seeing his mind so dotes on Gaveston,
Let him without controlment have his will.
The mightiest kings have had their minions: 390
Great Alexander loved Hephæstion,[2]
The conquering Hercules[3] for Hylas wept,[4]
And for Patroclus stern Achilles drooped.[5]
And not kings only but the wisest men:
The Roman Tully[6] loved Octavius;[7]   395

---

1 Anything.
2 The Macedonian Alexander the Great (356-23 BCE) established
   through conquest an empire stretching as far as India. Hephæstion,
   Alexander's friend, died in 325 BCE.
3 Hector in Q.
4 See note to 1.142.
5 Patroclus was the male companion of Achilles, the Greek hero of the
   Trojan War. When Hector killed Patroclus on the battlefield, however,
   Achilles responded not so much by drooping but by seeking and ultimately obtaining revenge by killing Hector. Along with the other figures
   he mentions in this speech, Mortimer Senior presents the friendship
   between Achilles and Patroclus as a model of noble male friendship, but
   for a different perspective see Shakespeare's *Troilus and Cressida*.
6 Marcus Tullius Cicero (106-43 BCE), a Roman orator whose treatises,
   orations, and epistles were considered exemplary by Renaissance
   humanists. In line 141 of the opening scene, the play echoes Cicero's
   treatise on friendship, *De amicitia*. In 43 BCE the Roman Empire's three
   rulers or triumvirs drew up a list of people to be executed. Cicero's
   name was on the list, and he was hunted down and executed.
7 Best known as the Emperor Augustus, Octavius (63 BCE-14 CE) was a
   member of the triumvirate that condemned Cicero to be executed.

Grave Socrates, wild Alcibiades.[1]
Then let his grace, whose youth is flexible
And promiseth as much as we can wish,
Freely enjoy that vain light-headed earl,
For riper years will wean him from such toys.   400

Mortimer Junior
Uncle, his wanton humour grieves not me,
But this I scorn, that one so basely born
Should by his sovereign's favour grow so pert[2]
And riot it with the treasure of the realm
While soldiers mutiny for want of pay.   405
He wears a lord's revenue on his back,
And Midas-like[3] he jets it in the court
With base outlandish[4] cullions[5] at his heels,
Whose proud fantastic liveries[6] make such show
As if that Proteus,[7] god of shapes, appeared.   410
I have not seen a dapper jack so brisk.
He wears a short Italian hooded cloak
Larded with pearl, and in his Tuscan[8] cap
A jewel of more value than the crown.
Whiles other walk below, the king and he   415
From out a window laugh at such as we
And flout our train[9] and jest at our attire.
Uncle, 'tis this that makes me impatient.

Mortimer Senior
But, nephew, now you see the king is changed.

---

1 As friends and lovers, Socrates (469-399 BCE) and Alcibiades (450-404
   BCE) might have seemed mismatched: the older, ugly philosopher and
   the younger, handsome nobleman. Plato has Alcibiades himself
   comment on the apparent incongruity when Alcibiades crashes the
   banquet at the end of the *Symposium* and delivers a eulogy on Socrates.
2 Impertinent.
3 Midas, a king famous for his wealth, was granted his foolish wish that all
   he touch turn into gold.
4 Extravagant, unfamiliar, foreign.
5 Rascals, knaves.
6 Uniform identifying the wearer as household servant of a particular aristocrat.
7 Shape-changing sea-god in classical mythology.
8 Tuscany is a region of Italy.
9 Retinue.

Mortimer Junior
    Then so am I, and live to do him service;   420
    But whiles I have a sword, a hand, a heart,
    I will not yield to any such upstart.
    You know my mind. Come, uncle, let's away.

Exit [the Mortimers]

[Scene 5]

Enter Spencer [Junior] and Baldock

Baldock
    Spencer,
    Seeing that our Lord th' earl of Gloucester's dead,
    Which of the nobles dost thou mean to serve?

Spencer Junior
    Not Mortimer, nor any of his side,
    Because the king and he are enemies.   5
    Baldock, learn this of me: a factious[1] lord
    Shall hardly do himself good, much less us;
    But he that hath the favour of a king
    May with one word advance us while we live.
    The liberal earl of Cornwall is the man   10
    On whose good fortune Spencer's hope depends.

Baldock
    What, mean you then to be his follower?

Spencer Junior
    No, his companion, for he loves me well
    And would have once preferred[2] me to the king.

Baldock
    But he is banished, there's small hope of him.   15

Spencer Junior
    Ay, for a while. But, Baldock, mark the end:
    A friend of mine told me in secrecy
    That he's repealed and sent for back again;

---

1 Divisive, seditious.
2 Recommended.

And even now a post came from the court
With letters to our lady from the King,   20
And as she read, she smiled, which makes me think
It is about her lover Gaveston.

Baldock

'Tis like enough, for since he was exiled,
She neither walks abroad nor comes in sight.
But I had thought the match had been broke off   25
And that his banishment had changed her mind.

Spencer Junior

Our Lady's first love is not wavering;
My life for thine she will have Gaveston.

Baldock

Then hope I by her means to be preferred,
Having read unto her since she was a child.   30

Spencer Junior

Then, Baldock, you must cast the scholar off
And learn to court it like a gentleman.
'Tis not a black coat and a little band,
A velvet-caped cloak, faced before with serge,[1]
And smelling to a nosegay[2] all the day,   35
Or holding of a napkin in your hand,
Or saying a long grace at a table's end,
Or making low legs to a noble man,
Or looking downward, with your eyelids close,
And saying, "Truly an't may please your honour,"   40
Can get you any favour with great men.
You must be proud, bold, pleasant, resolute,
And, now and then, stab as occasion serves.

Baldock

Spencer, thou knowest I hate such formal toys
And use them but of mere hypocrisy.   45
Mine old lord, whiles he lived, was so precise[3]
That he would take exceptions at my buttons,
And being like pins' heads, blame me for the bigness,
Which made me curate-like[4] in mine attire,

---

1 Durable woollen fabric.
2 Small bouquet of flowers.
3 Scrupulous.
4 Like a clergyman.

Though inwardly licentious enough 50
And apt for any kind of villainy.
I am none of these common pedants, I,
That cannot speak without *"propterea quod."*[1]

Spencer Junior
But one of those that saith *"quandoquidem"*[2]
And hath a special gift to form a verb.[3] 55

Baldock
Leave off this jesting, here my lady comes.

[Spencer Junior and Baldock withdraw]

Enter the Lady [Margaret de Clare, reading letters]

Lady Margaret
The grief for his exile was not so much
As is the joy of his returning home.
This letter came from my sweet Gaveston.
What needst thou, love, thus to excuse thyself? 60
I know thou couldst not come and visit me.
"I will not long be from thee, though I die":
This argues the entire love of my Lord;
"When I forsake thee, death seize on my heart."
But rest thee here where Gaveston shall sleep. 65
Now to the letter of my Lord the King.
He wills me to repair unto the court
And meet my Gaveston. Why do I stay,
Seeing that he talks thus of my marriage day?
Who's there? Baldock? 70

[Spencer Junior and Baldock step forward]

See that my coach be ready, I must hence.

Baldock
It shall be done, madam.

---

1 "Because of which" (Latin), a scholarly affectation when used in vernacular speech.
2 "Seeing that" (Latin), roughly synonymous with "propterea quod."
3 To form a verb is, in grammatical terms, to conjugate.

Lady Margaret
And meet me at the park pale[1] presently.

[Exit Baldock][2]

Spencer, stay you and bear me company,
For I have joyful news to tell thee of.   75
My lord of Cornwall is a-coming over
And will be at the court as soon as we.

Spencer Junior
I knew the King would have him home again.

Lady Margaret
If all things sort out, as I hope they will,
Thy service, Spencer, shall be thought upon.   80

Spencer Junior
I humbly thank your Ladyship.

Lady Margaret
Come, lead the way, I long till I am there.

[Exit Lady Margaret and Spencer Junior]

[Scene 6]

Enter Edward, the Queen [Isabella], Lancaster, Mortimer
[Junior], Warwick, Pembroke, Kent, and attendants

Edward
The wind is good. I wonder why he stays;
I fear me he is wracked[3] upon the sea.

Isabella
Look, Lancaster, how passionate he is,
And still his mind runs on his minion.

Lancaster
My Lord.   5

---

1 Fence, boundary.
2 Q places Baldock's exit immediately after Baldock's "It shall be done,
   madam."
3 Shipwrecked.

Edward
How now, what news? Is Gaveston arrived?

Mortimer Junior
Nothing but Gaveston! What means your grace?
You have matters of more weight to think upon:
The King of France sets foot in Normandy.[1]

Edward
A trifle, we'll expel him when we please.   10
But tell me, Mortimer, what's thy device[2]
Against the stately triumph we decreed?

Mortimer Junior
A homely one, my lord, not worth the telling.

Edward
Prithee[3] let me know it.

Mortimer Junior
But seeing you are so desirous, thus it is: 15
A lofty cedar tree fair flourishing,
On whose top-branches kingly eagles perch,
And by the bark a canker[4] creeps me up
And gets unto the highest bough of all.
The motto: *Æque tandem.*[5]   20

Edward
And what is yours, my lord of Lancaster?

Lancaster
My lord, mine's more obscure than Mortimer's.

---

1   Edward was also the Duke of Aquitaine (which included Gascony and
    Guienne) and as such owed homage to the French sovereign. Because of
    Edward's reluctance to perform homage to the French monarch in
    person, his French territories were throughout his reign threatened by
    French seizure. Edward was not, however, the Duke of Normandy:
    Henry III had renounced the English monarch's claim to the dukedom
    in 1259.
2   Emblematic figure often accompanied by an explanatory phrase or
    motto.
3   "I pray thee," please.
4   Caterpillar, which feeds on plant leaves before metamorphosing into a
    butterfly.
5   "Equal at last" (Latin).

Pliny[1] reports, there is a flying fish
Which all the other fishes deadly hate,
And therefore being pursued, it takes the air;   25
No sooner is it up, but there's a fowl
That seizeth it. This fish, my lord, I bear;
The motto this: *Undique mors est.*[2]

Edward
Proud Mortimer, ungentle Lancaster,
Is this the love you bear your sovereign?   30
Is this the fruit your reconcilement bears?
Can you in words make show of amity[3]
And in your shields display your rancorous[4] minds?
What call you this but private libelling
Against the Earl of Cornwall and my brother?   35

Isabella
Sweet husband, be content. They all love you.

Edward
They love me not that hate my Gaveston.
I am that cedar, shake me not too much;
And you the eagles, soar ye ne'er so high,
I have the jesses[5] that will pull you down;   40
And "*Æque tandem*" shall that canker cry
Unto the proudest peer of Brittany.[6]
Though thou compar'st him to a flying fish
And threat'nest death whether he rise or fall,

---

1 Pliny the Elder (23-79 CE), whose *Natural History* was treated by
   medieval and early modern readers and writers as a compendium of
   commonplaces about the natural world. Forker (1994) notes that the
   Natural History does not contain a description of flying fish and suggests
   that Marlowe may have garnered this bit of natural lore from contempo
   rary accounts of voyages to the Americas (190 n. 23). Bevington and
   Shapiro (1988) note that commentators on Alciati's emblem book,
   which contains Lancaster's emblem, attribute the natural lore to Pliny
   (270).
2 "Death is everywhere" (Latin).
3 Love, friendship.
4 Bitter, spiteful.
5 Short straps attached to the legs of a hawk, to which a falconer could
   attach a leash.
6 Britain.

'Tis not the hugest monster of the sea   45
Nor foulest harpy[1] that shall swallow him.

Mortimer Junior
If in his absence thus he favours him,
What shall he do whenas he shall be present?

Lancaster
That shall we see. Look where his lordship comes.

Enter Gaveston

Edward
My Gaveston!   50
Welcome to Tynemouth,[2] welcome to thy friend.
Thy absence made me droop and pine away,
For as the lovers of fair Danaë,[3]
When she was locked up in a brazen[4] tower,
Desired her more and waxed[5] outrageous,   55
So did it sure with me; and now thy sight
Is sweeter far than was thy parting hence
Bitter and irksome to my sobbing heart.

Gaveston
Sweet Lord and King, your speech preventeth mine,
Yet have I words left to express my joy: 60
The shepherd nipped with biting winter's rage
Frolics not more to see the painted spring
Than I do to behold your Majesty.

Edward
Will none of you salute my Gaveston?

Lancaster
Salute him? Yes, welcome, Lord Chamberlain.   65

---

1 In classical mythology, an obnoxious figure having the body of a woman
   and the wings of a bird. Harpies were often the agents of divine
   vengeance.
2 Located at the mouth of the River Tyne on the north-east coast of
   England.
3 Locked in a tower by her royal father because a prophecy declared she
   would have a son who would kill his grandfather, Danaë was impreg-
   nated by Jove, who entered the tower as a shower of gold.
4 Brass, bronze.
5 Grew.

Mortimer Junior
  Welcome is the good Earl of Cornwall.

Warwick
  Welcome, Lord governor of the Isle of Man.

Pembroke
  Welcome, master secretary.

Kent
  Brother, do you hear them?

Edward
  Still will these Earls and Barons use me thus?   70

Gaveston
  My Lord, I cannot brook these injuries.

Isabella
  [Aside] Ay me, poor soul, when these begin to jar.

Edward
  Return it to their throats, I'll be thy warrant.

Gaveston
  Base leaden Earls that glory in your birth,
  Go sit at home and eat your tenants' beef   75
  And come not here to scoff at Gaveston,
  Whose mounting thoughts did never creep so low
  As to bestow a look on such as you.

Lancaster
  Yet I disdain not to do this for you.

[Lancaster draws his sword]

Edward
  Treason, treason!

[Lancaster]
                    Where's the traitor?[1]

---

1 Q reads "Treason, treason: whers the traitor?" and attributes the line entirely
   to Edward. Given that Lancaster remains visible and entirely belligerent
   until Edward exits (i.e., he does not attempt to hide or flee), this attribution
   does not make complete sense. The compositor's error in the following line
   (see following note) suggests that a similar conflation of different speakers'
   lines has occurred here. The editor has conjecturally attributed "Where's the
   traitor?" to Lancaster as Lancaster's retort to Edward's accusation.

Pembroke
    [Gesturing to Gaveston]   Here, here.   80

Edward
    Convey hence Gaveston; they'll murder him.[1]

Gaveston
    [To Lancaster] The life of thee shall salve this foul disgrace.

Mortimer Junior
    Villain, thy life, unless I miss mine aim.

[Mortimer Junior stabs Gaveston]

Isabella
    Ah, furious Mortimer, what hast thou done?

Mortimer Junior
    No more than I would answer were he slain.   85

[Exit Gaveston and attendants]

Edward
    Yes, more than thou canst answer though he live.
    Dear shall you both aby[2] this riotous deed.
    Out of my presence, come not near the court!

Mortimer Junior
    I'll not be barred the court for Gaveston.

---

1   Q conflates this line, preceded by the speech prefix "King," with Pembroke's "Here, here." The line in Q reads "*Pen.* Heere here King: conuey
hence Gaueston, thaile murder him." The play's meter as well as the
sense indicates that this is an error by the compositor who set the type
for this page. The play is written primarily in iambic pentameter blank
verse, unrhymed lines of five units or feet of an unstressed syllable followed by a stressed syllable. Often one line of verse will carry over
several speakers, and Pembroke's "Here, here" clearly supplies the final,
fifth metrical foot to the line of verse begun by Edward and continued
by Lancaster. This indicates that "Convey hence Gaveston; they'll
murder him" should be a separate line; it is a complete and regular
iambic pentameter line if the preceding "King" is considered to be a
speech prefix rather than a part of the line itself.
2   Pay for.

Lancaster
We'll hale him by the ears unto the block.[1]   90

Edward
Look to your own heads, his is sure enough.

Warwick
Look to your own crown, if you back him thus.

Kent
Warwick, these words do ill beseem thy years.

Edward
Nay, all of them conspire to cross me thus;
But if I live, I'll tread upon their heads   95
That think with high looks thus to tread me down.
Come, Edmund, let's away and levy men.
'Tis war that must abate[2] these Barons' pride.

Exit the King [Edward] [with Isabella, and Kent]

Warwick
Let's to our castles, for the king is moved.

Mortimer Junior
Moved may he be and perish in his wrath.   100

Lancaster
Cousin, it is no dealing with him now.
He means to make us stoop by force of arms,
And therefore let us jointly here protest
To prosecute that Gaveston to the death.

Mortimer Junior
By heaven, the abject villain shall not live.   105

Warwick
I'll have his blood or die in seeking it.

Pembroke
The like oath Pembroke takes.

Lancaster
                                    And so doth Lancaster.

---

1 Executioner's chopping block.
2 Reduce, diminish.

Now send our heralds to defy the King
And make the people swear to pull him down.

Enter a post

Mortimer Junior
Letters—from whence? 110

Post
From Scotland, my lord.

Lancaster
Why how now, cousin, how fares all our friends?

Mortimer Junior
My uncle's taken prisoner by the Scots.

Lancaster
We'll have him ransomed, man. Be of good cheer.

Mortimer Junior
They rate his ransom at five thousand pound. 115
Who should defray the money but the King,
Seeing he is taken prisoner in his wars?
I'll to the King.

Lancaster
Do, cousin, and I'll bear thee company.

Warwick
Meantime my lord of Pembroke and myself 120
Will to Newcastle[1] here and gather head.

Mortimer Junior
About it then, and we will follow you.

Lancaster
Be resolute and full of secrecy.

Warwick
I warrant you.

Mortimer Junior
Cousin, and if he will not ransom him, 125
I'll thunder such a peal into his ears
As never subject did unto his King.

---

1 A city approximately 20 kilometres west of Tynemouth on the river
Tyne.

Lancaster
Content, I'll bear my part. Holla, who's there?

[Enter guard]

Mortimer Junior
Ay, marry, such a guard as this doth well.

Lancaster
Lead on the way.

Guard
                    Whither will your lordships?   130

Mortimer Junior
Whither else but to the King?

Guard
His highness is disposed to be alone.

Lancaster
Why, so he may, but we will speak to him.

Guard
You may not in, my lord.

Mortimer Junior
May we not?   135

[Enter Edward and Kent]

Edward
How now, what noise is this?
Who have we there? Is't you?

Mortimer Junior
Nay, stay my lord, I come to bring you news:
Mine uncle's taken prisoner by the Scots.

Edward
Then ransom him.   140

Lancaster
'Twas in your wars; you should ransom him.

Mortimer Junior
And you shall ransom him, or else.

Kent
What, Mortimer, you will not threaten him?

Edward
    Quiet yourself. You shall have the broad seal[1]
    To gather for him throughout the realm.   145

Lancaster
    Your minion Gaveston hath taught you this.

Mortimer Junior
    My lord, the family of the Mortimers
    Are not so poor but, would they sell their land,
    Would levy men enough to anger you.
    We never beg, but use such prayers as these.   150

[Mortimer Junior gestures at his sword]

Edward
    Shall I still be haunted thus?

Mortimer Junior
    Nay, now you are here alone, I'll speak my mind.

Lancaster
    And so will I, and then, my lord, farewell.

Mortimer Junior
    The idle triumphs, masques, lascivious[2] shows,
    And prodigal gifts bestowed on Gaveston   155
    Have drawn thy treasure dry[3] and made thee weak,
    The murmuring commons overstretchèd hath.

Lancaster
    Look for rebellion, look to be deposed.
    Thy garrisons are beaten out of France
    And, lame and poor, lie groaning at the gates;   160

---

1 A licence to collect alms or beg.
2 Sexually provocative, luxurious.
3 According to Holinshed, Gaveston "having the custody of the king's jewels and treasure, he took out of the jewel house a table and a pair of tressels of gold, which he delivered unto a merchant called Aymery de Friscobald, commanding him to convey them over the sea into Gascony. This table was judged of the common people to belong sometime unto King Arthur, and therefore men grudged the more that the same should thus be sent out of the realm" (320).

The wild O'Neill[1] with swarms of Irish kerns[2]
Live uncontrolled within the English Pale;[3]
Unto the walls of York the Scots made road
And unresisted drave away rich spoils.[4]

Mortimer Junior
The haughty Dane commands the narrow seas,   165
While in the harbour ride thy ships unrigged.

Lancaster
What foreign prince sends thee ambassadors?

Mortimer Junior
Who loves thee but a sort of flatterers?

Lancaster
Thy gentle Queen, sole sister to Valois,[5]
Complains that thou has left her all forlorn.   170

Mortimer Junior
Thy court is naked, being bereft of those
That makes a king seem glorious to the world,
I mean the peers, whom thou shouldst dearly love;
Libels are cast against thee in the street,
Ballads and rhymes made of thy overthrow.   175

Lancaster
The northern borderers,[6] seeing their[7] houses burnt,
Their wives and children slain, run up and down
Cursing the name of thee and Gaveston.

---

1 Edward II continued his father's project of conquering and "pacifying"
   Ireland. Irish resistance was led by prominent Irish nobility, including
   members of the O'Neill clan of Tir Eoghan (Tyrone). Irish resistance to
   English colonization was a major problem for Queen Elizabeth I during
   her reign, a problem exacerbated by Spanish support for the Catholic
   Irish. Hugh O'Neill, second Earl of Tyrone, led the Irish resistance in
   the last decades of the sixteenth century.
2 Irish foot-soldiers.
3 The area of English control in Ireland, centred on Dublin.
4 During Edward's reign the Scots frequently conducted border raids that
   pushed deep into northern England.
5 The French royal house.
6 English inhabitants of the area proximate to the border with Scotland.
7 The in Q; their in Q2-4.

Mortimer Junior

When wert thou in the field with banner spread?
But once, and then thy soldiers marched like
    players,[1]   180
With garish robes, not armour; and thyself,
Bedaubed with gold, rode laughing at the rest,
Nodding and shaking of thy spangled crest,
Where women's favours[2] hung like labels down.

Lancaster

And thereof came it that the fleering[3] Scots,   185
To England's high disgrace, have made this jig:
"Maids of England, sore may you mourn,
For your lemans[4] you have lost at Bannockburn.[5]
    With a heave and a ho!
What weeneth[6] the king of England   190
So soon to have won Scotland?
    With a rumbelow!"[7]

Mortimer Junior

Wigmore[8] shall fly to set my uncle free.

Lancaster

And when 'tis gone, our swords shall purchase more.
If ye be moved, revenge it as you can;   195
Look next to see us with our ensigns spread.

Exit Barons [Mortimer Junior and Lancaster]

---

1 Actors.
2 Items like handkerchiefs and gloves, given by ladies to knights as tokens of their favour.
3 Smirking, laughing scornfully.
4 Lovers.
5 Site of a crushing Scottish military victory over the English army led by Edward II in 1314. See Holinshed's description of the battle in Appendix A1(d).
6 Thinks.
7 Nonsense word used as the refrain in sailors' songs. Robert Fabyan records the song in his account of Bannockburn in *The Chronicle of Fabian whiche he Nameth the Concordaunce of Histories, Newly Perused. And Continued from the Beginnyng of Kyng Henry the Seuenth, to Thende of Queene Mary* (1559).
8 Mortimer Junior's estate.

Edward

My swelling heart for very anger breaks!
How oft have I been baited by these peers
And dare not be revenged, for their power is great?
Yet shall the crowing of these cockerels   200
Affright a lion? Edward, unfold thy paws
And let their lives' blood slake thy fury's hunger.
If I be cruel and grow tyrannous,
Now let them thank themselves and rue too late.

Kent

My lord, I see your love to Gaveston   205
Will be the ruin of the realm and you,
For now the wrathful nobles threaten wars;
And therefore, brother, banish him forever.

Edward

Art thou an enemy to my Gaveston?

Kent

Ay, and it grieves me that I favoured him.   210

Edward

Traitor, be gone! Whine thou with Mortimer.

Kent

So will I, rather than with Gaveston.

Edward

Out of my sight and trouble me no more.

Kent

No marvel though thou scorn thy noble peers
When I thy brother am rejected thus.   215

Edward

Away!

Exit [Kent]

Poor Gaveston, that hath no friend but me.[1]
Do what they can, we'll live in Tynemouth here;
And so I walk with him about the walls,
What care I though the Earls begirt[2] us round?   220

---

1 "Away! / Poor Gaveston ..." is one line in Q.
2 Encircle.

Here comes she that's cause of all these jars.

Enter the Queen [Isabella], three Ladies [Margaret de Clare
with two ladies in waiting], Baldock, and Spencer [Junior, and
Gaveston]

Isabella
My lord, 'tis thought the Earls are up in arms.

Edward
Ay, and 'tis likewise thought you favour him.

Isabella
Thus do you still suspect me without cause.

Lady Margaret
Sweet uncle, speak more kindly to the queen.   225

Gaveston
My lord, dissemble with her, speak her fair.

Edward
Pardon me, sweet, I forgot myself.

Isabella
Your pardon is quickly got of Isabel.

Edward
The younger Mortimer is grown so brave
That to my face he threatens civil wars.   230

Gaveston
Why do you not commit him to the Tower?

Edward
I dare not, for the people love him well.

Gaveston
Why then, we'll have him privily made away.

Edward
Would Lancaster and he had both caroused
A bowl of poison to each other's health.   235
But let them go, and tell me what are these?

Lady Margaret
Two of my father's servants whilst he lived;
May't please your grace to entertain them now.

Edward
Tell me, where wast thou born? What is thine arms?[1]

Baldock
My name is Baldock, and my gentry   240
I fetched from Oxford, not from heraldry.[2]

Edward
The fitter art thou, Baldock, for my turn.
Wait on me, and I'll see thou shalt not want.

Baldock
I humbly thank your majesty.

Edward
Knowest thou him, Gaveston?

Gaveston
                                   Ay, my lord.   245
His name is Spencer; he is well allied.[3]
For my sake let him wait upon your grace.
Scarce shall you find a man of more desert.[4]

Edward
Then, Spencer, wait upon me. For his sake
I'll grace thee with a higher style[5] ere long.   250

Spencer
No greater titles happen unto me
Than to be favoured of your majesty.

Edward
[To Lady Margaret] Cousin, this day shall be your
   marriage feast.
And, Gaveston, think that I love thee well
To wed thee to our niece, the only heir   255
Unto the Earl of Gloucester late deceased.

---

1 Heraldic insignia. "Tell me, where wast thou born? / What is thine
   arms?" in Q.
2 Baldock claims gentle status because of his university education, not his
   birth.
3 "Ay, my lord. / His name is Spencer ..." is one line in Q.
4 Merit, worth.
5 Title.

Gaveston
I know, my lord, many will stomach me,
But I respect neither their love nor hate.

Edward
The headstrong Barons shall not limit me:
He that I list[1] to favour shall be great.   260
Come, let's away, and when the marriage ends,
Have at the rebels and their complices.

Exit all

[Scene 7]

Enter Lancaster, Mortimer [Junior], Warwick, Pembroke, Kent

Kent
My lords, of love to this our native land
I come to join with you and leave the king,
And in your quarrel and the realm's behalf
Will be the first that shall adventure life.

Lancaster
I fear me you are sent of policy[2]   5
To undermine us with a show of love.

Warwick
He is your brother; therefore have we cause
To cast the worst and doubt of your revolt.

Kent
Mine honour shall be hostage of my truth;
If that will not suffice, farewell, my lords.   10

Mortimer Junior
Stay, Edmund. Never was Plantagenet[3]
False of his word, and therefore trust we thee.

Pembroke
But what's the reason you should leave him now?

---

1 Wish.
2 Political scheming. The word has Machiavellian connotations in the
   early modern period.
3 Family name of the English royal house.

Kent
    I have informed the Earl of Lancaster.

Lancaster
    And it sufficeth. Now, my lords, know this,   15
    That Gaveston is secretly arrived
    And here in Tynemouth frolics with the king.
    Let us with these our followers scale the walls
    And suddenly surprise them unawares.

Mortimer Junior
    I'll give the onset.

Warwick
               And I'll follow thee.   20

Mortimer Junior
    This tattered ensign of my ancestors,
    Which swept the desert shore of that Dead Sea[1]
    Whereof we got the name of Mortimer,[2]
    Will I advance upon this castle's[3] walls.
    Drums, strike alarum! Raise them from their sport   25
    And ring aloud the knell of Gaveston.

Lancaster
    None be so hardy[4] as to touch the King,
    But neither spare you Gaveston nor his friends.

Exit [all]

---

1 The Dead Sea, a salt lake situated between modern Israel and Jordan and in what used to be called the Holy Land, the geographical area in which Jesus Christ lived and died. In 1095 Western European leaders launched the first of a series of military expeditions or crusades whose ostensible purpose was to recover the Holy Land for Christendom.
2 Mortimer Junior's derivation of his family name from the Latin name for the Dead Sea (*Mortuum Mare*) is incorrect (Forker 1994 206 n. 23), but by linking his family with the crusades he is attempting to claim religious legitimacy for his rebellion against Edward.
3 These castle walls in Q.
4 Bold, rash.

[Scene 8]

Enter the king and Spencer [Junior]

Edward
O tell me, Spencer, where is Gaveston?

Spencer
I fear me he is slain, my gracious lord.

Edward
No, here he comes!

[Enter Gaveston, Lady Margaret, Isabella, and lords][1]

               Now let them spoil and kill.
Fly, fly, my lords, the earls have got the hold.
Take shipping and away to Scarborough;[2]   5
Spencer and I will post away by land.

Gaveston
O stay, my lord, they will not injure you.

Edward
I will not trust them, Gaveston. Away!

Gaveston
Farewell, my Lord.

Edward
Lady, farewell.   10

Lady Margaret
Farewell, sweet uncle, till we meet again.

Edward
Farewell, sweet Gaveston, and farewell, niece.

Isabella
No farewell to poor Isabel, thy Queen?

Edward
Yes, yes, for Mortimer your lover's sake.

---

1   Part of the opening stage directions in Q.
2   City on the north-east coast of England, south of Tynemouth.

Isabella
Heavens can witness I love none but you.   15

[Exit all except Isabella]

From my embracements thus he breaks away.
O that mine arms could close this isle about,
That I might pull him to me where I would,
Or that these tears that drizzle from mine eyes
Had power to mollify his stony heart,   20
That when I had him we might never part.

Enter the Barons [Lancaster, Mortimer Junior, and Warwick].
Alarums

Lancaster
I wonder how he 'scaped.

Mortimer Junior
                        Who's this, the Queen?

Isabella
Ay, Mortimer, the miserable Queen,
Whose pining heart her inward sighs have blasted,
And body with continual mourning wasted.   25
These hands are tired with haling[1] of my lord
From Gaveston, from wicked Gaveston,
And all in vain, for when I speak him fair
He turns away and smiles upon his minion.

Mortimer Junior
Cease to lament, and tell us where's the king?   30

Isabella
What would you with the king? Is't him you seek?

Lancaster
No, madam, but that cursèd Gaveston.
Far be it from the thought of Lancaster
To offer violence to his sovereign.
We would but rid the realm of Gaveston;   35
Tell us where he remains, and he shall die.

---

1 Pulling, tugging down.

Isabella
He's gone by water unto Scarborough.
Pursue him quickly and he cannot 'scape:
The king hath left him, and his train is small.

Warwick
Forslow[1] no time, sweet Lancaster, let's march.   40

Mortimer Junior
How comes it that the king and he is parted?

Isabella
That this your army going several ways
Might be of lesser force and with the power
That he intendeth presently to raise
Be easily suppressed; and therefore be gone.   45

Mortimer Junior
Here in the river rides a Flemish hoy.[2]
Let's all aboard and follow him amain.[3]

Lancaster
The wind that bears him hence will fill our sails.
Come, come aboard, 'tis but an hour's sailing.

[Exit Lancaster and Warwick]

Mortimer Junior
Madam, stay you within this castle here.   50

Isabella
No, Mortimer, I'll to my lord the king.

Mortimer Junior
Nay, rather sail with us to Scarborough.

Isabella
You know the king is so suspicious
As if he hear I have but talked with you,
Mine honour will be called in question;   55
And therefore, gentle Mortimer, be gone.

---

1 Waste.
2 Small boat.
3 At full speed, at once.

Mortimer Junior
Madam, I cannot stay to answer you,
But think of Mortimer as he deserves.

[Exit Mortimer Junior]

Isabella
So well hast thou deserved, sweet Mortimer,
As Isabel could live with thee forever.   60
In vain I look for love at Edward's hand,
Whose eyes are fixèd on none but Gaveston.
Yet once more I'll importune him with prayers;
If he be strange and not regard my words,
My son and I will over into France   65
And to the king my brother[1] there complain
How Gaveston hath robbed me of his love.
But yet I hope my sorrows will have end
And Gaveston this blessèd day be slain.

Exit [Isabella]

[Scene 9]

Enter Gaveston pursued

Yet, lusty lords, I have escaped your hands,
Your threats, your 'larums, and your hot pursuits;
And though divorcèd from king Edward's eyes,
Yet liveth Piers of Gaveston unsurprised,
Breathing in hope (*malgrado*[2] all your beards   5
That muster rebels thus against your king)
To see his royal sovereign once again.

Enter the Barons [Warwick, Mortimer Junior, Lancaster, Pembroke, soldiers, James, horse-boy, and Pembroke's men]

Warwick
Upon him, soldiers! Take away his weapons.

---

1 At this point, Isabella's father, Philip IV, is still on the French throne.
2 "In spite of" (Italian).

Mortimer Junior
Thou proud disturber of thy country's peace,
Corrupter of thy king, cause of these broils,   10
Base flatterer, yield. And were it not for shame,
Shame and dishonour to a soldier's name,
Upon my weapon's point here shouldst thou fall
And welter in thy gore.

Lancaster
                              Monster of men,
That like the Greekish strumpet[1] trained[2] to arms   15
And bloody wars so many valiant knights,[3]
Look for no other fortune, wretch, than death.
King Edward is not here to buckler thee.

Warwick
Lancaster, why talkst thou to the slave?
Go, soldiers, take him hence, for by my sword   20
His head shall off. Gaveston, short warning
Shall serve thy turn: it is our country's cause[4]
That here severely we will execute
Upon thy person. Hang him at a bough.

Gaveston
My Lord!

Warwick
                       Soldiers, have him away.   25
But for[5] thou wert the favourite of a King,
Thou shalt have so much honour at our hands.[6]

[Warwick gestures to indicate beheading]

Gaveston
I thank you all, my lords. Then I perceive

---

1 Helen of Troy.
2 Dragged, drew, led.
3 "Monster of men, that like the Greekish strumpet / Trained to arms and
   bloody wars / So many valiant knights" in Q.
4 "Go, soldiers, take him hence, / For by my sword his head shall off. /
   Gaveston, short warning shall serve thy turn: / It is our country's cause"
   in Q.
5 Because.
6 Beheading rather than hanging.

That heading is one and hanging is the other,
And death is all.   30

Enter earl of Arundel

Lancaster
How now, my lord of Arundel?

Arundel
My lords, king Edward greets you all by me.

Warwick
Arundel, say your message.

Arundel
                                        His majesty,
Hearing that you had taken Gaveston,[1]
Entreateth you by me, yet but[2] he may   35
See him before he dies; for why[3] he says
And sends you word, he knows that die he shall,
And if you gratify his grace so far,
He will be mindful of the courtesy.

Warwick
How now?

Gaveston
                    Renownèd Edward, how thy name   40
Revives poor Gaveston.

Warwick
                              No, it needeth not.
Arundel, we will gratify the king
In other matters; he must pardon us in this.
Soldiers, away with him.

Gaveston
Why, my Lord of Warwick,   45
Will not these delays beget my hopes?
I know it, lords, it is this life you aim at;
Yet grant king Edward this.

---

1   "His majesty / Hearing ..." is one line in Q.
2   That yet.
3   For which reason.

Mortimer Junior

                      Shalt thou appoint
What we shall grant? Soldiers, away with him.[1]
Thus we'll gratify the king: 50
We'll send his head by thee; let him bestow
His tears on that, for that is all he gets
Of Gaveston, or else his senseless trunk.

Lancaster

    Not so, my Lord, lest he bestow more cost
    In burying him than he hath ever earned.   55

Arundel

    My lords, it is his majesty's request,
    And in the honour of a king he swears
    He will but talk with him and send him back.

Warwick

    When, can you tell? Arundel, no. We wot,
    He that the care of realm remits[2]   60
    And drives his nobles to these exigents[3]
    For Gaveston will, if he seize him once,
    Violate any promise to possess him.

Arundel

    Then if you will not trust his grace in keep,
    My lords, I will be pledge for his return.   65

Mortimer Junior

    It is honourable in thee to offer this;
    But for we know thou art a noble gentleman,
    We will not wrong thee so,
    To make away a true man for a thief.

Gaveston

    How meanst thou, Mortimer? That is over-base.   70

Mortimer Junior

    Away, base groom, robber of kings' renown.
    Question with thy companions and thy mates.

---

1 "Shalt thou appoint what we shall grant? / Soldiers, away with him" in
   Q.
2 Gives up, abandons.
3 Desperate measures.

Pembroke
My lord Mortimer, and you my lords each one,
To gratify the king's request therein
Touching the sending of this Gaveston,   75
Because his majesty so earnestly
Desires to see the man before his death,
I will upon mine honour undertake
To carry him and bring him back again,
Provided this: that you, my lord of Arundel,   80
Will join with me.

Warwick
            Pembroke, what wilt thou do?
Cause yet more bloodshed? Is it not enough
That we have taken him, but must we now
Leave him on "had-I-wist"[1] and let him go?

Pembroke
My lords, I will not over-woo your honours,   85
But if you dare trust Pembroke with the prisoner,
Upon mine oath I will return him back.

Arundel
My lord of Lancaster, what say you in this?

Lancaster
Why, I say, let him go on Pembroke's word.

Pembroke
And you, lord Mortimer?   90

Mortimer Junior
How say you, my lord of Warwick?

Warwick
Nay, do your pleasures, I know how 'twill prove.[2]

Pembroke
Then give him me.

Gaveston
            Sweet sovereign, yet I come
To see thee ere I die.

---

1 "Had I known."
2 "Nay, do your pleasures, / I know how 'twill prove" in Q.

Warwick

[Aside] Yet not perhaps,
If Warwick's wit and policy prevail.   95

Mortimer Junior

My lord of Pembroke, we deliver him you;
Return him on your honour. Sound away.[1]

Exit [Mortimer Junior, Lancaster, and Warwick]

Pembroke, [Arundel],[2] Gavest[on], and Pembroke's men
[including the horse-boy, James, and three other soldiers]
remain

Pembroke

My Lord, you shall go with me.
My house is not far hence—out of the way
A little—but our men shall go along.   100
We that have pretty wenches to our wives,
Sir, must not come so near and balk at their lips.

Arundel

'Tis very kindly spoke, my lord of Pembroke.
Your honour hath an adamant[3] of power
To draw a prince.   105

Pembroke

So, my lord. Come hither, James.
I do commit this Gaveston to thee.
Be thou this night his keeper; in the morning
We will discharge thee of thy charge. Be gone.

Gaveston

Unhappy Gaveston, whither goest thou now?

---

1 Blow horn or trumpet to signal departure.
2 Mat. in Q. This clearly refers to Arundel, whom Pembroke has just
   invited to accompany him on his mission to bear Gaveston to Edward
   and back. Forker explains the confusion by suggesting that the parts of
   Arundel and Matrevis, one of Edward's keepers later in the play, were
   doubled (8-9). Speech prefixes have been altered accordingly for the rest
   of the scene.
3 Magnet, force of attraction.

Exit [Gaveston] with [James and the rest of] Pembroke's men
[except the horse-boy]

Horse-boy
    [To Arundel] My lord, we'll quickly be at Cobham.[1]   110

Exit Pembroke and Arundel [with attendants]

[Scene 10]

Enter Gaveston mourning, and the earl of Pembroke's men
[James and the other soldiers]

Gaveston
    O treacherous Warwick, thus to wrong thy friend!

James
    I see it is your life these arms[2] pursue.

Gaveston
    Weaponless must I fall and die in bands?
    O, must this day be period of my life,
    Centre[3] of all my bliss? And ye be men,   5
    Speed to the king.

Enter Warwick and his company

Warwick
            My lord of Pembroke's men,
    Strive you no longer. I will have that Gaveston.

James
    Your lordship doth dishonour to yourself
    And wrong our lord, your honourable friend

Warwick
    No, James, it is my country's cause I follow.   10
    Go, take the villain; soldiers, come away,

---

1 Forker (1994) notes that there are two villages named Cobham, one in
   Kent and one in Surrey, neither of which makes geographical sense in
   this context (217 n. 109).
2 Weapons, soldiers.
3 Point of contraction.

We'll make quick work. Commend me to your master,
My friend, and tell him that I watched it well.
[To Gaveston] Come, let thy shadow parley with king
    Edward.

Gaveston
Treacherous earl, shall I not see the king?   15

Warwick
The king of heaven perhaps, no other king.
Away.

Exit Warwick and his men with Gaveston

James and the other soldiers remain

[James][1]
Come, fellows, it booted[2] not for us to strive.
We will in haste go certify[3] our Lord.

Exit Pembroke's men

[Scene 11]

Enter king Edward and Spencer [Junior, and Baldock], with
drums and fifes[4]

Edward
    I long to hear an answer from the Barons
    Touching my friend, my dearest Gaveston.
    Ah, Spencer, not the riches of my realm
    Can ransom him; ah, he is marked to die.
    I know the malice of the younger Mortimer;   5
    Warwick I know is rough and Lancaster
    Inexorable; and I shall never see
    My lovely Piers, my Gaveston, again.
    The Barons overbear me with their pride.

Spencer Junior
    Were I king Edward, England's sovereign,   10

---

1 Speech prefix omitted in Q.
2 Profited, benefited.
3 Inform.
4 Flutes.

Son to the lovely Eleanor of Spain,[1]
Great Edward Longshanks'[2] issue, would I bear
These braves,[3] this rage, and suffer uncontrolled
These Barons thus to beard[4] me in my land,
In mine own realm? My lord, pardon my speech.   15
Did you retain your father's magnanimity,
Did you regard the honour of your name,
You would not suffer thus your majesty
Be counterbuffed of your nobility.
Strike off their heads and let them preach on poles.   20
No doubt, such lessons they will teach the rest
As by their preachments they will profit much
And learn obedience to their lawful king.

Edward
   Yea, gentle Spencer, we have been too mild,
   Too kind to them, but now have drawn our sword,   25
   And if they send me not my Gaveston,
   We'll steel it on their crest[5] and poll[6] their tops.

Baldock
   This haught[7] resolve becomes your majesty,
   Not to be tied to their affection
   As though your highness were a schoolboy still   30
   And must be awed and governed like a child.

Enter Hugh Spencer [Senior], an old man, father to the young
Spencer [Junior], with his truncheon, and soldiers

Spencer Senior
   Long live my sovereign, the noble Edward,
   In peace triumphant, fortunate in wars.

Edward
   Welcome, old man. Com'st thou in Edward's aid?
   Then tell thy prince of whence and what thou art.   35

---

1 Edward II's mother, daughter of Fernando III, king of Castile and Leon;
   she died 28 November 1290.
2 Edward I.
3 Insults, acts of defiance.
4 Defy, insult, mock.
5 We'll strike our swords on their helmets.
6 Cut off, prune.
7 Haughty, noble.

Spencer Senior

Lo, with a band of bowmen and of pikes,[1]
Brown bills[2] and targeteers,[3] four hundred strong,
Sworn to defend king Edward's royal right,
I come in person to your majesty,
Spencer, the father of Hugh Spencer there,   40
Bound to your highness everlastingly,
For favours done in him unto us all.

Edward

Thy father, Spencer?

Spencer Junior

True, and it like your grace,
That pours in lieu of all your goodness shown
His life, my lord, before your princely feet.   45

Edward

Welcome ten thousand times, old man, again.
Spencer, this love, this kindness to thy King,
Argues thy noble mind and disposition.
Spencer, I here create thee earl of Wiltshire[4]
And daily will enrich thee with our favour,   50
That as the sunshine shall reflect o'er thee.
Beside, the more to manifest our love,
Because we hear Lord Bruce doth sell his land[5]
And that the Mortimers are in hand withal,
Thou shalt have crowns[6] of us t'outbid the Barons;   55
And, Spencer, spare them not but lay it on.
Soldiers, a largesse,[7] and thrice welcome all.

---

1 Soldiers armed with spears with metal heads.
2 Soldiers armed with axe- or sword-like blades mounted on long poles.
3 Soldiers bearing shields.
4 Historically, the earldom of Wiltshire was never conferred on either
   Despenser. Holinshed records that Hugh Despenser the Elder possessed
   a manor in Wiltshire, which the barons ravaged in retaliation for the
   younger Despenser's acquisition of Bruce's lands. The Spencer whom
   Edward is addressing in this line, however, seems to be Spencer Junior.
5 William de Braose's lands were in Wales, where Hugh Despenser the
   Younger was seeking to expand his holdings and where the Mortimers
   had established territories (Haines 122).
6 Coins, money.
7 Gift.

Spencer Junior
My lord, here comes the Queen.

Enter the Queen [Isabella] and her son [Prince Edward], and
Levune, a Frenchman

Edward

Madam, what news?

Isabella
News of dishonour, lord, and discontent.
Our friend Levune, faithful and full of trust,   60
Informeth us by letters and by words
That lord Valois our brother, king of France,[1]
Because your highness hath been slack in homage,
Hath seizèd Normandy[2] into his hands.
These be the letters, this the messenger.   65

Edward
Welcome, Levune. Tush, Sib,[3] if this be all,
Valois and I will soon be friends again.
But to my Gaveston: shall I never see,
Never behold thee now? Madam, in this matter
We will employ you and your little son;   70
You shall go parley with the king of France.
Boy, see you bear you bravely to the king
And do your message with a majesty.

Prince Edward
Commit not to my youth[4] things of more weight
Than fits a prince so young as I to bear.   75
And fear not, lord and father: heaven's great beams
On Atlas'[5] shoulder shall not be more safe
Than shall your charge committed to my trust.

---

1 Charles IV (r. 1322-28).
2 Historically, Gascony, which Charles IV confiscated in 1324 (Keen 74).
3 Diminutive form of Isabella.
4 Born 13 November 1312, Prince Edward is in this scene not quite a
   teenager.
5 A titan who, for having fought against Zeus with the other Titans, was
   condemned to hold up the heavens.

Isabella

Ah, boy, this towardness[1] makes thy mother fear
Thou art not marked to many days on earth.   80

Edward

Madam, we will that you with speed be shipped,
And this our son; Levune shall follow you
With all the haste we can dispatch him hence.
Choose of our lords to bear you company
And go in peace; leave us in wars at home.   85

Isabella

Unnatural wars, where subjects brave their king.
God end them once. My lord, I take my leave
To make my preparation for France.[2]

[Exit Isabella and Prince Edward]

Enter Lord [Arundel][3]

Edward

What, Lord Arundel, dost thou come alone?

Arundel

Yea, my good lord, for Gaveston is dead.[4]   90

Edward

Ah traitors, have they put my friend to death?
Tell me, Arundel, died he ere thou cam'st,
Or didst thou see my friend to take his death?

Arundel

Neither, my lord, for as he was surprised,
Begirt with weapons and with enemies round,   95
I did your highness's message to them all,
Demanding him of them, entreating rather,
And said, upon the honour of my name,

---

1 Boldness, forwardness.
2 Isabella and Prince Edward departed for France in March 1325.
3 Matre. in Q but clearly Edward's messenger to the barons in scene 9.
   Speech prefixes and titles in the rest of the scene are modified accordingly. Cf. note 000.
4 Gaveston was executed on 19 June 1312 at Blacklow Hill. See Holinshed's account in Appendix A1(c).

That I would undertake to carry him
Unto your highness and to bring him back.   100

Edward
And tell me, would the rebels deny me that?

Spencer Junior
Proud recreants![1]

Edward
                    Yea, Spencer, traitors all.

Arundel
I found them at the first inexorable.
The earl of Warwick would not bide the hearing,
Mortimer hardly, Pembroke and Lancaster   105
Spake least; and when they flatly had denied,
Refusing to receive me pledge for him,
The earl of Pembroke mildly thus bespake:
"My lords, because our sovereign sends for him
And promiseth he shall be safe returned,   110
I will this undertake, to have him hence
And see him re-delivered to your hands."

Edward
Well, and how fortunes that he came not?

Spencer Junior
Some treason or some villainy was cause.

Arundel
The earl of Warwick seized him on his way,   115
For, being delivered unto Pembroke's men,
Their lord rode home, thinking his prisoner safe;
But ere he came, Warwick in ambush lay
And bare him to his death, and in a trench
Strake off his head and marched unto the camp.   120

Spencer Junior
A bloody part, flatly against law of arms.[2]

Edward
O, shall I speak, or shall I sigh and die?

---

1 Cowards, traitors.
2 Martial law and code of chivalric conduct.

Spencer Junior
> My lord, refer your vengeance to the sword
> Upon these Barons; hearten up your men.
> Let them not unrevenged murder your friends;   125
> Advance your standard,[1] Edward, in the field
> And march to fire them from their starting holes.[2]

Edward kneels

Edward
> By earth, the common mother of us all,
> By heaven and all the moving orbs[3] thereof,
> By this right hand and by my father's sword,   130
> And all the honours 'longing to my crown,
> I will have heads and lives for him as many
> As I have manors, castles, towns, and towers.
> Treacherous Warwick, traitorous Mortimer!
> If I be England's king, in lakes of gore   135
> Your headless trunks, your bodies will I trail,
> That you may drink your fill and quaff in blood,
> And stain my royal standard with the same,
> That so my bloody colours may suggest
> Remembrance of revenge immortally   140
> On your accursèd traitorous progeny,
> You villains that have slain my Gaveston.

[Edward rises]

> And in this place of honour and of trust,
> Spencer, sweet Spencer, I adopt thee here,
> And merely[4] of our love we do create thee   145
> Earl of Gloucester[5] and lord Chamberlain,
> Despite of times, despite of enemies.

---

1 Military ensign.
2 Hiding place of hunted animals or criminals.
3 Planets.
4 Purely, entirely.
5 Holinshed endows Hugh Despenser the Younger with the title of the earl
  of Gloucester, but in fact Despenser never attained the earldom
  although he attempted to acquire all the lands belonging to it (Haines
  96).

Spencer Junior
My lord, here's a messenger from the Barons
Desires access unto your majesty.

Edward
Admit him near.   150

Enter the herald from the Barons, with his coat of arms

Herald
Long live king Edward, England's lawful lord.

Edward
So wish not they, iwis,[1] that sent thee hither.
Thou com'st from Mortimer and his complices—
A ranker rout[2] of rebels never was.
Well, say thy message.   155

Herald
The Barons up in arms by me salute
Your highness with long life and happiness,
And bid me say as plainer[3] to your grace
That if without effusion of blood
You will this grief have ease and remedy,   160
That from your princely person you remove
This Spencer, as a putrifying branch
That deads the royal vine, whose golden leaves
Empale[4] your princely head, your diadem,
Whose brightness such pernicious upstarts dim;   165
Say they, and lovingly advise your grace
To cherish virtue and nobility,
And have old servitors in high esteem,
And shake off smooth dissembling flatterers.
This granted, they, their honours, and their lives   170
Are to your highness vowed and consecrate.

Spencer Junior
Ah traitors, will they still display their pride?

---

1 Truly, certainly.
2 Rabble, herd.
3 Complainant, plaintiff.
4 Crown, garland.

Edward
Away, tarry no answer but be gone.
Rebels, will they appoint their sovereign
His sports, his pleasures, and his company?   175
Yet ere thou go, see how I do divorce
Spencer from me.

Edward embraces Spencer [Junior]

Now get thee to thy lords
And tell them I will come to chastise them
For murdering Gaveston. Hie thee, get thee gone;
Edward with fire and sword follows at thy heels.   180

[Exit herald]

My lords,[1] perceive you how these rebels swell?
Soldiers, good hearts, defend your sovereign's right,
For now, even now, we march to make them stoop.
Away.

Exit [all]

[Scene 12][2]

Alarums, excursions, a great fight, and a retreat

Enter the king, Spencer [Senior], Spencer [Junior], and the
noblemen of the king's side

Edward
Why do we sound retreat? Upon them, lords!
This day I shall pour vengeance with my sword
On those proud rebels that are up in arms
And do confront and countermand their king.

Spencer Junior
I doubt it not, my lord. Right will prevail.   5

---

1   Lord in Q.
2   Marlowe here condenses a series of battles into one, fought at Borough-
    bridge, Yorkshire 16 March 1322.

Spencer Senior
'Tis not amiss, my liege,[1] for either part
To breathe a while. Our men, with sweat and dust
All choked well near, begin to faint for heat,
And this retire refresheth horse and man.

Spencer Junior
Here come the rebels.   10

Enter the Barons [Mortimer Junior, Lancaster, Warwick, Pembroke, and Kent, with others]

Mortimer Junior
Look, Lancaster,
Yonder is Edward among his flatterers.

Lancaster
And there let him be,
Till he pay dearly for their company.

Warwick
And shall, or Warwick's sword shall smite in vain.   15

Edward
What, rebels, do you shrink and sound retreat?

Mortimer Junior
No, Edward, no, thy flatterers faint and fly.

Lancaster
Th'ad[2] best betimes[3] forsake them and their trains,
For they'll betray thee, traitors as they are.

Spencer Junior
Traitor on thy face, rebellious Lancaster.   20

Pembroke
Away, base upstart! Brav'st thou nobles thus?

Spencer Senior
A noble attempt and honourable deed
Is it not, trow[4] ye, to assemble aid
And levy arms against your lawful king?

---

1 Lord, sovereign.
2 Contraction of "thou had."
3 Shortly, while you can.
4 Believe, trust.

Edward

For which ere long their heads shall satisfy   25
T'appease the wrath of their offended king.

Mortimer Junior

Then, Edward, thou wilt fight it to the last
And rather bathe thy sword in subjects' blood
Than banish that pernicious company?

Edward

Ay, traitors all, rather than thus be braved,   30
Make England's civil towns huge heaps of stones
And ploughs to go about our palace gates.

Warwick

A desperate and unnatural resolution.

[Alarum to the fight]¹

Saint George² for England and the Barons's right!

Edward

Saint George for England and king Edward's right!   35

[Exit all, fighting]

[Scene 13]

Enter Edward, [Spencer Senior, Spencer Junior, Levune,
Baldock, soldiers, and others], with the Barons [Kent, Lancaster, Warwick, Mortimer Junior, and others] captives

Edward

Now, lusty lords, now not by chance of war
But justice of the quarrel and the cause,
Vailed is your pride. Methinks you hang the heads,
But we'll advance them, traitors. Now 'tis time
To be avenged on you for all your braves   5
And for the murder of my dearest friend,

---

1 Part of the following line in Q: "Alarum to the fight! Saint George for
   England / And the barons' right."
2 Edward III made Saint George England's patron saint when he established the chivalric Order of the Garter in 1348.

To whom right well you knew our soul was knit,
Good Piers of Gaveston, my sweet favourite.
Ah rebels, recreants, you made him away!

Kent

Brother, in regard of thee and of thy land　　　　　　10
Did they remove that flatterer from thy throne.

Edward

So, sir, you have spoke. Away, avoid our presence.
Accursed wretches, was't in regard of us,
When we had sent our messenger to request
He might be spared to come to speak with us　　　　15
And Pembroke undertook for his return,
That thou, proud Warwick, watched the prisoner,
Poor Piers, and headed[1] him against law of arms?
For which thy head shall overlook the rest
As much as thou in rage outwent'st the rest.　　　　20

Warwick

Tyrant, I scorn thy threats and menaces;
'Tis but temporal[2] that thou canst inflict.

Lancaster

The worst is death, and better die to live
Than live in infamy under such a king.

Edward

[To Spencer Senior] Away with them, my lord
　　of Winchester,[3]　　　　　　　　　　　　　　25
These lusty leaders Warwick and Lancaster.
I charge you roundly, off with both their heads.
Away!

Warwick

Farewell, vain world.

Lancaster

Sweet Mortimer, farewell.　　　　　　　　　　　30

[Exit Warwick and Lancaster, guarded by Spencer Senior]

1　Beheaded.
2　Temporary, earthly harm as opposed to eternal, spiritual harm.
3　Hugh Despenser the Elder was created Earl of Winchester in 1322.

Mortimer Junior
    England, unkind to thy nobility,
    Groan for this grief; behold how thou art maimed.

Edward
    Go take that haughty Mortimer to the Tower.
    There see him safe bestowed, and for the rest,
    Do speedy execution on them all.   35
    Be gone.

Mortimer Junior
    What, Mortimer? Can ragged stony walls
    Immure[1] thy virtue[2] that aspires to heaven?
    Edward, England's scourge, it may not be;
    Mortimer's hope surmounts his fortune far.   40

[Exit Mortimer Junior under guard]

Edward
    Sound drums and trumpets! March with me, my friends.
    Edward this day hath crowned him king anew.

Exit [Edward, with others]

Spencer Junior, Levune, and Baldock remain

Spencer Junior
    Levune, the trust that we repose in thee
    Begets the quiet of king Edward's land.
    Therefore be gone in haste, and with advice   45
    Bestow that treasure on the lords of France,
    That therewith all enchanted, like the guard
    That suffered Jove to pass in showers of gold
    To Danaë,[3] all aid may be denied
    To Isabel the Queen, that now in France   50
    Makes friends, to cross the seas with her young son
    And step into his father's regiment.

Levune
    That's it these Barons and the subtle Queen
    Long levelled[4] at.

---

1 Wall up, enclose.
2 In a Machiavellian sense, courage and ambition.
3 See note to 6.53.
4 Levied in Q.

Baldock
              Yea, but Levune, thou seest
These Barons lay their heads on blocks together;   55
What they intend, the hangman frustrates clean.

Levune
    Have you no doubts, my lords, I'll clap so[1] close
    Among the lords of France with England's gold,
    That Isabel shall make her plaints in vain
    And France shall be obdurate with her tears.   60

Spencer Junior
    Then make for France amain, Levune. Away,
    Proclaim king Edward's wars and victories.

Exit all

[Scene 14]

Enter [Kent]

Kent
    Fair blows the wind for France. Blow, gentle gale,
    Till Edmund be arrived for England's good.
    Nature, yield to my country's cause in this.
    A brother? No, a butcher of thy friends!
    Proud Edward, dost thou banish me thy presence?   5
    But I'll to France and cheer the wrongèd Queen,
    And certify what Edward's looseness is.
    Unnatural king, to slaughter noble men
    And cherish flatterers.
    Mortimer, I stay[2] thy sweet escape;[3]   10
    Stand gracious, gloomy night, to his device.[4]

Enter Mortimer [Junior] disguised

---

1 Claps in Q.
2 Await.
3 Mortimer Junior escaped the Tower in August 1323.
4 "And cherish flatterers. Mortimer, I stay / Thy sweet escape; stand gracious, gloomy night, / To his device" in Q.

Mortimer Junior
Holla, who walketh there? Is't you, my lord?

Kent
Mortimer, 'tis I.
But hath thy potion wrought so happily?[1]

Mortimer Junior
It hath, my lord. The warders all asleep,   15
I thank them, gave me leave to pass in peace.
But hath your grace got shipping unto France?

Kent
Fear it not.

Exit [Kent and Mortimer Junior]

[Scene 15]

Enter the Queen [Isabella] and her son [Prince Edward]

Isabella
Ah boy, our friends do fail us all in France;
The lords are cruel and the king unkind.[2]
What shall we do?

Prince Edward
                    Madam, return to England
And please my father well, and then a fig[3]
For all my uncle's friendship here in France.   5
I warrant you, I'll win his highness quickly;
He loves me better than a thousand Spencers.

Isabella
Ah boy, thou art deceived at least in this,
To think that we can yet be tuned together.
No, no, we jar too far. Unkind Valois!   10
Unhappy Isabel, when France rejects,
Whither, O whither, dost thou bend thy steps?

---

1 "Mortimer, 'tis I. / But hath ..." is one line in Q.
2 With the additional connotation of "unbrotherly."
3 A proverbially worthless item.

Enter sir John of Hainault

Sir John
    Madam, what cheer?

Isabella
                   Ah, good sir John of Hainault,
    Never so cheerless nor so far distressed.

Sir John
    I hear, sweet lady, of the king's unkindness.   15
    But droop not, madam, noble minds contemn[1]
    Despair. Will your grace with me to Hainault
    And there stay time's advantage with your son?
    How say you, my Lord, will you go with your friends
    And shake off all our fortunes equally?   20

Prince Edward
    So pleaseth the Queen my mother, me it likes.
    The king of England nor the court of France
    Shall have me from my gracious mother's side
    Till I be strong enough to break a staff,
    And then have at the proudest Spencer's head.   25

Sir John
    Well said, my lord.

Isabella
    O my sweetheart, how do I moan thy wrongs
    Yet triumph in the hope of thee, my joy.
    Ah, sweet sir John, even to the utmost verge
    Of Europe or the shore of Tanaïs[2]   30
    Will we with thee; to Hainault, so we will.
    The Marquis[3] is a noble gentleman;
    His grace, I dare presume, will welcome me.
    But who are those?

Enter Kent and Mortimer [Junior]

---

1 Scorn.
2 The River Don in Russia, held to mark the boundary between Europe
  and Asia.
3 Sir John's brother.

Kent

                    Madam, long may you live

  Much happier than your friends in England do.   35

Isabella

  Lord Edmund and lord Mortimer alive!

  Welcome to France. The news was here, my lord,

  That you were dead or very near your death.

Mortimer Junior

  Lady, the last was truest of the twain;

  But Mortimer, reserved for better hap,   40

  Hath shaken off the thraldom[1] of the Tower

  And lives t'advance your standard, good my lord.

Prince Edward

  How mean you, and the king my father lives?

  No, my lord Mortimer, not I, I trow.

Isabella

  Not, son? Why not? I would it were no worse.   45

  But, gentle lords, friendless we are in France.

Mortimer Junior

  Monsieur le Grand, a noble friend of yours,

  Told us at our arrival all the news—

  How hard the nobles, how unkind the king

  Hath showed himself. But, madam, right makes room   50

  Where weapons want,[2] and though a many friends

  Are made away, as Warwick,[3] Lancaster,[4]

  And others of our party and faction,

  Yet have we friends, assure your grace, in England

  Would cast up caps and clap their hands for joy   55

  To see us there appointed[5] for our foes.

Kent

  Would all were well and Edward well reclaimed,

  For England's honour, peace, and quietness.

---

1 Captivity.
2 Are lacking.
3 Warwick died in 1315.
4 Thomas of Lancaster was beheaded 22 March 1322 on a hill outside
    Pontefract.
5 Equipped, dressed, prepared.

Mortimer Junior
But by the sword, my lord, it must be deserved.
The king will ne'er forsake his flatterers.   60

Sir John
My Lords of England, since the ungentle king
Of France refuseth to give aid of arms
To this distressèd Queen his sister here,
Go you with her to Hainault. Doubt ye not,
We will find comfort, money, men, and friends   65
Ere long to bid the English king a base.[1]
How say, young Prince, what think you of the match?

Prince Edward
I think king Edward will outrun us all.

Isabella
Nay son, not so; and you must not discourage
Your friends that are so forward in your aid.   70

Kent
Sir John of Hainault, pardon us, I pray.
These comforts that you give our woeful queen
Bind us in kindness all at your command.

Isabella
Yea, gentle brother; and the God of heaven
Prosper your happy motion,[2] good sir John.   75

Mortimer Junior
This noble gentleman forward in arms
Was born, I see, to be our anchor hold.
Sir John of Hainault, be it thy renown
That England's Queen and nobles in distress
Have been by thee restored and comforted.   80

Sir John
Madam, along, and you, my lord, with me,
That England's peers may Hainault's welcome see.

[Exit all]

---

1 Challenge the English king. The phrase comes from a children's game.
2 Plan.

[Scene 16]

Enter the king, Arundel,[1] the two Spencers, with others

Edward
Thus, after many threats of wrathful war,
Triumpheth England's Edward with his friends;
And triumph Edward with his friends uncontrolled.
My lord of Gloucester, do you hear the news?

Spencer Junior
What news, my lord?   5

Edward
Why, man, they say there is great execution
Done through the realm. My lord of Arundel,
You have the note, have you not?

Arundel
From the lieutenant of the Tower, my lord.

Edward
I pray let us see it. What have we there?   10
Read it, Spencer.

Spencer [Junior] reads their names[2]

Why so, they barked apace[3] a month ago;
Now, on my life, they'll neither bark nor bite.
Now, sirs, the news from France. Gloucester, I trow
The lords of France love England's gold so well   15
As Isabella[4] gets no aid from thence.
What now remains? Have you proclaimed, my lord,
Reward for them can bring in Mortimer?

Spencer Junior
My lord, we have, and if he be in England,
He will be had ere long, I doubt it not.   20

---

1 Matr. in Q, though Edward in line 7 refers to him as "my lord of
   Arundel." Speech prefixes have been altered accordingly throughout the
   scene.
2 See Appendix A1(e).
3 Rapidly.
4 Isabell in Q. Emended to preserve the line's meter.

Edward

> If, dost thou say? Spencer, as true as death,
> He is in England's ground. Our port-masters
> Are not so careless of their king's command.

Enter a post

> How now, what news with thee? From whence come these?

Post

> Letters, my lord, and tidings forth of France   25
> To you, my lord of Gloucester, from Levune.

Edward

> Read.

Spencer [Junior] reads the letter.

"My duty to your honour promised, *et cetera*, I have, according to instructions in that behalf, dealt with the king of France his lords and effected that the Queen, all discontented and discomforted, is gone—whither if you ask, with sir John of Hainault, brother to the Marquis, into Flanders. With them are gone lord Edmund and the lord Mortimer, having in their company diverse of your nation and others, and, as constant report goeth, they intend to give king Edward battle in England sooner than he can look for them. This is all the news of import. Your honour's in all service, Levune."

Edward

> Ah, villains! Hath that Mortimer escaped?   35
> With him is Edmund gone associate?
> And will sir John of Hainault lead the round?
> Welcome a God's name, Madam, and your son;
> England shall welcome you and all your rout.
> Gallop apace, bright Phoebus,[1] through the sky,   40
> And dusky night, in rusty iron car;
> Between you both, shorten the time, I pray,
> That I may see that most desirèd day,
> When we may meet these traitors in the field.
> Ah, nothing grieves me but my little boy   45

---

1 Apollo, god of the sun.

Is thus misled to countenance[1] their ills.
Come, friends, to Bristol,[2] there to make us strong;
And, winds, as equal be to bring them in
As you injurious were to bear them forth.

[Exit all]

[Scene 17][3]

Enter the Queen [Isabella], her son [Prince Edward], Edmund
[Kent], Mortimer [Junior], and sir John, [with soldiers]

Isabella
Now, lords, our loving friends, and countrymen,
Welcome to England all. With prosperous winds,
Our kindest friends in Belgia[4] have we left
To cope[5] with friends at home. A heavy case,
When force to force is knit, and sword and glaive[6]   5
In civil broils makes kin and countrymen
Slaughter themselves in others, and their sides
With their own weapons gored, but what's the help?
Misgoverned kings are cause of all this wrack,
And, Edward, thou art one among them all,   10
Whose looseness hath betrayed thy land to spoil
And made the channels overflow with blood.
Of thine own people patron shouldst thou be,
But thou—

Mortimer Junior
Nay, madam, if you be a warrior,   15
Ye must not grow so passionate in speeches.
Lords, since that we are by sufferance[7] of heaven
Arrived and armèd in this prince's right,
Here for our country's cause swear we to him

---

1 Approve, support.
2 City in south-west England.
3 Isabella and her forces landed on England's east coast at Orwell in
   Suffolk on 25 September 1326.
4 The Netherlands.
5 Engage, meet in battle.
6 Spear or sword.
7 Allowance, permission.

All homage, fealty,[1] and forwardness.   20
And for the open wrongs and injuries
Edward hath done to us, his Queen, and land,
We come in arms to wreak[2] it with the sword,
That England's queen in peace may repossess
Her dignities and honours, and withal   25
We may remove these flatterers from the king,
That havocks[3] England's wealth and treasury.

Sir John
Sound trumpets, my lord, and forward let us march.
Edward will think we come to flatter him.

Kent
I would he never had been flattered more.   30

[Exit all]

[Scene 18]

Enter the King, Baldock, and Spencer [Junior], flying about the
stage

Spencer Junior
Fly, fly, my Lord, the Queen is overstrong;
Her friends do multiply and yours do fail.
Shape we our course to Ireland, there to breathe.

Edward
What, was I born to fly and run away,
And leave the Mortimers conquerors behind?   5
Give me my horse, and let's r'enforce our troops
And in this bed of honour die with fame.

Baldock
O no, my lord, this princely resolution
Fits not the time. Away, we are pursued.

[Exit Edward, Baldock, and Spencer Junior]

---

1 Fidelity.
2 Redress, punish. Wrecke in Q.
3 Wastes.

[Enter] Kent alone with a sword and target

Kent
    This way he fled, but I am come too late.   10
    Edward, alas, my heart relents for thee.
    Proud traitor Mortimer, why dost thou chase
    Thy lawful king, thy sovereign, with thy sword?
    Vile wretch, and why hast thou, of all unkind,
    Borne arms against thy brother and thy king?   15
    Rain showers of vengeance on my cursèd head,
    Thou God, to whom in justice it belongs
    To punish this unnatural revolt.
    Edward, this Mortimer aims at thy life—
    O fly him, then! But, Edmund, calm this rage;   20
    Dissemble or thou diest, for Mortimer
    And Isabel do kiss while they conspire.
    And yet she bears a face of love, forsooth—
    Fie on that love that hatcheth death and hate!
    Edmund, away. Bristol to Longshanks' blood[1]   25
    Is false.[2] Be not found single[3] for suspect:[4]
    Proud Mortimer pries near into thy walks.

Enter the Queen [Isabella], Mortimer [Junior], the young
Prince [Edward,] and Sir John of Hainault, [with soldiers]

Isabella
    Successful battles gives the God of kings
    To them that fight in right and fear his wrath.
    Since, then, successfully we have prevailed,   30
    Thanks be heaven's great architect and you.
    Ere farther we proceed, my noble lords,
    We here create our well belovèd son,
    Of love and care unto his royal person,
    Lord warden[5] of the realm; and since the fates   35
    Have made his father so infortunate,
    Deal you, my lords, in this, my loving lords,
    As to your wisdoms fittest seems in all.

---

1   Edward, son of Edward Longshanks (Edward I).
2   The city of Bristol, which Edward considered to be a stronghold, turned
    the king's forces stationed there over to the invaders.
3   Alone.
4   For fear of suspicion.
5   Governor of the kingdom during a monarch's minority or absence.

Kent
Madam, without offence if I may ask,
How will you deal with Edward in his fall?   40

Prince Edward
Tell me, good uncle, what Edward do you mean?

Kent
Nephew, your father; I dare not call him king.

Mortimer Junior
My lord of Kent, what needs these questions?
'Tis not in her controlment nor in ours;
But as the realm and parliament shall please,   45
So shall your brother be disposèd of.
[Aside to Isabella] I like not this relenting mood in
    Edmund.
Madam, 'tis good to look to him betimes.

Isabella
My lord, the Mayor of Bristol knows our mind?

Mortimer Junior
Yea, madam, and they 'scape not easily   50
That fled the field.

Isabella
                    Baldock is with the king.
A goodly chancellor is he not, my lord?

Sir John
So are the Spencers, the father and the son.

Kent
[Aside] This Edward is the ruin of the realm.

Enter Rhys ap Howell,[1] and the Mayor of Bristol, with Spencer
[Senior]

Rhys ap Howell
God save Queen Isabel and her princely son.   55
Madam, the Mayor and citizens of Bristol,

---

1   One of Mortimer Junior's Welsh clients, Rhys ap Hwyel had his lands
    confiscated and was imprisoned at Dover and then in the Tower of
    London for his part in the barons' rebellion of 1321-22. He was
    released from the Tower upon Isabella's return to England.

In sign of love and duty to this presence,
Present by me this traitor to the state,
Spencer, the father to that wanton Spencer
That, like the lawless Catiline[1] of Rome,   60
Revelled in England's wealth and treasury.

Isabella
We thank you all.

Mortimer Junior
                                    Your loving care in this
Deserveth princely favours and rewards.
But where's the king and the other Spencer fled?

Rhys ap Howell
Spencer the son, created earl of Gloucester,   65
Is with that smooth-tongued scholar Baldock gone
And shipped but late for Ireland with the king.

Mortimer Junior
Some whirlwind fetch them back or sink them all.
They shall be started[2] thence, I doubt it not.

Prince Edward
Shall I not see the king my father yet?   70

Kent
[Aside] Unhappy Edward, chased from England's bounds.

Sir John
Madam, what resteth?[3] Why stand ye in a muse?[4]

Isabella
I rue my lord's ill fortune, but alas,
Care of my country called me to this war.

Mortimer Junior
Madam, have done with care and sad complaint.   75
Your king hath wronged your country and himself,
And we must seek to right it as we may.
Meanwhile, have hence this rebel to the block.
Your lordship cannot privilege your head.

---

1 First-century BCE Roman aristocrat whose conspiracy against the
   Roman Republic was exposed by Cicero.
2 Chased.
3 Remains [to be done].
4 Why are you so contemplative?

Spencer Senior
> Rebel is he that fights against his prince;　　　　　80
> So fought not they that fought in Edward's right.

Mortimer Junior
> Take him away, he prates.[1]

[Exit Spencer Senior under guard]

> 　　　　　You, Rhys ap Howell,
> Shall do good service to her Majesty,
> Being of countenance[2] in your country[3] here,
> To follow these rebellious runagates.[4]　　　　　85
> We in meanwhile, madam, must take advice
> How Baldock, Spencer, and their complices
> May in their fall be followed to their end.

Exit all

[Scene 19][5]

Enter the Abbot, monks, [King] Edward, Spencer [Junior], and Baldock

Abbot
> Have you no doubt, my lord, have you no fear.
> As silent and as careful will we be
> To keep your royal person safe with us,
> Free from suspect[6] and fell[7] invasion
> Of such as have your majesty in chase,　　　　　5
> Yourself and those your chosen company,
> As danger of this stormy time requires.

1　Prattles, speaks to no purpose. Hugh Despenser the Elder, who was in charge of Bristol's defence, was executed 27 October 1326.
2　Credit, reputation, weight.
3　Wales.
4　Fugitives, runaways.
5　At the Abbey at Neath, in Wales.
6　Suspicion.
7　Fierce, ruthless, dreadful.

Edward
  Father, thy face should harbour no deceit.
  O hadst thou ever been a king, thy heart,
  Pierced deeply with sense of my distress,   10
  Could not but take compassion of my state.
  Stately and proud in riches and in train
  Whilom[1] I was, powerful and full of pomp.
  But what is he whom rule and empery[2]
  Have not in life or death made miserable?[3]   15
  Come Spencer, come Baldock, come sit down by me;
  Make trial now of that philosophy
  That in our famous nurseries of arts[4]
  Thou sucked'st from Plato and from Aristotle.
  Father, this life contemplative[5] is heaven;   20
  O that I might this life in quiet lead.
  But we, alas, are chased; and you, my friends,
  Your lives and my dishonour they pursue.
  Yet, gentle monks, for treasure, gold nor fee,
  Do you betray us and our company.   25

Monks
  Your grace may sit secure, if none but we
  Do wot[6] of your abode.[7]

Spencer Junior
  Not one alive, but shrewdly[8] I suspect
  A gloomy fellow in a mead[9] below.

---

1 Once.
2 Imperial power.
3 The fall of princes from their high position is in this period a common
   definition of tragedy. George Puttenham in *The Arte of English Poesie*
   (1589) states that tragic poets "set forth the dolefull falls of unfortunate
   and afflicted Princes" (20). Holinshed uses the commonplace to round
   out his account of Edward's deposition: "Ah lamentable ruin from
   royalty to miserable calamity, procured by them chiefly that should have
   been the pillars of the king's estate, and not hooked engines to pull him
   down from his throne" (Appendix A1[h]).
4 Universities of Cambridge and Oxford.
5 Life of religious devotion, in contrast to the active life of worldly affairs.
6 Know.
7 "Your grace ... / ... Do wot ..." is one line in Q.
8 Fearfully, grievously.
9 Meadow.

He gave a long look after us, my lord, 30
And all the land, I know, is up in arms,
Arms that pursue our lives with deadly hate.

Baldock
We were embarked for Ireland, wretched we,
With awkward winds and sore tempests driven
To fall on shore and here to pine in fear 35
Of Mortimer and his confederates.

Edward
Mortimer, who talks of Mortimer?
Who wounds me with the name of Mortimer,
That bloody man? Good father, on thy lap
Lay I this head, laden with mickle[1] care. 40
O might I never open these eyes again,
Never again lift up this drooping head,
O never more lift up this dying heart!

Spencer Junior
Look up, my lord. Baldock, this drowsiness
Betides no good. Here even we are betrayed. 45

Enter with Welsh hooks,[2] Rhys ap Howell, a mower,[3] *and the
Earl of Leicester, [with soldiers]*

Mower
Upon my life, those be the men ye seek.

Rhys ap Howell
Fellow, enough. My lord, I pray be short;
A fair commission warrants what we do.

Leicester
[Aside] The Queen's commission, urged by Mortimer.
What cannot gallant Mortimer with the Queen? 50
Alas, see where he sits and hopes unseen
T'escape their hands that seek to reave[4] his life.
Too true it is, *quem dies vidit veniens superbum,*

---

1 Great, much.
2 Halberd-like weapons, but also farming implements. The sharp hook at
  the end of its long pole could be used for fighting or pruning trees.
3 One who mows grass or stacks hay.
4 Deprive of, rob.

Hunc dies vidit fugiens iacentem.[1]
But, Leicester, leave to grow so passionate.   55
[To Spencer and Baldock] Spencer and Baldock, by no
    other names
I arrest you of high treason here.
Stand not on titles, but obey th'arrest;
'Tis in the name of Isabel the Queen.
My lord, why droop you thus?   60

Edward
O day! The last of all my bliss on earth,
Centre of all misfortune. O my stars!
Why do you lour[2] unkindly on a king?
Comes Leicester then in Isabella's name
To take my life, my company, from me?   65
Here, man, rip up this panting breast of mine
And take my heart in rescue of my friends.

Rhys ap Howell
Away with them.

Spencer Junior
                It may become thee yet
To let us take our farewell of his grace.

Abbot
My heart with pity earns[3] to see this sight,   70
A king to bear these words and proud commands.

Edward
Spencer, ah sweet Spencer, thus then must we part.

Spencer Junior
We must, my lord; so will the angry heavens.

Edward
Nay, so will hell and cruel Mortimer;
The gentle heavens have not to do in this.   75

---

1 "Whom the morning sees raised up, that one the evening sees laid low."
  The Latin quotation is from Roman dramatist Seneca's revenge tragedy
  Thyestes. In Jasper Heywood's translation, first published in 1560 and
  republished in 1581 in Thomas Newton's *Seneca His Tenne Tragedies*, the
  lines read "Whom dawn of day hath seen in pride to reign, / Him overthrown hath seen the evening late" (31).
2 Frown.
3 Grieves, laments.

Baldock

My lord, it is in vain to grieve or storm.
Here humbly of your grace we take our leaves.
Our lots are cast; I fear me so is thine.

Edward

In heaven we may, in earth never shall we meet.
And, Leicester, say, what shall become of us?   80

Leicester

Your majesty must go to Killingworth.[1]

Edward

Must! 'Tis somewhat hard when kings must go.

Leicester

Here is a litter ready for your grace
That waits your pleasure, and the day grows old.

Rhys ap Howell

As good be gone as stay and be benighted.   85

Edward

A litter hast thou? Lay me in a hearse
And to the gates of hell convey me hence.
Let Pluto's[2] bells ring out my fatal knell
And hags howl for my death at Charon's[3] shore,
For friends hath Edward none but these, and these,   90
And these must die under a tyrant's sword.

Rhys ap Howell

My lord, be going; care not for these,
For we shall see them shorter by the heads.

Edward

Well, that shall be shall be. Part we must,
Sweet Spencer, gentle Baldock, part we must.   95
Hence, feignèd weeds;[4] unfeignèd are my woes.
Father, farewell. Leicester, thou stay'st for me,
And go I must. Life, farewell with my friends.

---

1 Kenilworth.
2 God of the underworld in classical mythology.
3 The ferryman who transported the souls of the dead across the river
   Styx into the underworld.
4 Clothes.

Exit Edward and Leicester

Spencer Junior
> O, is he gone? Is noble Edward gone,
> Parted from hence, never to see us more?　　　　　100
> Rend,[1] sphere of heaven,[2] and fire forsake thy orb;
> Earth melt to air. Gone is my sovereign,
> Gone, gone alas, never to make return.

Baldock
> Spencer, I see our souls are fleeted hence;
> We are deprived the sunshine of our life.　　　　　105
> Make for a new life, man; throw up thy eyes
> And heart and hand to heaven's immortal throne;
> Pay nature's debt[3] with cheerful countenance.
> Reduce we all our lessons unto this:
> To die, sweet Spencer, therefore live we all;　　　　110
> Spencer, all live to die and rise to fall.

Rhys ap Howell
> Come, come, keep these preachments till you come to the
> place appointed.[4] You, and such as you are, have made wise
> work in England. Will your Lordships away?

Mower
> Your worship, I trust, will remember me?

Rhys ap Howell
> Remember thee, fellow? What else?　　　　　　　　115
> Follow me to the town.

[Exit all]

1　Rent in Q.
2　The sun.
3　Death.
4　The place of execution.

[Scene 20]

Enter the king, Leicester, with a Bishop [of Winchester, and Trussel] for the crown

Leicester

> Be patient, good my lord, cease to lament.
> Imagine Killingworth castle were your court
> And that you lay for pleasure here a space,
> Not of compulsion or necessity.

Edward

> Leicester, if gentle words might comfort me,   5
> Thy speeches long ago had eased my sorrows,
> For kind and loving hast thou always been.
> The griefs of private men are soon allayed,
> But not of kings. The forest deer, being struck,
> Runs to an herb that closeth up the wounds;   10
> But when the imperial lion's flesh is gored,
> He rends and tears it with his wrathful paw,
> And[1] highly scorning that the lowly earth
> Should drink his blood, mounts up into the air.[2]
> And so it fares with me, whose dauntless mind   15
> Th' ambitious Mortimer would seek to curb,
> And that unnatural Queen, false Isabel,
> That thus hath pent[3] and mewed[4] me in a prison.
> For such outrageous passions cloy[5] my soul
> As with the wings of rancour and disdain   20
> Full often am I soaring up to heaven
> To plain me to the gods against them both;
> But when I call to mind I am a king,
> Methinks I should revenge me of the wrongs
> That Mortimer and Isabel have done.   25
> But what are kings when regiment is gone

---

1 And is not in Q.

2 Versions of the lore about deer and lions in these lines can be found in Book VIII of Pliny's *Natural History*. Compare also to Holinshed's "the anger and displeasure of the king is as the roaring of a lion, and his revenge inevitable" (Appendix A1 [e]) and the *Homily against Disobedience*'s "the anger and displeasure of the prince is as the roaring of a lion and the very messenger of death" (Appendix F1).

3 Penned.

4 Confined.

5 Pierce.

But perfect shadows in a sunshine day?
My nobles rule, I bear the name of king;
I wear the crown but am controlled by them,
By Mortimer and my unconstant Queen,   30
Who spots my nuptial[1] bed with infamy
Whilst I am lodged within this cave of care,
Where sorrow at my elbow still attends
To company my heart with sad laments,
That bleeds within me for this strange exchange.   35
But tell me, must I now resign my crown
To make usurping Mortimer a king?

Bishop of Winchester
Your grace mistakes. It is for England's good
And princely Edward's right we crave the crown.

Edward
No, 'tis for Mortimer, not Edward's head,   40
For he's a lamb encompassèd by wolves
Which in a moment will abridge his life.
But if proud Mortimer do wear this crown,
Heavens turn it to a blaze of quenchless fire,
Or like the snaky wreath of Tisiphon[2]   45
Engirt[3] the temples of his hateful head.
So shall not England's vines be perishèd,
But Edward's name survive,[4] though Edward dies.

Leicester
My lord, why waste you thus the time away?
They stay[5] your answer. Will you yield your crown?   50

Edward
Ah, Leicester, weigh how hardly I can brook
To lose my crown and kingdom without cause,
To give ambitious Mortimer my right,
That like a mountain overwhelms my bliss,
In which extreme my mind here murdered is.   55
But what the heavens appoint, I must obey.

---

1 Marriage.
2 Tisiphone, one of the Furies, who had snakes for hair. See note to 4.315.
3 Encircle.
4 Survives in Q.
5 Wait for.

[Edward removes his crown]

Here, take my crown, the life of Edward too;
Two kings in England cannot reign at once.
But stay awhile, let me be king till night,
That I may gaze upon this glittering crown.   60
So shall my eyes receive their last content,
My head, the latest honour due to it,
And jointly both yield up their wishèd right.
Continue ever, thou celestial sun,
Let never silent night possess this clime;[1]   65
Stand still, you watches of the element;[2]
All times and seasons, rest you at a stay,
That Edward may be still fair England's king.
But day's bright beams doth vanish fast away,
And needs I must resign my wishèd crown.   70
Inhuman creatures nursed with tiger's milk,
Why gape you for your sovereign's overthrow?
My diadem, I mean, and guiltless life.
See, monsters, see, I'll wear my crown again!

[Edward puts back on his crown]

What, fear you not the fury of your king?   75
But, hapless Edward, thou art fondly[3] led.
They pass[4] not for thy frowns as late they did
But seek to make a new-elected king,
Which fills my mind with strange despairing thoughts,
Which thoughts are martyred with endless torments.   80
And in this torment, comfort find I none
But that I feel the crown upon my head,
And therefore let me wear it yet a while.

Trussel
My Lord, the parliament must have present news,
And therefore say, will you resign or no?   85

The king rageth

---

1 Region, climate.
2 Planets in the heavens.
3 Foolishly.
4 Care.

Edward
I'll not resign, not[1] whilst I live!
Traitors, be gone and join you with Mortimer;
Elect, conspire, install, do what you will,
Their blood and yours shall seal these treacheries.

Bishop of Winchester
This answer we'll return, and so farewell.   90

Leicester
Call them again, my lord, and speak them fair,
For if they go, the prince shall lose his right.

Edward
Call thou them back, I have no power to speak.

Leicester
My lord, the king is willing to resign.

Bishop of Winchester
If he be not, let him choose—   95

Edward
O would I might, but heavens and earth conspire
To make me miserable. Here, receive my crown.

[Edward removes his crown]

Receive it? No, these innocent hands of mine
Shall not be guilty of so foul a crime.
He of you all that most desires my blood   100
And will be called the murderer of a king,
Take it. What, are you moved, pity you me?
Then send for unrelenting Mortimer
And Isabel, whose eyes, being[2] turned to steel,
Will sooner sparkle fire than shed a tear.   105
Yet stay, for rather than I will look on them,
Here, here.

[Edward gives the crown to the bishop of Winchester]

Now, sweet God of heaven,
Make me despise this transitory pomp

---

1 But in Q; Q3 and 4 emend to not.
2 Been in Q.

And sit for aye enthronizèd in heaven.
Come, death, and with thy fingers close my eyes,   110
Or if I live let me forget myself.

Bishop of Winchester[1]
My lord.

Edward
Call me not lord. Away, out of my sight!
Ah, pardon me, grief makes me lunatic.
Let not that Mortimer protect my son;   115
More safety is there in a tiger's jaws
Than his embracements.

[Edward gives a handkerchief]

                    Bear this to the queen,
Wet with my tears and dried again with sighs.
If with the sight thereof she be not moved,
Return it back and dip it in my blood.   120
Commend me to my son and bid him rule
Better than I. Yet how have I transgressed,
Unless it be with too much clemency?

Trussel
And thus most humbly do we take our leave.

[Exit Trussel and the Bishop of Winchester]

Edward
Farewell. I know the next news that they bring   125
Will be my death, and welcome shall it be.
To wretched men death is felicity.

[Enter Berkeley, with a letter][2]

---

1   Bartley in Q. This is clearly a misattribution because Bartley (or Berke-
    ley, in the modernized form used in this edition) does not enter this
    scene until immediately before line 128, when Leicester announces
    "Another post." In the following line Edward addresses the post as
    Bartley. Winchester, to whom Edward has just given the crown, is line
    112's most likely speaker.
2   In Q the stage direction "Enter Bartley" is placed after line 111. Without
    having given Bartley (or Berkeley, in the modernized form used in this
    edition) an exit or a reason to exit and return, however,   *(continued)*

Leicester
Another post. What news brings he?

Edward
Such news as I expect. Come, Berkeley, come,
And tell thy message to my naked breast.   130

Berkeley
My lord, think not a thought so villainous
Can harbour in a man of noble birth.
To do your highness service and devoir[1]
And save you from your foes, Berkeley would die.

Leicester
[Reading the letter] My lord, the council of the Queen
    commands   135
That I resign my charge.

Edward
And who must keep me now? Must you, my lord?

Berkeley
Ay, my most gracious lord, so 'tis decreed.

Edward
[Taking the letter] By Mortimer, whose name is
    written here.
Well may I rend[2] his name, that rends my heart!   140

[Edward rips up the letter]

This poor revenge hath something eased my mind;
So may his limbs be torn, as is this paper.
Hear me, immortal Jove, and grant it too.

Berkeley
Your grace must hence with me to Berkeley straight.

Edward
Whither you will. All places are alike,   145
And every earth is fit for burial.

---

the play calls for his entrance on stage again shortly thereafter, at line
127s.d. This has led the editor to move the stage direction and emend
the speech prefix of line 112. See note to line 112.
1 Duty.
2 Rent in Q.

Leicester
Favour him, my lord, as much as lieth in you.

Berkeley
Even so betide my soul as I use him.

Edward
Mine enemy hath pitied my estate,[1]
And that's the cause that I am now removed.　　150

Berkeley
And thinks your grace that Berkeley will be cruel?

Edward
I know not, but of this am I assured,
That death ends all, and I can die but once.
Leicester, farewell.

Leicester
Not yet, my lord. I'll bear you on your way.　　155

Exit all

[Scene 21]

Enter Mortimer [Junior], and Queen Isabella

Mortimer Junior
Fair Isabel, now have we our desire.
The proud corrupters of the light-brained king
Have done their homage to the lofty gallows,
And he himself lies in captivity.
Be ruled by me, and we will rule the realm.　　5
In any case, take heed of childish fear,
For now we hold an old wolf by the ears,
That if he slip[2] will seize upon us both
And gripe[3] the sorer, being griped[4] himself.
Think therefore, madam, that imports us much[5]　　10

1　State, condition.
2　Escape, free himself.
3　Clutch, grip.
4　Gripped in Q.
5　That it is very important for us.

To erect[1] your son with all the speed we may
And that I be protector[2] over him,
For our behoof[3] will bear the greater sway
When as a king's name shall be underwrit.[4]

Isabella
Sweet Mortimer, the life of Isabel,   15
Be thou persuaded that I love thee well,
And therefore, so the prince my son be safe,
Whom I esteem as dear as these mine eyes,
Conclude against his father what thou wilt,
And I myself will willingly subscribe.   20

Mortimer Junior
First would I hear news that he were deposed,
And then let me alone to handle him.

Enter messenger

Mortimer Junior
Letters, from whence?

Messenger
                              From Killingworth, my lord.

Isabella
How fares my lord the king?

Messenger
In health, madam, but full of pensiveness.   25

Isabella
Alas poor soul, would I could ease his grief.

[Enter the bishop of Winchester with the crown]

Thanks, gentle Winchester; sirrah, be gone.

[Exit messenger]

---

1 Establish as monarch.
2 While a monarch was a minor, a protector was appointed to govern on
   his or her behalf.
3 Advantage.
4 Mortimer's commands will carry more weight when accompanied by
   Edward III's signature.

Bishop of Winchester
The king hath willingly resigned his crown.[1]

Isabella
O happy news! Send for the prince my son.

Bishop of Winchester
Further, ere this letter was sealed, Lord Berkeley came,   30
So that he now is gone from Killingworth;
And we have heard that Edmund laid a plot
To set his brother free. No more but so.
The lord of Berkeley is so pitiful
As Leicester that had charge of him before.   35

Isabella
Then let some other be his guardian.

[Exit the Bishop of Winchester]

Mortimer Junior
Let me alone—here is the privy seal.[2]
Who's there? Call hither Gurney and Matrevis.[3]
To dash the heavy-headed Edmund's drift,
Berkeley shall be discharged, the king removed,   40
And none but we shall know where he lieth.

Isabella
But, Mortimer, as long as he survives
What safety rests for us or for my son?

Mortimer Junior
Speak, shall he presently be dispatched and die?

Isabella
I would he were, so it were not by my means.   45

Enter Matrevis and Gurney

---

1 Edward II was deposed by parliament and abdicated in January 1327.
 See Holinshed's account in Appendix A1(h).
2 The official royal seal.
3 Following Forker and others, this editor has adopted the position that
 Matrevis, whom John Stow describes as a knight (Appendix A2[b]), is
 distinct from the Earl of Arundel of scenes 9, 11, and 16. Wiggins and
 Lindsey conflate the two in their edition.

Mortimer Junior

Enough. Matrevis, write a letter presently
Unto the Lord of Berkeley from ourself,
That he resign the king to thee and Gurney;
And when 'tis done we will subscribe our name.

Matrevis

It shall be done, my lord.

Mortimer Junior

Gurney.

Gurney

My Lord.   50

Mortimer Junior

As thou intendest to rise by Mortimer,
Who now makes Fortune's wheel[1] turn as he please,
Seek all the means thou canst to make him droop
And neither give him kind word nor good look.

Gurney

I warrant you, my lord.   55

Mortimer Junior

And this above the rest, because we hear
That Edmund casts to work his liberty,
Remove him still from place to place by night,
Till[2] at the last he come to Killingworth,
And then from thence to Berkeley back again.   60
And by the way to make him fret the more
Speak curstly[3] to him, and in any case
Let no man comfort him if he chance to weep,
But amplify his grief with bitter words.

Matrevis

Fear not, my Lord, we'll do as you command.   65

---

1 The goddess Fortune, who spins the wheel of human affairs, is a commonplace figure in early modern literature. In *The Prince* Machiavelli
writes that "fortune is a woman, and it is necessary, if you wish to
master her, to conquer her by force" (94).
2 And in Q. Till in Q2-Q4.
3 Harshly.

Mortimer Junior
So now away, post thitherwards amain.[1]

Isabella
Whither goes this letter? To my lord the king?
Commend me humbly to his Majesty
And tell him that I labour all in vain
To ease his grief and work his liberty.   70
And bear him this as witness of my love.

[Isabella gives Matrevis a jewel]

Matrevis
I will, madam.

Exit Matrevis and Gurney

Isabella and Mortimer [Junior] remain

Enter the young Prince [Edward], and the Earl of Kent talking
with him

Mortimer Junior
Finely dissembled; do so still, sweet Queen.
Here comes the young prince with the Earl of Kent.

Isabella
Something he whispers in his childish ears.   75

Mortimer Junior
If he have such access unto the prince,
Our plots and stratagems will soon be dashed.

Isabella
Use Edmund friendly, as if all were well.

Mortimer Junior
How fares my honourable lord of Kent?

Kent
In health, sweet Mortimer. How fares your grace?   80

Isabella
Well, if my Lord your brother were enlarged.

---

1   Ride there immediately.

Kent
I hear of late he hath deposed himself.

Isabella
The more my grief.

Mortimer Junior
And mine.

Kent
[Aside] Ah, they do dissemble.   85

Isabella
Sweet son, come hither. I must talk with thee.

Mortimer Junior
Thou, being his uncle and the next of blood,
Do look to be protector over the prince.

Kent
Not I, my lord. Who should protect the son
But she that gave him life, I mean the Queen?   90

Prince Edward
Mother, persuade me not to wear the crown.
Let him be king; I am too young to reign.

Isabella
But be content, seeing it his highness's pleasure.

Prince Edward
Let me but see him first, and then I will.

Kent
Ay, do, sweet nephew.   95

Isabella
Brother, you know it is impossible.

Prince
Why, is he dead?

Isabella
No, God forbid.

Kent
I would these words proceeded from your heart.

Mortimer Junior
Inconstant Edmund, dost thou favour him,   100
That wast a cause of his imprisonment?

Kent
The more cause have I now to make amends.

Mortimer Junior
I tell thee, 'tis not meet[1] that one so false
Should come about the person of a prince.
My lord, he hath betrayed the king his brother,   105
And therefore trust him not.

Prince Edward
But he repents and sorrows for it now.

Isabella
Come, son, and go with this gentle Lord and me.

Prince
With you I will, but not with Mortimer.

Mortimer Junior
Why youngling, 'sdain'st[2] thou so of Mortimer?   110
Then I will carry thee by force away.

Prince Edward
Help, uncle Kent! Mortimer will wrong me.

[Exit Mortimer Junior with Prince Edward]

Isabella
Brother Edmund, strive not. We are his friends;
Isabel is nearer than the earl of Kent.

Kent
Sister, Edward is my charge. Redeem him.[3]   115

Isabella
Edward is my son, and I will keep him.

[Exit Isabella]

Kent
Mortimer shall know that he hath wronged me.
Hence will I haste to Killingworth castle

---

1 Fitting, appropriate.
2 Disdainest.
3 Return.

And rescue agèd Edward from his foes
To be revenged on Mortimer and thee.   120

[Exit Kent]

[Scene 22]

Enter Matrevis and Gurney with the king, [and soldiers]

Matrevis
My lord, be not pensive. We are your friends.
Men are ordained to live in misery.
Therefore come; dalliance¹ dangereth our lives.

Edward
Friends, whither must unhappy Edward go?
Will hateful Mortimer appoint no rest?   5
Must I be vexèd like the nightly bird²
Whose sight is loathsome to all wingèd fowls?
When will the fury of his mind assuage?³
When will his heart be satisfied with blood?
If mine will serve, unbowel straight this breast   10
And give my heart to Isabel and him—
It is the chiefest mark they level⁴ at.

Gurney
Not so, my liege. The Queen hath given this charge⁵
To keep your grace in safety.
Your passions make your dolours⁶ to increase.   15

Edward
This usage makes my misery increase.
But can my air of life continue long
When all my senses are annoyed with stench?
Within a dungeon England's king is kept,
Where I am starved for want of sustenance;   20
My daily diet is heartbreaking sobs

---

1 Delay, loitering.
2 The owl.
3 Abate, diminish.
4 Aim.
5 Order.
6 Sorrows.

That almost rends[1] the closet of my heart.
Thus lives old Edward, not relieved by any,
And so must die, though pitièd by many.
O water, gentle friends, to cool my thirst   25
And clear my body from foul excrements.[2]

Matrevis

Here's channel water,[3] as our charge is given.
Sit down, for we'll be barbers to your grace.

Edward

Traitors, away! What, will you murder me
Or choke your sovereign with puddle water?   30

Gurney

No, but wash your face and shave away your beard,
Lest you be known and so be rescued.

Matrevis

Why strive you thus? Your labour is in vain.

Edward

The wren may strive against the lion's strength,
But all in vain; so vainly do I strive   35
To seek for mercy at a tyrant's hand.

They wash him with puddle water, and shave his beard away[4]

Immortal powers, that knows the painful cares
That waits upon my poor distressèd soul,
O level all your looks upon these daring men
That wrongs their liege and sovereign, England's king.   40
O Gaveston, it is for thee that I am wronged;
For me, both thou and both the Spencers died,
And for your sakes a thousand wrongs I'll take.
The Spencers's ghosts, wherever they remain,
Wish well to mine; then tush, for them I'll die.   45

---

1 Rents in Q.
2 Harmful substances.
3 Water from an open sewer or ditch.
4 Many of the details of Edward's mistreatment in this scene, including
   the shaving with puddle water, can be found in John Stow's *The Annales
   of England* (1592). See Appendix A2(b).

Matrevis
'Twixt theirs and yours shall be no enmity.
Come, come, away. Now put the torches out;
We'll enter in by darkness to Killingworth.

Enter Edmund [Kent]

Gurney
How now, who comes there?

Matrevis
Guard the king sure! It is the earl of Kent.   50

Edward
O gentle brother, help to rescue me.

Matrevis
Keep them asunder; thrust in the king.

Kent
Soldiers, let me but talk to him one word.

Gurney
Lay hands upon the earl for this assault.

Kent
Lay down your weapons; traitors, yield the king.   55

Matrevis
Edmund, yield thou thyself, or thou shalt die.

Kent
Base villains, wherefore do you grip me thus?

Gurney
Bind him, and so convey him to the court.

Kent
Where is the court but here? Here is the king,
And I will visit him. Why stay you me?   60

Matrevis
The court is where lord Mortimer remains.
Thither shall your honour go, and so farewell.

Exit Matrevis and Gurney, with the king

Edmund [Kent] and the soldiers remain

Kent
O miserable is that commonweal, where lords
Keep courts and kings are locked in prison!

Soldier
Wherefore stay we? On, sirs, to the court.   65

Kent
Ay, lead me whither you will, even to my death,
Seeing that my brother cannot be released.[1]

Exit all

[Scene 23]

Enter Mortimer [Junior] alone

Mortimer Junior
The king must die, or Mortimer goes down:
The commons[2] now begin to pity him.
Yet he that is the cause of Edward's death
Is sure to pay for it when his son is of age,
And therefore will I do it cunningly.   5
This letter, written by a friend[3] of ours,
Contains his death yet bids them save his life:
"*Edwardum occidere nolite timere, bonum est,*"
"Fear not to kill the king, 'tis good he die."
But read it thus, and that's another sense: 10
"*Edwardum occidere nolite, timere bonum est,*"
"Kill not the king, 'tis good to fear the worst."
Unpointed[4] as it is, thus shall it go,

---

1 Although Kent and others did plot to release Edward from captivity
   before his death, Kent was executed only after Edward's murder. Believ-
   ing that Edward was still alive at Corfe Castle, Kent wrote incriminating
   letters attempting to gather support for plans to free Edward. These
   letters were discovered, and Kent was beheaded for treason on 19
   March 1330 (Haines 211-12).
2 Common people.
3 Adam Orleton, Bishop of Hereford, according to Holinshed.
4 The difference between the two versions of the Latin sentence lies solely
   in the placement of the comma. "Unpointed" or unpunctuated, the sentence is ambiguous, leaving the reader to choose which of the two
   meanings the writer intended.

That, being dead,[1] if it chance to be found,
Matrevis and the rest may bear the blame,   15
And we be quit[2] that caused it to be done.
Within this room is locked the messenger
That shall convey it and perform the rest,
And by a secret token that he bears
Shall he be murdered when the deed is done.   20
Lightborn,[3] come forth.

[Enter Lightborn]

                              Art thou as resolute as thou wast?

Lightborn
What else, my lord? And far more resolute.

Mortimer Junior
And hast thou cast how to accomplish it?

Lightborn
Ay, ay, and none shall know which way he died.

Mortimer Junior
But at his looks, Lightborn, thou wilt relent.   25

Lightborn
Relent! Ha, ha, I use[4] much to relent.

Mortimer Junior
Well, do it bravely and be secret.

Lightborn
You shall not need to give instructions;
'Tis not the first time I have killed a man.
I learned in Naples how to poison flowers,   30
To strangle with a lawn[5] thrust through the throat,
To pierce the windpipe with a needle's point,
Or, whilst one is asleep, to take a quill
And blow a little powder in his ears,

---

1 Once Edward is dead.
2 Acquitted, free of blame.
3 "Lightborn" is a rough English translation of "Lucifer" and is the name
   of a devil in the medieval Chester cycle dramas (Levin 101).
4 Am accustomed (Lightborn is being ironic).
5 A piece of linen.

Or open his mouth and pour quicksilver down.   35
But yet I have a braver way than these.

Mortimer Junior
What's that?

Lightborn
Nay, you shall pardon me, none shall know my tricks.

Mortimer Junior
I care not how it is, so it be not spied.
Deliver this to Gurney and Matrevis.   40

[Mortimer Junior gives Lightborn the letter]

At every ten miles' end thou hast a horse.
Take this.

[Mortimer Junior gives Lightborn the token]

Away, and never see me more.

Lightborn
No?

Mortimer Junior
No, unless thou bring me news of Edward's death.

Lightborn
That will I quickly do. Farewell, my lord.   45

[Exit Lightborn]

Mortimer Junior
The prince I rule, the queen do I command,
And with a lowly congé[1] to the ground
The proudest lords salute me as I pass;
I seal,[2] I cancel, I do what I will.
Feared am I more than loved; let me be feared,[3]   50
And when I frown make all the court look pale.

---

1 Bow.
2 Approve into law, make official.
3 A Machiavellian maxim. Machiavelli's *The Prince* was not translated
   into English until 1640, but Innocent Gentillet's widely read *Anti-
   Machiavell*, published in French in 1576 and translated   (*continued*)

I view the prince with Aristarchus'[1] eyes,
Whose looks were as a breeching[2] to a boy.
They thrust upon me the Protectorship
And sue[3] to me for that that I desire,   55
While at the council table, grave enough,
And not unlike a bashful Puritan,[4]
First I complain of imbecility,
Saying it is *onus quam gravissimum*,[5]
Till, being interrupted by my friends,   60
Suscepi[6] that *provinciam*,[7] as they term it.
And to conclude, I am Protector now;
Now all is sure. The Queen and Mortimer
Shall rule the realm, the king, and none rule us.
Mine enemies will I plague, my friends advance,   65
And what I list[8] command, who dare control?
Maior sum quam cui possit fortuna nocere,[9]
And that this be the coronation day,
It pleaseth me and Isabel the Queen.
The trumpets sound, I must go take my place.   70

---

into English in 1602, provided a (not entirely accurate) summary of
Machiavelli's thought in the form of a series of maxims, which the
author then attempted to refute. Gentillet's ninth "maxim of policy" is:
"It is better for a Prince to be feared than loved" (216).
1   Librarian, grammarian, and literary critic who established a school at
    Alexandria in the second century BCE.
2   Whipping.
3   Petition.
4   A term that by the end of the sixteenth century denominated radical
    English Protestants unhappy with what they perceived to be the laxness
    and impurity of the established Elizabethan Church. The label is most
    frequently used pejoratively, and Puritans were often satirized for their
    hypocrisy.
5   "Most weighty burden" (Latin).
6   "I undertake" (Latin).
7   "Office" (Latin).
8   Wish to.
9   "I am beyond Fortune's ability to harm." The Latin quotation is from
    Ovid's *Metamorphoses*. Golding (1567) translates the Latin as "I am
    greater than that frowarde fortune may / Empeache me" (VI.248-49).
    The quotation is ironic: Niobe, queen of Thebes, makes this boast
    immediately before all her children are killed by Apollo and Diana
    because she had the presumption to consider herself their mother Leto's
    equal.

Enter the young King [Edward III], Bishop [of Canterbury],
Champion, Nobles, Queen

Bishop of Canterbury
    Long live king Edward, by the grace of God
    King of England and lord of Ireland.[1]

Champion
    If any Christian, Heathen, Turk, or Jew
    Dares but affirm that Edward's not true king
    And will avouch his saying with the sword,   75
    I am the Champion that will combat him.

Mortimer Junior
    None comes. Sound trumpets.

King Edward III
                            Champion, here's to thee.

[Edward III toasts the champion and gives him the cup]

Isabella
    Lord Mortimer, now take him to your charge.

Enter soldiers with the Earl of Kent prisoner

Mortimer Junior
    What traitor have we there with blades and bills?

Soldier
    Edmund the Earl of Kent.

King Edward III
                            What hath he done?   80

Soldier
    He would have taken the king away perforce[2]
    As we were bringing him to Killingworth.

Mortimer Junior
    Did you attempt his rescue, Edmund? Speak.

---

1   Prince Edward was crowned Edward III 1 February 1327.
2   By force.

Kent
Mortimer, I did. He is our king,
And thou compell'st this prince to wear the crown. 85

Mortimer Junior
Strike off his head. He shall have martial law.

Kent
Strike off my head? Base traitor, I defy thee.

King Edward III
My lord, he is my uncle and shall live.

Mortimer Junior
My lord, he is your enemy and shall die.

Kent
Stay, villains. 90

King Edward III
Sweet mother, if I cannot pardon him,
Entreat my lord Protector for his life.

Isabella
Son, be content, I dare not speak a word.

King Edward III
Nor I, and yet methinks I should command;
But seeing I cannot, I'll entreat for him. 95
My lord, if you will let my uncle live,
I will requite it when I come to age.

Mortimer Junior
'Tis for your highness' good and for the realm's.
[To soldiers] How often shall I bid you bear him hence?

Kent
Art thou king? Must I die at thy command? 100

Mortimer Junior
At our command. Once more, away with him.

Kent
Let me but stay and speak; I will not go.
Either my brother or his son is king,
And none of both them thirst for Edmund's blood.
And therefore, soldiers, whither will you hale me? 105

They [soldiers] hale Edmund [Kent] away, and carry him to be beheaded

[Exit all except Edward III and Isabella]

King Edward III
> What safety may I look for at his hands,
> If that my uncle shall be murdered thus?

Isabella
> Fear not, sweet boy, I'll guard thee from thy foes.
> Had Edmund lived, he would have sought thy death.
> Come, son, we'll ride a-hunting in the park.   110

King Edward III
> And shall my uncle Edmund ride with us?

Isabella
> He is a traitor, think not on him. Come.

[Exit Edward III and Isabella]

[Scene 24]

Enter Matrevis and Gurney

Matrevis
> Gurney, I wonder the king dies not,
> Being in a vault[1] up to the knees in water,
> To which the channels[2] of the castle run,
> From whence a damp continually ariseth
> That were enough to poison any man,   5
> Much more a king brought up so tenderly.[3]

Gurney
> And so do I, Matrevis. Yesternight
> I opened but the door to throw him meat,
> And I was almost stifled with the savour.[4]

---

1 Dungeon.
2 Sewers.
3 Some of the details of Edward's treatment while imprisoned can be found in Holinshed's account. See Appendix A1(i).
4 Smell.

Matrevis

He hath a body able to endure   10
More than we can inflict, and therefore now
Let us assail his mind another while.

Gurney

Send for him out thence, and I will anger him.

Matrevis

But stay, who's this?

Enter Lightborn

Lightborn

                    My lord protector greets you.

[Lightborn gives them Mortimer Junior's letter]

Gurney

What's here? I know not how to conster[1] it.   15

Matrevis

Gurney, it was left unpointed for the nonce.[2]
"Edwardum occidere nolite timere,"
That's his meaning.

Lightborn

Know you this token? I must have the king.

Matrevis

Ay, stay a while; thou shalt have answer straight.   20
[Aside to Gurney] This villain's sent to make away the king.

Gurney

[Aside to Matrevis] I thought as much.

Matrevis

[Aside to Gurney]   And when the murder's done,
See how he must be handled for his labour:
Pereat iste.[3] Let him have the king.
[To Lightborn] What else? Here is the keys, this is
    the lake;   25
Do as you are commanded by my lord.

---

1 Construe, interpret.
2 For the occasion, on purpose.
3 "Let this man die" (Latin).

Lightborn
    I know what I must do, get you away.
    Yet be not far off, I shall need your help.
    See that in the next room I have a fire,
    And get me a spit and let it be red hot.   30

Matrevis
    Very well.

Gurney
        Need you anything besides?

Lightborn
    What else? A table and a featherbed.

Gurney
    That's all?

Lightborn
    Ay, ay. So when I call you, bring it in.

Matrevis
    Fear not you that.   35

Gurney
    Here's a light to go into the dungeon.

[Exit Matrevis and Gurney]

Lightborn
    So now must I about this gear. Ne'er was there any
    So finely handled as this king shall be.
    Foh, here's a place indeed with all my heart.

[Enter Edward]

Edward
    Who's there? What light is that? Wherefore comes thou?   40

Lightborn
    To comfort you and bring you joyful news.

Edward
    Small comfort finds poor Edward in thy looks.
    Villain, I know thou com'st to murder me.

Lightborn
    To murder you, my most gracious lord?
    Far is it from my heart to do you harm.   45

The Queen sent me to see how you were used,
For she relents at this your misery.
And what eyes can refrain from shedding tears
To see a king in this most piteous state?

Edward

    Weep'st thou already? List awhile to me,   50
    And then thy heart, were it as Gurney's is
    Or as Matrevis', hewn from the Caucasus,[1]
    Yet will it melt ere I have done my tale.
    This dungeon where they keep me is the sink[2]
    Wherein the filth of all the castle falls.   55

Lightborn

    O villains!

Edward

    And there in mire and puddle have I stood
    This ten days' space, and lest that I should sleep,
    One plays continually upon a drum.
    They give me bread and water, being a king,   60
    So that for want of sleep and sustenance
    My mind's distempered and my body's numbed,
    And whether I have limbs or no, I know not.
    O would my blood dropped out from every vein,
    As doth this water from my tattered robes!   65
    Tell Isabel the Queen I looked not thus
    When for her sake I ran at tilt[3] in France
    And there unhorsed the duke of Cleremont.

Lightborn

    O speak no more, my lord, this breaks my heart.
    Lie on this bed and rest yourself awhile.   70

Edward

    These looks of thine can harbour naught but death;
    I see my tragedy written in thy brows.
    Yet stay awhile. Forbear thy bloody hand
    And let me see the stroke before it comes,
    That even then when I shall lose my life,   75
    My mind may be more steadfast on my God.

---

1 The Caucasus mountains, considered to mark the boundary between
   Europe and Asia.
2 Cesspit.
3 In a joust.

Lightborn
What means your highness to mistrust me thus?

Edward
What means thou to dissemble with me thus?

Lightborn
These hands were never stained with innocent blood,
Nor shall they now be tainted with a king's.   80

Edward
Forgive my thought, for having such a thought.
One jewel have I left, receive thou this.
Still fear I and know not what's the cause,
But every joint shakes as I give it thee.
O if thou harbour'st murder in thy heart,   85
Let this gift change thy mind and save thy soul.
Know that I am a king. O, at that name
I feel a hell of grief! Where is my crown?
Gone, gone—and do I remain alive?

Lightborn
You're overwatched,[1] my lord. Lie down and rest.   90

[Edward lies down on the bed]

Edward
But that grief keeps me waking, I should sleep,
For not these ten days have these eyes' lids closed.
Now as I speak they fall, and yet with fear
Open again. O wherefore sits thou here?

Lightborn
If you mistrust me I'll be gone, my lord.   95

Edward
No, no, for if thou mean'st to murder me,
Thou wilt return again, and therefore stay.

[Edward falls asleep]

Lightborn
He sleeps.

---

1 Overtired.

Edward
O let me not die! Yet stay, O stay a while.

Lightborn
How now, my Lord.   100

Edward
Something still buzzeth in mine ears
And tells me if I sleep I never wake.
This fear is that which makes me tremble thus,
And therefore tell me, wherefore art thou come?

Lightborn
To rid thee of thy life. Matrevis, come.   105

[Enter Matrevis]

Edward
I am too weak and feeble to resist.
Assist me, sweet God, and receive my soul.[1]

Lightborn
Run for the table.

[Exit Matrevis. He and Gurney return with the table]

Edward
O spare me or dispatch me in a trice.

Lightborn
So, lay the table down and stamp on it,   110
But not too hard, lest that you bruise his body.

[Edward screams as Lightborn, Matrevis, and Gurney murder
him][2]

---

1 Compare to Christ's last words in Luke 23:46: "And when Jesus had
   cried with a loud voice, he said, Father, into thy hands I commend my
   spirit: and having said thus, he gave up the ghost."
2 Q includes no stage directions to specify exactly how Edward is to be
   murdered. Editors and critics are divided on whether just the featherbed
   and table are used or whether the hot spit, thrust into Edward's bowels
   through his anus, is the murder weapon. Holinshed's account in Appendix A1(i) states that a hot spit or something analogous was used. In the
   play itself the lines immediately preceding Edward's murder focus on
   the featherbed and table while the screaming that Matrevis mentions
   immediately afterward suggests the pain of the hot spit.

Matrevis
I fear me that this cry will raise the town,[1]
And therefore let us take horse and away.

Lightborn
Tell me, sirs, was it not bravely done?
Gurney
Excellent well. Take this for thy reward.   115

Then Gurney stabs Lightborn

Come, let us cast the body in the moat
And bear the king's to Mortimer our lord.
Away!

[Exit Matrevis and Gurney with the bodies]

[Scene 25]

Enter Mortimer [Junior] and Matrevis

Mortimer Junior
Is't done, Matrevis, and the murderer dead?

Matrevis
Ay, my good Lord; I would it were undone.

Mortimer Junior
Matrevis, if thou now growest penitent,
I'll be thy ghostly father.[2] Therefore choose
Whether thou wilt be secret in this   5
Or else die by the hand of Mortimer.

Matrevis
Gurney, my lord, is fled and will, I fear,
Betray us both. Therefore let me fly.

---

1 Berkeley. In Appendix A1(i), Holinshed reports that "His cry did move
   many within the castle and town of Berkeley to compassion, plainly
   hearing him utter a wailful noise, as the tormentors were about to
   murder him, so that diverse being awakened therewith (as they themselves confessed) prayed heartily to God to receive his soul, when they
   understood by his cry what the matter meant."
2 Confessor.

Mortimer Junior
    Fly to the savages.

Matrevis
    I humbly thank your honour.   10

[Exit Matrevis]

Mortimer Junior
    As for myself, I stand as Jove's huge tree,[1]
    And others are but shrubs compared to me.
    All tremble at my name, and I fear none;
    Let's see who dare impeach[2] me for his death.

Enter the Queen [Isabella]

Isabella
    Ah, Mortimer, the king my son hath news   15
    His father's dead and we have murdered him.

Mortimer Junior
    What if he have? The king is yet a child.

Isabella
    Ay, ay, but he tears his hair and wrings his hands
    And vows to be revenged upon us both.
    Into the council chamber he is gone   20
    To crave the aid and succour of his peers.
    Ay me, see where he comes, and they with him.
    Now, Mortimer, begins our tragedy.

Enter the king [Edward III], with the lords [and attendants]

First Lord
    Fear not, my lord. Know that you are a king.

King Edward III
    Villain.   25

Mortimer Junior
    How now, my lord?

King Edward III
    Think not that I am frighted with thy words.
    My father's murdered through thy treachery,

1 The oak.
2 Challenge.

And thou shalt die; and on his mournful hearse
Thy hateful and accursèd head shall lie   30
To witness to the world that by thy means
His kingly body was too soon interred.

Isabella
Weep not, sweet son.

King Edward III
Forbid me not to weep. He was my father,
And had you loved him half so well as I,   35
You could not bear his death thus patiently.
But you, I fear, conspired with Mortimer.

First Lord
Why speak you not unto my lord the king?

Mortimer Junior
Because I think scorn to be accused.
Who is the man dare say I murdered him?   40

King Edward III
Traitor, in me my loving father speaks
And plainly saith, 'twas thou that murd'redst him.

Mortimer Junior
But hath your grace no other proof than this?

King Edward III
Yes, if this be the hand of Mortimer.

[Edward shows the letter]

Mortimer Junior
[Aside to Isabella] False Gurney hath betrayed me
and himself.   45

Isabella
[Aside to Mortimer Junior] I feared as much. Murder
cannot be hid.

Mortimer Junior
'Tis my hand.[1] What gather you by this?

---

1 If this is the unpointed Latin letter of scenes 23 and 24, then Marlowe
seems to have forgotten that it was "written by a friend" (23.6).

King Edward III
That thither thou didst send a murderer.

Mortimer Junior
What murderer? Bring forth the man I sent.

King Edward III
Ah, Mortimer, thou knowst that he is slain,   50
And so shalt thou be too. Why stays he here?
Bring him unto a hurdle,[1] drag him forth,
Hang him, I say, and set his quarters[2] up.
But bring his head back presently to me.

Isabella
For my sake, sweet son, pity Mortimer.   55

Mortimer Junior
Madam, entreat not. I will rather die
Than sue for life unto a paltry boy.

King Edward III
Hence with the traitor, with the murderer.

Mortimer Junior
Base Fortune, now I see that in thy wheel
There is a point to which, when men aspire,   60
They tumble headlong down. That point I touched,
And seeing there was no place to mount up higher,
Why should I grieve at my declining fall?[3]
Farewell, fair Queen. Weep not for Mortimer,
That scorns the world and as a traveller   65
Goes to discover countries yet unknown.

King Edward III
What, suffer you the traitor to delay?

[Exit Mortimer Junior guarded by the first lord]

---

1 Frame on which traitors were dragged to execution.
2 Arms and legs.
3 These lines possibly echo the account of Mortimer's fall contained in
  William Baldwin's popular *Mirror for Magistrates* (London, 1578):
  "Fortune brought [Mortimer] from boote [succees] to extreme bale
  [misery]," the narrator states, later adding that "whom she [Fortune]
  heaves, she hurleth down as fast" (B3r).

Isabella

As thou receivèd'st thy life from me,
Spill not the blood of gentle Mortimer.

King Edward III

This argues that you spilt my father's blood;   70
Else would you not entreat for Mortimer.

Isabella

I spill his blood? No.

King Edward III

Ay, madam, you, for so the rumour runs.

Isabella

That rumour is untrue. For loving thee
Is this report raised on poor Isabel.   75

King Edward III

I do not think her so unnatural.

Second Lord

My lord, I fear me it will prove too true.

King Edward III

Mother, you are suspected for his death,
And therefore we commit you to the Tower
Till further trial may be made thereof.   80
If you be guilty, though I be your son
Think not to find me slack or pitiful.

Isabella

Nay, to my death, for too long have I lived
When as my son thinks to abridge my days.

King Edward III

Away with her. Her words enforce these tears,   85
And I shall pity her if she speak again.

Isabella

Shall I not mourn for my belovèd lord
And with the rest accompany him to his grave?

Second Lord

Thus, madam, 'tis the king's will you shall hence.

Isabella

He hath forgotten me. Stay, I am his mother.   90

Second Lord
That boots not; therefore, gentle madam, go.

Isabella
Then come, sweet death, and rid me of this grief.

[Exit Isabella guarded by the second lord]

[Enter the first lord with Mortimer Junior's head]

First Lord
My lord, here is the head of Mortimer.[1]

King Edward III
Go fetch my father's hearse, where it shall lie,
And bring my funeral robes.

[Exit attendants]

       Accursèd head,   95
Could I have ruled thee then as I do now,
Thou hadst not hatched this monstrous treachery.

[Enter attendants with funeral robes and King Edward II's hearse]

Here comes the hearse. Help me to mourn, my lords.[2]
Sweet father, here unto thy murdered ghost
I offer up this wicked traitor's head.   100
And let these tears distilling from mine eyes
Be witness of my grief and innocency.

[Exit all]

FINIS

---

1 Mortimer was hanged and drawn (rather than beheaded, the usual sentence for aristocratic traitors) on 29 November 1330. See Stow's account of Mortimer's capture and execution in Appendix A2(c).
2 Edward II's funeral was held 20 December 1327, three months after his death on 21 September 1327 (22 September according to Holinshed).

Appendix A: Marlowe's Historical Sources

1. From Raphael Holinshed, *The Third Volume of Chronicles of England, Scotland, and Ireland* (1587)

[Raphael Holinshed (c. 1525-80) was an English historian and translator. He is most famously known for *The Chronicles of England, Scotland, and Ireland*, first published in 1577 and published after his death in an expanded edition in 1587. Holinshed's text includes historical, sociological, and geographical descriptions of each country from the biblical flood to the reign of Queen Elizabeth. Most of the 1587 edition's third volume, which narrates English history from William the Conqueror to Queen Elizabeth, was written by Holinshed and revised and updated by Abraham Fleming and John Stow. The histories in the first two volumes—of Scotland, Ireland, and England before the Conquest—were written by various collaborators. Holinshed's history also draws heavily from two earlier works: Edward Hall's *The Union of the Two Noble and Illustrious Families of Lancaster and York* (1548) and John Leland's *Itinerary*. Holinshed's *Chronicles*, however, are the most complete history of England written in the English vernacular. They are the major historical source for Shakespeare's history plays as well as Marlowe's *Edward the Second*. The passages excerpted here include descriptions of Edward's death and coronation, Gaveston's reception in court and his death, the battle of Bannockburn, the Earl of Lancaster's execution, and Edward's political relationship with Queen Isabella.]

(a) [The beginning of Edward's reign.] Edward, the second of that name, the son of Edward the First, born at Caernarfon in Wales, began his reign over England the seventh day of July, in the year of our Lord 1307, of the world 5273, of the coming of the Saxons 847, after the conquest 241, about the tenth year of Albert emperor of Rome, and the two and twentieth of the fourth Philip, surnamed Le Beau, as then King of France, and in the third year after that Robert the Bruce had taken upon him the crown and government of Scotland.[1] His father's

---

1 Holinshed dated God's creation of the world to 3966 BCE and the arrival of
   the Saxons in Britain to 460 CE. The "conquest" refers to the Norman Conquest in 1066 CE, which saw Franco-Norman rule replace Saxon kingship in
   England. Albert I was Holy Roman Emperor from 1298 to 1308, (*continued*)

corpse was conveyed from Burgh upon Sands, unto the abbey of Waltham, there to remain till things were ready for the burial, which was appointed at Westminster.

Within three days after, when the Lord Treasurer Walter de Langton bishop of Coventry and Lichfield (through whose complaint Piers de Gaveston had been banished the land) was going towards Westminster to make preparation for the same burial, he was upon commandment from the new king arrested, committed to prison, and after delivered to the hands of the said Piers, being then returned again into the realm, who sent him from castle to castle as a prisoner. His lands and tenements were seized to the king's use, but his movables were given to the aforesaid Piers. Walter Reynolds that had been the king's tutor in his childhood, was then made Lord Treasurer, and after when the see[1] of Worcester was void, at the king's instance he was by the pope to that bishopric preferred. Also, Rafe bishop of London was deposed from the office of Lord Chancellor, and John Langton bishop of Chichester was thereto restored. Likewise, the barons of the exchequer were removed, and others put in their places. And Aymer de Valence earl of Pembroke was discharged of the wardenship of Scotland, and John de Britaine[2] placed in that office, whom he also made earl of Richmond.

But now concerning the demeanour of this new king, whose disordered manners brought himself and many others unto destruction: we find that in the beginning of his government, though he was of nature given to lightness,[3] yet being restrained with the prudent advertisements[4] of certain of his counsellors, to the end he might show some likelihood of good proof, he counterfeited a kind of gravity, virtue, and modesty; but yet he could not thoroughly be so bridled but that forthwith he began to play diverse wanton and light parts, at the first indeed not outrageously, but by little and little, and that covertly. For having revoked again into England his old mate the said Piers de Gaveston, he received him into most high favour, creating him earl of Cornwall, and Lord of Man, his principal secretary, and Lord Chamberlain of the realm, through whose company and society he was suddenly so corrupted that he burst out into most heinous vices; for then using the said Piers as a procurer of his disordered doings, he began

---

and Philip IV, Edward's father-in-law, reigned from 1285 to 1314. Holinshed is mistaken about Robert Bruce: Bruce crowned himself King of Scotland at Scone in 1306, not 1304 (Prestwich 53).

1 Diocese.
2 Edward II's cousin.
3 Frivolity, sexual promiscuity.
4 Warnings.

to have his nobles in no regard, to set nothing by their instructions, and to take small heed unto the good government of the commonwealth, so that within a while he gave himself to wantonness, passing his time in voluptuous pleasure and riotous excess. And to help them forward in that kind of life, the foresaid Piers, who (as it may be thought, he had sworn to make the king forget himself and the state, to which he was called) furnished his court with companies of jesters, ruffians, flattering parasites, musicians, and other vile and naughty ribalds, that the king might spend both days and nights in jesting, playing,[1] banqueting, and in such other filthy and dishonourable exercises; and moreover, desirous to advance those that were like to himself, he procured for them honourable offices, all which notable preferments and dignities, since they were ill bestowed, were rather to be accounted dishonourable than otherwise, both to the giver and the receiver.

(b) [Description of Gaveston.] The malice which the lords had conceived against the earl of Cornwall still increased, the more indeed through the high bearing of him, being now advanced to honour. For being a goodly gentleman and a stout, he would not once yield an inch to any of them, which worthily procured him great envy amongst the chiefest peers of all the realm, as Sir Henry Lacy earl of Lincoln, Sir Guy earl of Warwick, and Sir Aymer de Valence earl of Pembroke, the earls of Gloucester, Hereford, Arundel, and others, which upon such wrath and displeasure as they had conceived against him, thought it not convenient to suffer the same any longer, in hope that the king's mind might happily be altered into a better purpose, being not altogether converted into a venomous disposition, but so that it might be cured, if the corrupter thereof were once banished from him.

(c) [Gaveston's death.] The same night it chanced that Guy earl of Warwick came to the very place where the earl of Cornwall was left, and taking him from his keepers, brought him unto Warwick, where incontinently[2] it was thought best to put him to death, but that some doubting the king's displeasure advised the residue[3] to stay; and so they did, till at length an ancient grave man amongst them exhorted them to use the occasion now offered and not to let slip the mean to deliver the realm of such a dangerous person, that had wrought so much mischief and might turn them all to such peril as afterwards

---

1 Acting.
2 Immediately.
3 Rest, remainder.

they should not be able to avoid nor find shift how to remedy it. And thus persuaded by his words they caused him straightaway to be brought forth to a place called Blacklow, otherwise named by most writers Gaversley Heath, where he had his head smitten from his shoulders, the twentieth day of June being Tuesday. A just reward for so scornful and contemptuous a merchant, as in respect of himself (because he was in the prince's favour) esteemed the nobles of the land as men of such inferiority as that in comparison of him they deserved no little jot or mite of honour. But lo the vice of ambition, accompanied with a rabble of other outrages, even a reproachful end, with an everlasting mark of infamy, which he pulled by violent means on himself with the cords of his own lewdness and could not escape this fatal fall.

(d) [Bannockburn.] King Edward to be revenged hereof,[1] with a mighty army bravely[2] furnished and gorgeously apparelled, more seemly for a triumph than meet[3] to encounter with the cruel enemy in the field, entered Scotland in purpose specially to rescue the castle of Sterling, as then besieged by the Scottishmen. But at his approaching near to the same, Robert Bruce was ready with his power to give him battle. To the which King Edward, nothing doubtful of loss, had so unwisely ordered his people and confounded their ranks that even at the first joining they were not only beaten down and overthrown by those that coped with them at hand, but also were wounded with a shot afar off by those their enemies which stood behind to succour their fellows when need required, so that in the end the Englishmen fled to save their lives and were chased and slain by the Scots in great number.

(e) [Commentary on Lancaster's execution.] Thus the king seemed to be revenged of the displeasure done to him by the earl of Lancaster for the beheading of Piers de Gaveston earl of Cornwall, whom he so dearly loved, and because the earl of Lancaster was the chief occasioner of his death the king never loved him entirely after. So that here is verified the censure of the Scripture expressed by the wisdom of Solomon, that the anger and displeasure of the king is as the roaring of a lion,[4] and his revenge inevitable. Wherefore it is an high point of

---

1 Robert Bruce had just forcibly expelled the English from a number of their strongholds in Scotland.
2 Finely.
3 Fit, appropriate.
4 Proverbs 19:12.

discretion in such as are mighty to take heed how they give edge unto the wrath of their sovereign, which if it be not by submission made blunt, the burden of the smart[1] ensuing will lie heavy upon the offender, even to his utter undoing and loss (perhaps) of life. In this sort came the mighty earl of Lancaster to his end, being the greatest peer in the realm and one of the mightiest earls in Christendom. For when he began to levy war against the king, he was possessed of five earldoms, Lancaster, Lincoln, Salisbury, Leicester, and Derby, beside other seigniories, lands, and possessions, great to his advancement in honour and puissance.[2] But all this was limited within prescription of time, which being expired, both honour and puissance were cut off with dishonour and death, for (O mutable state!)

> *Invida fatorum series, summisque negatum*
> *Stare diu.*[3]

On the same day [as Lancaster's execution], the Lord William Tucket, the Lord William fitz William, the Lord Warren de Lisle, the Lord Henry Bradborne, and the Lord William Chenie, barons, with John Page, an esquire, were drawn[4] and hanged at Pomfret aforesaid, and then shortly after, Roger Lord Clifford, John Lord Mowbray, and Sir Gosein d'Evill, barons, were drawn and hanged at York. At Bristol in like manner were executed Sir Henry de Willington and Sir Henry Montfort, baronets; and at Gloucester, the Lord John Gifford and Sir William Elmebridge, knight; and at London, the Lord Henry Teies, baron; at Winchelsea, Sir Thomas Culpepper, knight; at Windsor, the Lord Francis de Aldham, baron; and at Canterbury, the Lord Bartholomew de Badalisemere, and the Lord Bartholomew de Ashbornham, barons. Also at Cardiff in Wales, Sir William Fleming, knight, was executed. Diverse were executed in their countries, as Sir Thomas Mandit and others.

(f) [Commentary on Isabella's reluctance to return to England.] A lamentable case, that such division should be between a king and his queen, being lawfully married and having issue of their bodies, which ought to have made that their copulation more comfortable. But (alas) what will not a woman be drawn and allured unto if by evil counsel she be once assaulted? And what will she leave undone,

---

1 Pain, wound.
2 Power.
3 Lines 70-71 of Book I of Lucan's *Belli Civilis*. In Marlowe's pithy translation, "The Fates are envious, high seats quickly perish" (*Lucan's First Book* 70).
4 Disembowelled.

though never so inconvenient to those that should be most dear unto her, so her own fancy and will be satisfied? And how hardly is she revoked from proceeding in an evil action if she have once taken a taste of the same? As very truly is reported by the comedy-writer, saying,

> Malè quod mulier incœpit nisi efficere id perpetrat,
> Id illi morbo, id illi senio est; ea illi misera miseria est:
> Si bene facere incœpit, eius eam citó odium percipit,
> Nimisq, pauca sunt defessa, malè qua facere occœperint;
> Nimisq, pauca efficiunt, si quid ocœperint benefacere;
> Mulieri nimiò malefacere melius est onus, quàm benè.[1]

(g) [Competing interests.] At the time of the queen's landing he [Edward] was at London, and being sore amazed with the news, he required aid of the Londoners. They answered that they would do all the honour they might unto the king, the queen, and to their son the lawful heir of the land, but as for the strangers and traitors to the realm, they would keep them out of their gates and resist them with all their forces. But to go forth of the city further than that they might return before sun-setting, they refused, pretending certain liberties in that behalf to them granted in times past as they alleged.

The king not greatly liking of this answer, fortified the Tower, and leaving within it his younger son John of Eltham and the wife of the Lord Chamberlain Hugh Spenser the Younger that was his niece, he departed towards the marches of Wales, there to raise an army against the queen. Before his departure from London, he set forth a proclamation that every man under pain of forfeiting of life and goods should resist them that were thus landed, assail, and kill them, the queen, his son Edward, and his brother the earl of Kent only excepted; and whosoever could bring the head or dead corpse of the Lord Mortimer of Wigmore should have for his labour a thousand marks. The queen's proclamations on the other part willed all men to hope for peace, the Spensers public enemies of the realm and the Lord Robert Baldock with their assistants only excepted, through whose means the present trouble was happened to the realm. And it was forbidden that no man should take aught from any person, and whosoever could

---

1 "What wickedness a woman undertakes, unless she is able to complete it, / It is a disease to her, it is old age, it is the most miserable of miseries. / If she begin to do well, soon hatred of it takes hold of her. / Very few who have begun wickedly are tired, / And very few complete if they have begun to do good. / For a woman it is by far a better burden to do evil than good" (Plautus, *Truculentus* II.v.465-70; editor's translation).

bring to the queen the head of Hugh Spenser the Younger should have two thousand pounds of the queen's gift.

The king at his departure from London left Master Walter Stapleton the bishop of Exeter behind him to have the rule of the city of London. Then shortly after, the queen, with her son making towards London, wrote a letter to the mayor and the citizens, requiring to have assistance for the putting down of the Spensers, not only known enemies of theirs but also common enemies to the realm of England. To this letter no answer at the first was made, wherefore another was sent, dated at Baldocke the first day of October, under the names of *Isabel by the grace of God Queen of England, lady of Ireland, and countess of Ponthieu, and of Edward eldest son to the King of England, duke of Guienne, earl of Chester, of Ponthieu and of Montreuil.* This letter being directed to the mayor and communality of London, containing in effect that the cause of their landing and entering into the realm at that time was only for the honour of the king and wealth of the realm, meaning hurt to no manner of person but to the Spensers, was fastened upon the cross in Cheape,[1] then called the new cross in Cheape, on the night before the ninth day of October. Diverse copies of the same letter were set up and fastened upon windows and doors in other places of the city, and one of the same copies was tacked upon the Lord Mayor's gates.

(h) [Edward's deposition.] After Christmas, the queen with her son and such lords as were then with them removed to London, where at their coming thither, which was before the feast of Epiphany,[2] they were received with great joy, triumph, and large gifts, and so brought to Westminster, where the morrow after the same feast, the parliament which before hand had been summoned began, in which it was concluded and fully agreed by all the states[3] (for none durst[4] speak to the contrary) that for diverse articles which were put up against the king, he was not worthy longer to reign and therefore should be deposed, and withal they willed to have his son Edward duke of Aquitaine to reign in his place. This ordinance was openly pronounced in the great hall at Westminster by one of his lords, on the feast day of Saint Hilary[5] being Tuesday, to the which all the people consented. The archbishop of Canterbury taking his theme, *Vox*

---

1 A cross erected in Cheapside, a major market street in London, by Edward I in 1290 to commemorate his dead wife Eleanor.
2 6 January.
3 Estates: the commons, the nobility, and the clergy.
4 Dared.
5 14 January.

populi, vox Dei,[1] made a sermon, exhorting the people to pray to God to bestow of his grace upon the new king. And so when the sermon was ended, every man departed to his lodging. But the duke of Aquitaine, when he perceived that his mother took the matter heavily in appearance, for that her husband should be thus deprived of the crown, he protested that he would never take it on him without his father's consent, and so thereupon it was concluded that certain solemn messengers should go to Killingworth[2] to move the king to make resignation of his crown and title of the kingdom unto his son.

There were sent on this message (as some write) three or (as others have) two bishops, two earls, two abbots, two or (as Thomas de la More and Walsingham have) four barons, and for every county, city, and borough, and likewise for the Cinque Ports,[3] certain knights and burgesses.[4] The bishops that were sent were these (as Thomas de la More noteth): John de Stratford bishop of Winchester, Adam de Torleton bishop of Hereford, and Henry bishop of Lincoln. The two earls (as Southwell hath) were Lancaster and Warwick; the two barons, Rose and Courtney. Beside these (as he saith) there were two abbots, two priors, two justices, two friars of the order of preachers, two of the Carmelites,[5] two knights for the commons on the north side of Trent,[6] and two for the other on the south side of the same river; two citizens for London, two burgesses for the Cinque Ports, so as in all there went of this message (as Southwell saith) three and twenty or rather four and twenty persons of one degree[7] and the other.

None of the friar minors[8] went, because they would not be the bringers of so heavy tidings, since he [Edward] had ever borne them great good will. The bishops of Winchester and Lincoln went before and, coming to Killingworth, associated with them the earl of Leicester, of some called the earl of Lancaster, that had the king in keeping. And having secret conference with the king, they sought to frame his mind so as he might be contented to resign the crown to his son, bearing him in hand[9] that, if he refused so to do, the people in respect

---

1 "The voice of the people is the voice of God" (Latin).
2 Kenilworth.
3 Hastings, Romney, Hythe, Sandwich, and Dover, ports on the southeast coast of England enjoying considerable economic and political autonomy in return for maintaining a navy for royal service.
4 Member of parliament for a borough or town.
5 Order of mendicant (begging) friars.
6 River flowing through the English Midlands.
7 Rank, social status.
8 Franciscans.
9 Making it clear to him.

of the evil will which they had conceived against him would not fail but proceed to the election of some other that should happily[1] not touch him in lineage.[2] And since this was the only mean to bring the land in quiet, they willed him to consider how much he was bound in conscience to take that way that should be beneficial to the whole realm.

The king, being sore troubled to hear such displeasant news, was brought into a marvellous agony, but in the end, for the quiet of the realm and doubt of further danger to himself, he determined to follow their advice, and so when the other commissioners were come and that the bishop of Hereford had declared the cause wherefore[3] they were sent, the king in presence of them all, notwithstanding his outward countenance, discovered how much it inwardly grieved him; yet after he was come to himself, he answered that he knew that he was fallen into this misery through his own offences, and therefore he was contented patiently to suffer it, but yet it could not (he said) but grieve him that he had in such wise run into the hatred of all his people; notwithstanding, he gave the lords most hearty thanks that they had so forgotten their received injuries and ceased not to bear so much good will towards his son Edward as to wish that he might reign over them. Therefore to satisfy them, since otherwise it might not be, he utterly renounced his right to the kingdom and to the whole administration thereof. And lastly he besought the lords now in his misery to forgive him such offences as he had committed against them. Ah lamentable ruin from royalty to miserable calamity, procured by them chiefly that should have been the pillars of the king's estate and not hooked engines to pull him down from his throne!

(i) [The murder.] They lodged the miserable prisoner in a chamber over a foul filthy dungeon full of dead carrion, trusting so to make an end of him with the abominable stench thereof; but he bearing it out strongly, as a man of a tough nature, continued still in life, so as it seemed he was very like to escape that danger, as he had by purging either up or down avoided the force of such poison as had been ministered to him sundry[4] times before of purpose so to rid him.

Whereupon when they saw that such practices would not serve their turn, they came suddenly one night into the chamber where he lay in bed fast asleep, and with heavy featherbeds or a table (as some

---

1 Perhaps.
2 Not come from his blood line.
3 Why.
4 Various, several.

write) being cast upon him, they kept him down and withal put into his fundament[1] an horn, and through the same they thrust up into his body an hot spit, or (as others have) through the pipe of a trumpet a plumber's instrument of iron made very hot, the which passing up into his entrails and being rolled to and fro, burnt the same, but so as no appearance of any wound or hurt outwardly might be once perceived. His cry did move many within the castle and town of Berkeley to compassion, plainly hearing him utter a wailful noise as the tormentors were about to murder him, so that diverse being awakened therewith (as they themselves confessed) prayed heartily to God to receive his soul when they understood by his cry what the matter meant.

The queen, the bishop, and others, that their tyranny might be hid, outlawed and banished the Lord Matravers and Thomas Gurney, who flying unto Marseille, three years after, being known, taken, and brought toward England, was beheaded on the sea lest he should accuse the chief doers, as the bishop and others. John Matravers, repenting himself, lay long hidden in Germany and in the end died penitently. Thus was King Edward murdered in the year 1327 on the 22 of September. The fame went that by this Edward the Second, after his death, many miracles were wrought. So that the like opinion of him was conceived as before had been of earl Thomas of Lancaster, namely amongst the common people. He was known to be of a good and courteous nature, though not of most pregnant wit.

And albeit in his youth he fell into certain light crimes, and after by the company and counsel of evil men was induced unto more heinous vices, yet was it thought that he purged the same by repentance, and patiently suffered many reproofs and finally death itself (as before ye have heard) after a most cruel manner. He had surely good cause to repent his former trade of living, for by his indiscreet and wanton misgovernance there were headed and put to death during his reign (by judgement of law) to the number of 28 barons and knights, over and beside such as were slain in Scotland by his unfortunate conduct.

2. From John Stow, *The Annals of England* (1592)

[John Stow (c. 1525-1605) assisted Raphael Holinshed in the preparation of his *Chronicles*. He was also a collector of manuscripts and a historian in his own right, producing three major texts: a collection of Chaucer's works, the *Survey of London and Westminster* (1565), and the *Annals; or, a General Chronicle of England*. The *Annals*, first published in 1580 (the year of Holinshed's death) are drawn from a systematic

---

1 Anus.

study of public records and histories. The excerpts here are from the 1592 revised edition of the *Annals* and describe the barons' petition against Gaveston, Edward's mistreatment during his imprisonment, and the fall of Mortimer Junior.]

(a) [The barons' petition.] The king gave unto Piers of Gaveston all such gifts and jewels as had been given to him, with the crowns of his father, his ancestors' treasure, and many other things, affirming that if he could, he should succeed him in the kingdom, calling him brother, not granting anything without his consent. The lords therefore envying him, told the king that the father of this Piers was a traitor to the King of France and was for the same executed, and that his mother was burned for a witch, and that the said Piers was banished for consenting to his mother's witchcraft, and that he had now bewitched the king himself. They besought the king to hear therefore their petitions, which should be both for his own honour and for the wealth of his people.

First, that he would confirm and use such ancient laws and customs as are contained in the charters of the kings his predecessors; and for that they would grant him the twentieth part of their goods and be his true subjects.

Secondly, that he would take nothing of any man but at the price of the owner of the same, to be paid for to the uttermost.

Thirdly, that whatsoever was alienated from the Crown[1] since his father's death might be restored thereunto again.

Fourthly, that he would observe the oath he made before his father, as of the revoking of Piers Gaveston, the prosecuting of the Scottish War, and that all that was amiss should be amended, lest his enemies rejoice at it, etc.

[Fifthly,] that justice and judgement might be done in the land, as well to the rich as to the poor, according to the ancient and approved laws and customs of England, and that no man should be restrained by the king's writ from prosecuting his right or to defend himself by law.

(b) [Edward's mistreatment.] This Edward of Caernarfon, now deprived of his royal crown and dignity, remained with Henry earl of Leicester his kinsman, lacking but liberty, where he being shut up led his life as if he had been a monk. But the fierce and cruel woman[2] being troubled with many things, taking counsel of her wicked school-

---

1 Whatever Crown estates (which were sources of revenue) had been sold off.
2 Isabella.

master Adam de Orleton bishop of Hereford, she had an answer of him which did not grieve her a little, that was that the earl of Leicester did take pity upon Edward his cousin. Moreover, there was talk throughout the land that there were covenants made amongst many to take King Edward by force out of the castle of Kenilworth, to the which one friar preacher, named Thomas Dunhed, and one clerk were assenting, for which cause he and others were imprisoned at York. It was therefore decreed by the cruel woman the queen, through the subtle device of her said schoolmaster, that Thomas of Gurney and John Maltravers, knights, having received him from the keeping of the earl of Lancaster, should carry Edward the old king about whither they would so that none of his well-willers should have access unto him or understand where he made any long abode.

And to these two wicked traitors authority was given by the highest sort that into whatsoever part of the kingdom they bent themselves, that all governors and keepers of castles should suffer them to enjoy their offices and rooms during their pleasure, upon pain of forfeiture of goods, lands, and life, if any should deny them. By means of which authority Henry earl of Leicester, through commandment of King Edward the Third, delivered the old king by indenture to Sir Thomas Berkeley and Sir John Maltravers, and they brought him from Kenilworth to the Castle of Corfe, then to Bristol, where for a season he was kept shut up in the castle, until it was understood by certain burgesses of the town, who for his deliverance conveyed themselves over sea. Wherefore in a dark night the keepers of Edward convey him thence to Berkeley.

These tormentors of Edward exercised towards him many cruelties, unto whom it was not permitted to ride unless it were by night, neither to see any man or to be seen of any. When he rode, they forced him to be bareheaded; when he would sleep, they would not suffer him; neither when he was hungry would they give him such meats as he desired, but such as he loathed. Every word that he spake was contraried by them, who gave it out most slanderously that he was mad. And shortly to speak, in all matters they were quite contrary to his will, that either by cold, watching, or unwholesome meats, for melancholy, by some infirmity, he might languish and die. But this man being by nature strong to suffer pains and patient through God's grace to abide all griefs, he endured all the devices of his enemies, for as touching poisons, which they gave him often to drink, by the benefit of nature he dispatched away.

These champions bring Edward towards Berkeley, being guarded with a rabble of hell-hounds, along by the grange[1] belonging to the

---

1   Barn, granary.

castle of Bristol, where that wicked man Gurney, making a crown of hay, put it on his head, and the soldiers that were present scoffed and mocked him beyond all measure, saying, "Tprut, avaunt[1] Sir King," making a kind of noise with their mouths as though they had farted. They feared to be met of any that should know Edward, they bent their journey therefore towards the left hand, riding along over the marshy grounds lying by the river of Severn.[2] Moreover, devising to disfigure him that he might not be known, they determine for to shave as well the hair of his head as also of his beard, wherefore, as in their journey they travelled by a little water which ran in a ditch, they commanded him to light from his horse to be shaven, to whom, being set on a mole hill, a barber came unto him with a basin of cold water taken out of the ditch, to shave him withal, saying unto the king that that water should serve for that time. To whom Edward answered that, would they, nould they,[3] he would have warm water for his beard, and, to the end that he might keep his promise, he began to weep and to shed tears plentifully. At length they came to Berkeley castle, where Edward was shut up close like an anchor.[4]

(c) [Mortimer's fall.] There was a parliament holden at Nottingham, where Roger Mortimer was in such glory and honour that it was without comparison. No man durst name him any other than the earl of March. A greater rout of men waited at his heels than on the king's person. He would suffer the king to rise to him and would walk with the king equally, step by step and cheek by cheek, never preferring[5] the king, but would go foremost himself with his officers. He greatly rebuked the earl of Lancaster, cousin to the king, for that without his consent he appointed certain lodgings for noblemen in the town, demanding who made him so bold to take up lodgings so nigh unto the queen ... By which means a contention rose among the noblemen and great murmuring among the common people, who said that Roger Mortimer, the queen's paragon[6] and the king's master, sought all the means he could to destroy the king's blood and to usurp the regal majesty. Which report troubled much the king's friends, to wit William Montacute and others, who for the safeguard of the king swore themselves to be true to his person and drew unto them Robert

---

1 Move! Go on!
2 River flowing through southwest England and Wales.
3 Whether they liked it or not.
4 Anchorite, hermit.
5 Giving precedence to.
6 Equal, match; prized jewel.

de Holland, who had of long time been chief keeper of the castle,[1] unto whom all secret corners of the same were known. Then upon a certain night, the king lying without the castle, both he and his friends were brought by torch light through a secret way underground, beginning far off from the said castle, till they came even to the queen's chamber, which they by chance found open. They therefore, being armed with naked swords in their hands, went forwards, leaving the king also armed without the door of the chamber, lest his mother should espy him. They which entered in slew Hugh Turpinton knight, who resisted them, Master John Nevill of Hornby giving him his deadly wound. From thence they went toward the queen mother, whom they found with the earl of March, ready to have gone to bed. And having taken the said earl, they led him out into the hall, after whom the queen followed, crying "Bel fils, bel fils, ayez pitie de gentil Mortimer, Good son, good son, take pity upon gentle Mortimer," for she suspected that her son was there though she saw him not. Then are the keys of the castle sent for and every place with all the furniture is yielded up unto the king's hands, but in such secret wise that none without the castle except the king's friends understood thereof. The next day in the morning very early, they bring Roger Mortimer and his other friends taken with him with a horrible shout and crying (the earl of Lancaster, then blind, being one of them that made the shout for joy) towards London, where he was committed to the Tower and afterward condemned at Westminster in presence of the whole parliament on Saint Andrew's next following,[2] and then drawn to the Elms[3] and there hanged on a common gallows, whereupon he hung two days and two nights by the king's commandment and then was buried in the Gray Friars' Church. He was condemned by his peers and yet never was brought to answer before them, for it was not then the custom, after the death of the earls of Lancaster, Winchester, Gloucester, and Kent, wherefore this earl had that law himself which he appointed for others.

---

1 Nottingham Castle.
2 November 30.
3 Tyburn, a site in London commonly used for executions.

Appendix B: From Michael Drayton, Mortimeriados: The Lamentable Civil Wars of Edward the Second and the Barons (1596)

[Michael Drayton (1563-1631) was a prolific early modern English poet and playwright. Much of his poetry retells English history, often with particular interest in the nobility of England. Among his longer poems are *Idea*, nine eclogues to Robert Dudley (1595), *The Tragical Legend of Robert, Duke of Normandy* (1596), and *The Legend of Thomas Cromwell, Earl of Essex* (1607). Drayton's interest in Edward II's reign is evident in early works such as *Piers Gaveston, Earl of Cornwall* (1593) and *Mortimeriados* (1596 and later republished as *The Barons' Wars* in 1603). The excerpts from the latter included here display the influence of Marlowe's play, and the reader will find it instructive to compare Marlowe's and Drayton's treatment of Edward, Isabella, and Mortimer. Nonetheless, Drayton's poem provides a very different historical perspective from Marlowe's play. The poem thematizes, and is a contribution to, the making of a heroic national English history. Edward is a blot on that history, the "eclipse of England's fame," and it is not surprising that Drayton has Edward say "O let that name ... from books be torn" (2007) when he encounters the record of his own birth while reading a chronicle history of England. Mortimer, in contrast, is the hero to be rescued from oblivion and given his proper place in English history. In 1597 Drayton published *England's Heroical Epistles*, a collection of verse letters based on Ovid's *Heroides*. Drayton's epistolary poems draw more from history than myth, however, recounting the correspondence between famous lovers in English history. The *Epistles* includes a pair of letters between Isabella and Mortimer, sent after Mortimer has escaped the Tower of London and fled into France. In 1603, *England's Heroical Epistles* were republished in the same volume as *The Barons'Wars*.]

1. [Lines 1-7: Edward's birth.]

The louring heaven had masked her in a cloud,
Dropping sad tears upon the sullen earth,
Bemoaning in her melancholy shroud,
The angry star which reigned at Edward's birth,
     With whose beginning ended all our mirth.   5
Edward the Second, but the first of shame,
Scourge of the crown, eclipse of England's fame.

2. [Lines 29-49: Mortimer.]

The rageful fire which burnt Caernarfon's[1] breast,
Blown with revenge of Gaveston's disgrace,   30
Awakes the barons from their nightly rest,
And maketh way to give the Spensers place,
      Whose friendship Edward only doth embrace;
By whose allurements he is fondly[2] led,
To leave his queen, and fly his lawful bed.   35

This planet stirred up by that tempestuous blast
By which our fortune's anchorage was torn,
The storm wherewith our spring was first defaced,
Whereby all hope unto the ground was borne:
      Hence came the grief, the tears, the cause to mourn.   40
This bred the blemish which her beauty stained,
Whose ugly scars, to after-times remained.

In all this heat his greatness first began,
The serious subject of my sadder vein,
Great Mortimer, the wonder of a man,   45
Whose fortunes here my Muse must entertain,
      And from the grave his grief must yet complain,
To show our vice nor virtues never die,
Though under ground a thousand years we lie.

3. [Lines 624-58: Isabella as witch.]

For Mortimer the wind yet rightly blew,
Darkening their eyes which else perhaps might see,   625
Whilst Isabel who all advantage knew,
Is closely plotting his delivery,
      Now fitly drawn by Torlton's[3] policy:
Thus by a queen, a bishop, and a knight,
To check a king, in spite of all despite.   630

A drowsy potion she by skill hath made,
Whose secret working had such wondrous power,
As could the sense with heavy sleep invade,

---

1 Edward II's.
2 Foolishly.
3 Adam Orleton, Bishop of Hereford.

And mortify the patient in one hour,
        As though pale death the body did devour;   635
Nor for two days might opened be his eyes,
By all means art or physic[1] could devise.

Thus sits the great enchantress in her cell,
Environed with spirit-commanding charms,
Her body censed[2] with most sacred smell,   640
With holy fires her liquors now she warms,
        Then her with sorcering instruments she arms.
And from her herbs the powerful juice she wrung,
To make the poison forcible and strong.

Reason might judge, doubts better might advise,   645
And as a woman, fear her hand have stayed;[3]
Weighing the strangeness of the enterprise,
The danger well might have her sex dismayed,
        Fortune, distrust, suspect, to be betrayed;
But when they leave[4] of virtue to esteem,   650
They greatly err which think them as they seem.

Their plighted[5] faith, when as they list[6] they leave,
Their love is cold, their lust, hot, hot their hate;
With smiles and tears these serpents do deceive,
In their desires they be insatiate,   655
        Their will no bound, and their revenge no date.
All fear exempt, where they at ruin aim,
Covering their sin with their discovered shame.

4. [Lines 940-74. Mortimer's aspiring mind.]

Never saw France, no never till this day,   940
A mind more great, more free, more resolute,
Let all our Edwards say, what Edwards may,

---

1 Medicine.
2 Perfumed.
3 Restrained.
4 Cease.
5 Pledged.
6 Wish.

Our Henries, Talbot,[1] or our Mountacute,[2]
    To whom our royal conquests we impute:
That Charles[3] himself, oft to the peers hath sworn,   945
This man alone the Destinies did scorn.

Virtue can bear, what can on virtue fall,
Who cheapeneth honour, must not stand on price,
Who beareth heaven (they say) can well bear all,
A yielding mind doth argue cowardice,   950
    Our haps do turn as chances on the dice.
Nor never let him from his hope remove,
That under him hath mould,[4] the stars above.

Let dull-brained slaves contend for mud and earth,
Let blocks and stones, sweat but for blocks and stones,   955
Let peasants speak of plenty and of dearth,[5]
Fame never looks so low as on these drones,
    Let courage manage empires, sit on thrones.
And he that Fortune at command will keep,
He must be sure, he never let her sleep.   960

Who wins her grace, must with achievements woo her,
As she is blind, so never had she ears,
Nor must with puling[6] eloquence go to her,
She understands not sighs, she hears not prayers,
    Flattered she flies, controlled she ever fears;   965
And though a while she nicely[7] do forsake it,
She is a woman, and at length will take it.

---

1 John Talbot (1388-1453), Earl of Shrewsbury, who won renown during the reigns of Henry V and Henry VI in the Hundred Years War between France and England. He and his army were destroyed in the battle of Castillon, which ended the Hundred Years War and any realistic English claims to the French throne.

2 Thomas Montacute (1388-1428), Earl of Salisbury, who died in 1428 at the siege of Orleans.

3 Charles VII of France (1403-61).

4 Earth.

5 Scarcity, famine.

6 Whining.

7 Coyly.

Nor never let him dream once of a crown,
For one bad cast, that will give up his game,
And though by ill hap he be overthrown,   970
Yet let him manage her, till she be tame,
    The path is set with danger leads to fame:
When Minos[1] did the Grecian's[2] flight deny,
He made him wings and mounted through the sky.

5. [Lines 1688-1778: Edward's abdication speech.]

He takes the crown, and closely hugs it to him,
And smiling in his grief he leans upon it;
Then doth he frown because it would forgo him,   1690
Then softly stealing, lays his vesture[3] on it;
    Then snatching at it, loath to have forgone it,
He put it from him, yet he will not so,
And yet retains what fain[4] he would forgo.

Like as a mother overcharged with woe,   1695
Her only child now labouring in death,
Doing to help it, nothing yet can do,
Though with her breath, she fain would give it breath,
    Still saying, yet forgetting what she say'th:
Even so with poor King Edward doth it fare,   1700
Leaving his crown, the firstborn of his care.

In this confusèd conflict of the mind,
Tears drowning sighs, and sighs confounding tears,
Yet whenas neither any ease could find,
And extreme grief doth somewhat harden fears,   1705
    Sorrow grows senseless when too much she bears,
Whilst speech and silence, strives which place should take,
With words half spoke, he silently bespake.

---

1 King of Crete whose wife Pasiphaë gave birth to the Minotaur after having
    intercourse with a bull.
2 Daedalus, who made wings and flew across the Aegean to escape imprison-
    ment by Minos for his involvement in Pasiphaë's bestial affair.
3 Clothing.
4 Gladly, willingly.

I claim no crown, quoth he, by vile oppression,
Nor by the law of nature have you chose me,   1710
My father's title groundeth my succession,
Nor in your power is colour[1] to depose me,
    By heaven's decree I stand, they must dispose me;
A lawless act, in an unlawful thing,
Withdraws allegiance, but uncrowns no king.   1715

What God hath said to one, is only due,
Can I usurp by tyrannizing might?
Or take what by your birthright falls to you?
Root out your houses? Blot your honour's light?
    By public rule, to rob your public right?   1720
Then can you take, what he could not that gave it,
Because the heavens commanded I should have it.

My lords, quoth he, commend me to the king,
Here doth he pause, fearing his tongue offended,
Even as in childbirth forth the word doth bring,   1725
Sighing a full point, as he there had ended,
    Yet striving, as his speech he would have mended;
Things of small moment[2] we can scarcely hold,
But griefs that touch the heart, are hardly told.

Here doth he weep, as he had spoke in tears,   1730
Calming this tempest with a shower of rain,
Whispering, as he would keep it from his ears,
Do my allegiance to my sovereign;
    Yet at this word, here doth he pause again:
Yes say even so, quoth he, to him you bear it,   1735
If it be Edward that you mean shall wear it.

Keep he the crown, with me remain the curse,
A hapless father, have a happy son,
Take he the better, I endure the worse,
The plague to end in me, in me begun,   1740
    And better may he thrive than I have done;
Let him be second Edward, and poor I,
For ever blotted out of memory.

---

1 Legitimate reason.
2 Importance.

Let him account his bondage from the day
That he is with the diadem invested,   1745
A glittering crown doth make the hair soon grey,
Within whose circle he is but arrested,
        In all his feasts, he's but with sorrow feasted;
And when his feet disdain to touch the mould,
His head a prisoner, in a jail of gold.   1750

In numb'ring of his subjects, numb'ring care,
And when the people do with shouts begin,
Then let him think their only prayers are,
That he may 'scape the danger he is in,
        The multitude, be multitudes of sin;   1755
And he which first doth say, God save the king,
He is the first doth news of sorrow bring.

His commons' ills shall be his private ill,
His private good is only public care,
His will must only be as others will: 1760
Himself not as he is, as others are,
        By Fortune dared to more than Fortune dare:
And he which may command an empery,[1]
Yet can he not entreat his liberty.

Appeasing tumults, hate cannot appease,   1765
Soothed with deceits, and fed with flatteries,
Displeasing to himself, others to please,
Obeyed as much as he shall tyrannize,
        Fear forcing friends, enforcing enemies:
And when he sitteth under his estate,   1770
His foot-stool danger, and his chair is hate.

He king alone, no king that once was one,
A king that was, unto a king that is;
I am unthroned, and he enjoys my throne,
Nor should I suffer that, nor he do this: 1775
        He takes from me what yet is none of his.
Young Edward climbs, old Edward falleth down,
Kinged and unkinged, he crowned, farewell my crown.

---

1 Empire.

6. [Lines 1793-1855: Gurney and Matravers's abuse of Edward.]

To Gurney and Matravers he is given;
O let their act be odious to all ears,
And being spoke, stir clouds to cover heav'n,   1795
And be the badge the wretched murd'rer bears,
     The wicked oath whereby the damned swears:
But Edward, in thy hell thou must content thee,
These be the devils which must still torment thee.

He on a lean ill-favoured beast is set,   1800
Death upon Famine moralizing right;
His cheeks with tears, his head with rain bewet,
Night's very picture, wand'ring still by night;
     When he would sleep, like dreams they him affright;
His food torment, his drink a poisoned bane,[1]   1805
No other comfort but in deadly pain.

And yet because they fear to have him known,
They shave away his princely tressèd hair,
And now become not worth a hair of's own,
Body and fortune now be equal bare;   1810
     Thus void of wealth, O were he void of care.
But O, our joys are shadows, and deceive us,
But cares, even to our deaths do never leave us.

A silly molehill is his kingly chair,
With puddle water must he now be dressed,[2]   1815
And his perfume, the loathsome fenny air,
An iron skull, a basin fitting best,
     A bloody workman, suiting with the rest;
His loathed eyes, within this filthy glass,[3]
Truly behold how much deformed he was.   1820

The drops which from his eyes' abundance fall,
A pool of tears still rising by this rain,
Even fighting with the water, and withal,

---

1 Cause of death or destruction.
2 Shaved.
3 Mirror.

A circled compass makes it to retain,
    Billowed with sighs, like to a little main;[1]   1825
Water with tears, contending whether should
Make water warm, or make the warm tears cold.

Vile traitors, hold off your unhallowed hands,
The cruellest beast the lion's presence fears:
And can you keep your sovereign then in bands?   1830
How can your eyes behold th'annointed tears?
    Are not your hearts even pierced through your ears?
The mind is free, whate'er afflict the man,
A king's a king, do Fortune what she can.

Who's he can take what God himself hath given?   1835
Or spill that life his holy spirit infused?
All powers be subject to the powers of heaven,
Nor wrongs pass unrevenged, although excused;
    Weep majesty to see thyself abused.
O whither shall authority be take,   1840
When she herself, herself doth so forsake.

A wreath of hay they on his temples bind,
Which when he felt, (tears would not let him see),
Nature (quoth he) now art thou only kind,
Thou giv'st, but Fortune taketh all from me.   1845
    I now perceive, that were it not for thee,
I should want water, clothing for my brain,
But earth gives hay, and mine eyes give me rain.

My self deformed, like my deformed state,
My person made like to mine infamy,   1850
Alt'ring my favour, could you alter fate,
And blotting beauty, blot my memory,
    You might fly slander, I indignity·
My golden crown, took golden rule away,
A crown of hay, well suit a king of hay.   1855

7. [Lines 1926-46, 1996-2016: Edward and the English chronicle.]

Within a deep vault under where he lay,
Under buried filthy carcasses they keep,
Because the thick walls hearing kept away,

---

1 Open sea.

His feeling feeble, seeing ceas'd in sleep,
    This loathsome stink comes from the dungeon deep,   1930
As though before they fully did decree,
No one sense should from punishment be free.

He haps our English chronicle[1] to find,
On which to pass the hours he falls to read,
For minutes yet to recreate his mind,   1935
If any thought one uncared thought might feed,
    But in his breast new conflicts this doth breed:
For when sorrow is seated in the eyes,
Whate'er we see, increaseth miseries.

Opening the book, he chanced first of all   1940
On conquering William's[2] glorious coming in,
The Normans' rising, and the Britons' fall,
Noting the plague ordained for Harold's[3] sin,
    How much, in how short time this duke did win;
Great Lord (quoth he) thy conquests placed thy throne,   1945
I to mine own, have basely lost mine own.

[Lines 1947-95 describe Edward reading and moralizing upon the
reigns of a series of English kings down to the reign of his father,
Edward I.]

Then to great Longshanks'[4] mighty victories,
Who in the Orcads[5] fixed his country's mears,[6]
And dared in fight our faith's proud enemies,[7]
Which to his name eternal trophies rears,
    Whose graceful favours yet fair England wears: 2000
Be't deadly sin (quoth he) once to defile
This father's name with me, a son so vile.

---

1 History.
2 William the Conqueror (r. 1066-87), Duke of Normandy, who successfully
    invaded England in 1066.
3 Crowned in January 1066, Harold was the English king William defeated at
    the Battle of Hastings in 1066; his sin was to have violated an oath of alle-
    giance he allegedly made to William in 1064.
4 Edward I (r. 1272-1307).
5 Orkney Islands, off the northern coast of Scotland.
6 Boundaries.
7 Edward left England on crusade in 1270, returning to England in 1274.

Following the leaf,[1] he findeth unaware,
What day young Edward Prince of Wales was born,
Which letters seem like magic characters,   2005
Or to despite him they were made in scorn.
　　　O let that name (quoth he) from books be torn,
Lest that in time, the very grieved earth,
Do curse my mother's womb and ban[2] my birth.

Say that King Edward never had such child,   2010
Or was devoured as he in cradle lay,
Be all men from my place of birth exiled,
Let it be sunk, or swallowed with some sea,
　　　Let course of years devour that dismal day,
Let all be done that power can bring to pass,   2015
Only be it forgot that e'er I was.

8. [Lines 2052-79: Edward's death.]

Betwixt two beds these devils straight enclosed him;
Thus done, uncovering of his secret part,
When for his death they fitly had disposed him,
With burning iron thrust him to the heart.   2055
　　　O pain beyond all pain, how much thou art!
Which words, as words, may verbally confess,
But never pen precisely could express.

O let his tears even freezing as they light,[3]
By the impression of his monstrous pain,   2060
Still keep this odious spectacle in sight,
And show the manner how the king was slain,
　　　That it with ages may be new again;
That all may thither come that have been told it,
And in the mirror of his griefs behold it.   2065

Still let the building sigh his bitter groans,
And with a hollow cry his woes repeat,
That senseless things even moving senseless stones,

1　Page.
2　Curse.
3　Drop.

With agonizing horror still may sweat;
      And as consuming in their furious heat, 2070
Like boiling cauldrons be the drops that fall,
Even as that blood for vengeance still did call.

O let the woeful Genius of the place,
Still haunt the prison where his life was lost:
And with torn hair, and swollen ill-favoured face, 2075
Become the guide to his revengeful ghost,
      And night and day still let them walk the coast:
And with incessant howling terrify,
Or move with pity all that travel by.

Appendix C: The Diana-Actæon Myth

1. From The Third Book of Arthur Golding's *The XV Books of P. Ovidius Naso, Entitled Metamorphosis, Translated out of Latin into English Meter* (1567)

[The works of the classical Latin poet Ovid (43 BCE-17 CE) exercised enormous influence on the imaginations of early modern English poets. Perhaps the most influential of Ovid's works was his *Metamorphoses*, an epic collection of tales of transformation beginning with the universe's creation and ending with the apotheosis of Julius Caesar. Elizabethan schoolboys studied Ovid in the original in school, but Arthur Golding's translation of the *Metamorphoses* made the work even more accessible. Golding's was the first translation from Latin to English: earlier translations, like the printer William Caxton's 1480 translation, were translated from French editions of the poem. Marlowe, Shakespeare, and many other lesser Elizabethan poets and playwrights were familiar with it, echoing not just Ovid but Golding's translation in their verse. Gaveston's allusion to the myth of Diana and Actæon in scene one of Marlowe's play draws particularly from book three of Golding's translation.]

> Now Thebes stood in good estate, now Cadmus might thou
>   say   150
> That when thy father banished thee it was a lucky day.
> To join alliance both with Mars and Venus was thy chance,
> Whose daughter[1] thou hadst ta'en to wife, who did thee much
>   advance,
> Not only through her high renown, but through a noble race
> Of sons and daughters that she bare: whose children in like case 155
> It was thy fortune for to see all men and women grown.
> But ay the end of everything must marked be and known.
> For none the name of blessedness deserveth for to have
> Unless the tenor of his life last blessed to his grave.
> Among so many prosp'rous haps[2] that flowed with good success, 160
> Thine eldest nephew[3] was a cause of care and sore distress.

---

1 Harmonia.
2 Happenings, events.
3 Actæon, Cadmus's grandson.

Whose head was armed with palmed[1] horns, whose own hounds in
  the wood
Did pull their master to the ground and fill them with his blood.
But if you sift the matter well, ye shall not find desert[2]
But cruel fortune to have been the cause of this his smart.[3]   165
For who could do, with oversight?[4] Great slaughter had been made
Of sundry sorts of savage beasts one morning, and the shade
Of things was waxed very short. It was the time of day
That mid between the east and west the sun doth seem to stay,
Whenas[5] the Theban stripling thus bespake his company,   170
Still ranging in the wayless woods some further game to spy.
Our weapons and our toils are moist and stained with blood of deer;
This day hath done enough as by our quarry[6] may appear.
As soon as with her scarlet wheels next morning bringeth light,
·We will about our work again. But now Hyperion[7] bright   175
Is in the middes of heaven, and sears the fields with fiery rays.
Take up your toils, and cease your work, and let us go our ways.
They did even so, and ceased their work. There was a valley thick
With pineapple and cypress trees that armed be with prick.[8]
Gargaphie hight[9] this shady plot, it was a sacred place   180
To chaste Diana[10] and the nymphs that waited on her grace.
Within the furthest end thereof there was a pleasant bower
So vaulted with the leafy trees the sun had there no power,
Not made by hand nor man's devise, and yet no man alive
A trimmer piece of work than that could for his life contrive.   185
With flint and pommy[11] was it walled by nature half about,
And on the right side of the same full freshly flowed out
A lively spring with crystal stream, whereof the upper brim
Was green with grass and matted herbs that smelled very trim.
When Phœbe[12] felt herself wax faint, of following of her game,   190
It was her custom for to come and bathe her in the same.

---

1 Flattened.
2 Deserving.
3 Pain.
4 In retrospect, who could have done otherwise?
5 When.
6 Hunted animal; heap of animal corpses.
7 The sun.
8 Thorn, prickle.
9 Was called.
10 Moon goddess, goddess of chastity, goddess of hunting.
11 Pumice.
12 Diana.

That day she having timely left her hunting in the chase,
Was entered with her troupe of nymphs within this pleasant place.
She took her quiver and her bow the which she had unbent,
And eke[1] her javelin to a nymph that served that intent.   195
Another nymph to take her clothes among her train she chose,
Two loosed her buskins[2] from her legs and pulled off her hose.
The Theban ladie Crocale more cunning than the rest
Did truss her tresses handsomely which hung behind undressed.
And yet her own hung waving still. Then Niphe neat and clean   200
With Hiale glitt'ring like the grass in beauty fresh and sheen,[3]
And Rhanis clearer of her skin than are the rainy drops,
And little bibbling[4] Phyale, and Pseke that pretty mops,[5]
Poured water into vessels large to wash their lady with.
Now while she keeps this wont, behold, by wand'ring in the
     frith[6]   205
He wist[7] not whither (having stayed his pastime till the morrow)
Comes Cadmus' nephew to this thick: and ent'ring in with sorrow
(Such was his cursed cruel fate) saw Phœbe where she washed.
The damsels at the sight of man quite out of count'nance dashed,[8]
(Because they everyone were bare and naked to the quick)   210
Did beat their hands against their breasts, and cast out such a
     shriek,
That all the wood did ring thereof, and clinging to their dame
Did all they could to hide both her and eke themselves from
     shame.
But Phœbe was of personage so comely and so tall,
That by the middle of her neck she overpeered them all.   215
Such colour as appears in heaven by Phœbus' broken rays
Directly shining on the clouds, or such as is always
The colour of the morning clouds before the sun doth show,
Such sanguine colour in the face of Phœbe gan to glow
There standing naked in his sight. Why though she had her
     guard   220
Of nymphs about her, yet she turned her body from him ward[9]

---

1 Also.
2 Hunting boots.
3 Shining.
4 Drinking.
5 Moppet, darling.
6 Woods.
7 Knew.
8 Surprised and embarrassed.
9 Away from him.

And, casting back an angry look like as she would have sent
An arrow at him had she had her bow there ready bent,
So raught[1] she water in her hand and for to wreak[2] the spite
Besprinkled all the head and face of this unlucky knight,   225
And thus forespake the heavy lot that should upon him light.
Now make thy vaunt[3] among thy mates, thou sawest Diana bare.
Tell if thou can: I give thee leave: tell hardly:[4] do not spare.
This done she makes no further threats, but by and by doth spread
A pair of lively old hart's[5] horns upon his sprinkled head.   230
She sharps his ears, she makes his neck both slender, long and lank.
She turns his fingers into feet, his arms to spindle shank.[6]
She wraps him in a hairy hide beset with speckled spots,
And planteth in him fearfulness. And so away he trots,
Full greatly wond'ring to himself what made him in that case   235
To be so wight[7] and swift of foot. But when he saw his face
And hornèd temples in the brook, he would have cried alas,
But as for then no kind of speech out of his lips could pass.
He sighed and brayed: for that was then the speech that did
    remain,
And down the eyes that were not his, his bitter tears did rain.   240
No part remained (save his mind) of that he earst[8] had been.
What should he do? Turn home again to Cadmus and the queen?
Or hide himself among the woods? Of this he was afraid,
And of the other ill ashamed. While doubting thus he stayed,
    His hounds espied him where he was, and Blackfoot
        first of all   245
    And Stalker special good of scent began aloud to call.

[Lines 247 to 272 provide a catalogue of Actæon's hounds.]

These fellows over hill and dale in hope of prey do climb,
Through thick and thin and craggy cliffs where was no way to go;
He flies through grounds where oftentimes he chased had ere
    tho.[9]   275

---

1 Snatched.
2 Revenge.
3 Boast.
4 Vigorously.
5 Stag's.
6 Legs.
7 Quick.
8 Once.
9 Before then.

Even from his own folk is he fain[1] (alas) to flee away.
He strained oftentimes to speak and was about to say,
I am Actæon: know your lord and master sirs I pray,
But use of words and speech did want[2] to utter forth his mind.
Their cry did ring through all the wood redoubled with the
  wind,   280
First Slo did pinch him by the haunch, and next came Kildeere in,
And Hylbred fastened on his shoulder, bit him through the shin.
These came forth later than the rest, but coasting thwart[3] a hill,
They did gaincope[4] him as he came, and held their master still
Until that all the rest came in, and fastened on him to.   285
No part of him was free from wound. He could no other do
But sigh, and in the shape of hart with voice as harts are wont,
(For voice of man was none now left to help him at the brunt)
By braying show his secret grief among the mountains high
And kneeling sadly on his knees with dreary tears in eye,   290
As one by humbling of himself that mercy seemed to crave,
With piteous look instead of hands his head about to wave.
Not knowing that it was their lord, the huntsmen cheer their
  hounds
With wonted noise and for Actæon look about the grounds.
They hallow who could loudest cry still calling him by name,   295
As though he were not there, and much his absence they do
  blame
In that he came not to the fall,[5] but slacked to see the game.
As often as they named him he sadly shook his head,
And fain he would have been away thence in some other stead.
But there he was. And well he could have found in heart to see 300
His dogs' fell[6] deeds, so that to feel in place he had not be.
They hem him in on every side, and in the shape of stag,
With greedy teeth and griping paws their lord in pieces drag.
So fierce was cruel Phœbe's wrath, it could not be allayed,
Till all of his fault by bitter death the ransom he had paid.   305
     Much mutt'ring was upon this fact. Some thought there was
       extended
     A great deal more extremity than needed. Some commended

---

1 Willing, glad.
2 Lack.
3 Across.
4 Intercept, overtake.
5 Kill.
6 Savage, fearsome.

Diana's doing, saying that it was but worthely[1]
For safeguard of her womanhood. Each party did apply
Good reasons to defend their case.   310

2. Sonnet V of Samuel Daniel's Sonnet Sequence *Delia* (1592)

[Harkening back to sonnet 23 of Italian poet Petrarch's *Rime Sparse*, the following sonnet by early modern poet and playwright Samuel Daniel (1563-1619) uses the Diana-Actæon myth as a conceit for the transformative and self-devouring nature of the speaking voice's desire for the beloved, a common theme in Petrarchan love poetry. Duke Orsino, for example, presents a shorter version of the conceit in 1.1.18-22 of Shakespeare's *Twelfth Night*. Daniel's sonnet is the fifth in the larger sonnet sequence *Delia* (published in 1592 and republished with 29 additional sonnets in 1600). Like the sonnet itself, and unlike Shakespeare's play, the Delia sequence ends with the speaker's love tragically unrequited and the lover himself in despair and silence. Daniel's psychological use of the myth suggests another layer of meaning in Marlowe's use of the myth in *Edward the Second*. Edward's passions are not merely politically destructive but also psychologically self-destructive. Like Actæon, Edward is devoured by his own passion.]

Whilst youth and error led my wand'ring mind
And set my thoughts in heedless ways to range,
All unawares a goddess chaste I find,
Diana-like, to work my sudden change.
    For her no sooner had my view bewrayed,[2]
But with disdain to see me in that place,
With fairest hand, the sweet unkindest maid,
Casts water-cold disdain upon my face.
    Which turned my sport into a hart's[3] despair,
Which still is chased, whilst I have any breath,
By mine own thoughts; set on me by my fair,
My thoughts like hounds pursue me to my death.
        Those that I fostered of mine own accord
        Are made by her to murder thus their lord.

---

1 Honourable.
2 Betrayed.
3 Stag's; heart's.

Appendix D: On Friendship

1. Thomas Elyot, "The True Description of Amity or Friendship," from *The Book Named the Governor* (1580)

[The English historian and humanist Sir Thomas Elyot (c. 1490-1546) wrote *The Book Named the Governor* (first published in 1531), a conduct book for the monarch and his nobles. The text, which was frequently reprinted in the sixteenth century, reiterates arguments from the works of Plato and Aristotle, and particularly the Italian writer Castiglione's *Book of the Courtier*. It is divided into three parts or chapters. The first chapter begins by defining the commonwealth or republic and asserting the necessity for the commonwealth to be governed by a monarch to maintain order; it proceeds to discuss the proper education of future governors. Elyot emphasizes a classical education, but does not neglect to include instruction in music, dancing, and hunting. The second and third chapters discuss the virtues ideally found in governors, with ample illustration from both classical Greek and Roman history and English history. The virtues discussed in the second chapter might be grouped very broadly under the heading of mercy or love, while the virtues discussed in the third chapter are such sterner virtues as justice and fortitude. The excerpt printed here is taken from the second chapter and is largely Elyot's summary of the classical rhetorician Cicero's *De amicitia* ("On Friendship") and *De officiis* ("On Duty"). Structured as an attempt to define friendship, or "amity," the excerpt uncovers the inestimable value of friendship while also exposing its fragility in worlds of political and social competition. It is preceded by sections on humanity, benevolence, and liberality, and followed by sections on ingratitude and on how to choose one's friends wisely. Elyot's book was itself written in the context of the relationship between friendship and politics: Elyot dedicated *The Book Named the Governor* to Henry VIII, and many scholars suspect that this dedication, along with the sections on the virtues of monarchy, was responsible for Elyot's appointment as ambassador to the court of Emperor Charles V. Marlowe's play is similarly concerned with the relationship between friendship and politics. The word "friend" recurs frequently in the play and is used in ways that suggest that friendship and politics are inextricable.]

I have already treated of benevolence[1] and beneficence[2] generally, but forasmuch as friendship, called in Latin *amicitia*, comprehendeth both those virtues more specially and in a higher degree, and is now so infrequent or strange among mortal men by the tyranny of covetousness or ambition which have long reigned, and yet do, that amity may now unneth[3] be known or found throughout the world by them that seek for her as diligently as a maiden would seek for a small silver pin in a great chamber strawed with white rushes.

I will therefore borrow so much of the gentle reader, though he be nigh weary of this long matter, barren of eloquence and pleasant sentence, and declare somewhat by the way of very and true friendship, which perchance may be an allective[4] to good men to seek for their semblable on whom they may practice amity. For as Tully[5] saith, "Nothing is more to be loved or to be joined together than similitude of good manners or virtues; wherein be the same or semblable studies, the same wills or desires, in them it happeneth that one in another as much delighteth as in himself."[6] But now let us unearth what friendship or amity is.

Aristotle saith: friendship is a virtue or joineth with virtue.[7] Which is affirmed by Tully, saying, "friendship cannot be without virtue, neither but in good men only."[8] Who be good men, he after declareth to be those persons which do bear themselves and in such wise do live that their faith, surety, equality, and liberality be sufficiently proved; neither that there is in them any covetousness, wilfulness or foolhardiness, and that in them is great stability or constancy. Them suppose I, as they be taken, to be called good men, which do follow, as much as men may, Nature the chief captain or guard of man's life. Moreover, the same Tully defineth friendship in this manner, saying, "It is none other thing but a perfect consent of all things appertaining[9] as well to God as to man, with benevolence and charity,"[10] and that he knoweth nothing given of God except sapience[11] to man more commodious.[12]

---

1 Well-willing.
2 Well-doing.
3 Scarcely.
4 Something with the power to attract.
5 Marcus Tullius Cicero. Cf. notes to 1.141 and 4.395 of the play.
6 *De amicitia* xiv.49-50.
7 Aristotle, *Ethics* VIII.i.1.
8 *De amicitia* iv.18.
9 Belonging.
10 *De amicitia* vi.20.
11 Wisdom.
12 Helpful, convenient.

Which definition is excellent and very true. For in God and all thing that cometh of God, nothing is of more greater estimation than love, called in Latin *amor*, whereof *amicitia* cometh, named in English friendship or amity; the which taken away from the life of man, no house shall abide standing, no field shall be in culture.[1] And that is lightly perceived, if a man do remember what cometh of dissention and discord. Finally he seemeth to take the sun from the world that taketh friendship from a man's life.

Since friendship cannot be but in good men, nor may not be without virtue, we may be assured that thereof none evil may proceed or therewith any evil thing may participate. Wherefore, in as much as it may be but in a few persons (good men being in a small number) and also it is rare and seldom, as all virtues be commonly, I will declare, after the opinion of philosophers and partly by common experience, who among good men be of nature inoft[2] apt to friendship.

Between all men that be good cannot always be amity, but it also requireth that they be of semblable or much like manners or study, and especially of manners. For gravity and affability, be every of them laudable[3] qualities, so be severity and placability. Also magnificence and liberality be noble virtues, and yet frugality, which is a soberness or moderation in living, is, and that for good cause of all wise men extolled.[4] Yet where these virtues and qualities be separately in sundry persons assembled, may well be perfect concord, but friendship is there seldom or never. For that which one for a virtue embraceth, the other contemneth[5] or at the least neglecteth. Wherefore it seemeth, that it, wherein the one delighteth, is repugnant to the other's nature; and where is any repugnance may be none amity, since friendship is an entire consent of wills and desires. Therefore it is seldom seen that friendship is between these persons: a man sturdy of opinion, inflexible, and of sour countenance and speech, with him that is tractable and with reason persuaded and of sweet countenance and entertainment. Also between him which is elevate in authority and another of a very base estate or degree. Yea, and if they be both in an equal dignity, if they be desirous to climb, as they do ascend so friendship for the more part decayeth. For as Tully saith in his first book of offices, "What thing so ever it be, in the which many cannot excel or have therein superiority, therein oftentimes is such a contention that it is a thing of all other most difficult to keep among them good or virtuous

1 Cultivation.
2 Infrequently.
3 Praiseworthy.
4 Praised.
5 Scorns.

company,"[1] that is as much to say, as to retain among them friendship and amity. And it is oftentimes seen that divers[2] which, before they came in authority, were of good and virtuous conditions, being in their prosperity were utterly changed and, despising their old friends, set all their study and pleasure on their new acquaintance. Wherein men shall perceive to be a wonderful[3] blindness or (as I might say) a madness, if they note diligently all that I shall hereafter write of friendship. But now to resort to speak of them in whom friendship is most frequent and they also thereto be most aptly disposed.[4]

Undoubtedly it is specially[5] they which be wise and of nature inclined to beneficence, liberty, and constancy. For by wisdom is marked and substantially discerned the words, acts, and demeanour of all men between whom happeneth to be any intercourse or familiarity, whereby is engendered a favour or disposition of love. Beneficence, that is to say mutually putting to their study and help in necessary affairs, induceth love. They that be liberal do withhold or hide nothing from them whom they love, whereby love increaseth. And in them that be constant is never mistrust or suspicion or any surmise or evil report can withdraw them from their affection. And hereby friendship is made perpetual and stable. But if similitude of study or learning be joined unto the said virtues, friendship much rather happeneth, and the mutual interview and conversation is much more pleasant, specially if the studies have in them any delectable[6] affection or motion. For where they be too serious or full of contention, friendship is oftentimes assaulted, whereby it is often in peril. Where the study is elegant, and the matter illecebrous,[7] that is to say, sweet to the reader, the course whereof is rather gentle persuasion and quick reasonings than over-subtle argument or litigious controversies, there also it happeneth that the students do delight one in another, and without envy or malicious contention.

Now let us try out what is that friendship that we suppose to be in good men. Verily it is a blessed and stable connection of sundry[8] wills, making of two persons one in having and suffering. And therefore a friend is properly named of philosophers "the other I,"[9] for that in

---

1 *De officiis* I.viii.26.
2 Many or diverse people.
3 Amazing, startling.
4 And those also who are best fitted or inclined to friendship.
5 Especially.
6 Delightful.
7 Alluring.
8 Separate, distinct, individual.
9 Alter idem (Cicero, *De amicitia* xxi.80). See note to 1.141 of the play.

them is but one mind and one possession and that, which more is, a man more rejoiceth at his friend's good fortune than at his own.

Orestes and Pylades,[1] being wonderful like in all features, were taken together and presented unto a tyrant, who deadly hated Orestes. But when he beheld them both and would have slain Orestes only, he could not discern the one from the other. And also Pylades, to deliver his friend, affirmed that he was Orestes; on the other part Orestes, to save Pylades, denied and said that he was Orestes (as the truth was). Thus a long time they together contending the one to die for the other, at the last so relented the fierce and cruel heart of the tyrant that, wondering at their marvellous friendship, he suffered[2] them freely to depart without doing to them any damage.

[The example of Orestes and Pylades is followed by that of Pythias and Damon, two friends who offer to be executed for each other and for this display of true friendship are released by the tyrant who gave their death sentence, Dionysius of Syracuse. The story is related in Cicero's *De officiis* III.x.45.]

Undoubtedly that friendship which doth depend either on profit or else on pleasure, if the ability of the person which might be profitable do fail or diminish, or the disposition of the person which should be pleasant do change or appayre,[3] the ferventness[4] of love ceaseth, and then is there no friendship.

2. From Francis Bacon, Essay XXVII, "Of Friendship," *The Essays or Counsels Civil and Moral* (1625)

[Francis Bacon (1561-1626), known as the father of the empirical scientific method, was a prominent lawyer and the writer of several major works, including *The Advancement of Learning* (1605) and the *Novum Organum* (1620), both of which attempted to rectify earlier Aristotelian methods of acquiring and organising knowledge. Among his major literary achievements are the *Essays*. The first publication of this work was in 1597, and included ten entries, whose style carried some of the objective quality in Bacon's "philosophical" works. By 1625 (its last printing in Bacon's lifetime), the work had expanded to 58 essays. The essay excerpted here, "Of Friendship," is from the 1625 edition of the *Essays*. Although typically aphoristic, it is somewhat more

---

1 Cicero relates this story in *De amicitia* vii.24.
2 Permitted.
3 Worsen, weaken.
4 Ardour, intensity.

unified than some of Bacon's other essays. Bacon treats the theme of friendship from both a medical and a historical approach. He emphasizes the importance of "fellowship" as a means of restoring bodily health and order, yet balances the restorative qualities of friendship with reports of the political disruption that can occur when monarchs place too great a value on friendship, raising, as Edward does, their companions to an equal footing. In 1621 Bacon, who had been Attorney-General and was currently Lord Chancellor under James I, was impeached by parliament for bribery. After his impeachment, a number of his contemporaries added to the cloud of ill-repute under which Bacon lived his final years by circulating rumours that Bacon had engaged in sodomitical relations with his male servants (Jardine and Stewart 464-66).]

It had been hard for him that spoke it, to have put more truth and untruth together, in few words, than in that speech, "whosoever is delighted in solitude is either a wild beast or a god."[1] For it is most true that a natural and secret hatred and aversation[2] towards society in any man hath somewhat of the savage beast. But it is most untrue that it should have any character at all of the divine nature, except it proceed, not out of a pleasure in solitude, but out of a love and desire to sequester a man's self, for a higher conversation. Such as is found to have been falsely and fainedly[3] in some of the heathen: as Epimenides the Candian,[4] Numa the Roman,[5] Empedocles the Sicilian,[6] and Apollonius of Tyana;[7] and truly and really in divers of the ancient hermits and Holy Fathers of the Church. But little do men perceive what solitude is and how far it extendeth. For a crowd is not company, and faces are but a gallery of pictures, and talk but a "tinkling cymbal, where there is no love."[8] The Latin adage meeteth with it a little: *magna civitas, magna solitudo.*[9] Because in a great town, friends are scattered, so that there is not that fellowship, for the most part, which

---

1 Aristotle, *Politics* I.i.12.
2 Aversion.
3 In pretence, deceptively, falsely.
4 Cretan poet and prophet who is fabled to have fallen asleep in a cave as a boy and woken up fifty-seven years later.
5 Legendary second king of Rome, founder of Rome's religion.
6 Fifth-century BCE Sicilian philosopher.
7 First-century CE Pythagorean philosopher and miracle-worker.
8 See 1 Corinthians 13:1, "Though I speak with the tongues of men and of angels, and have not charity, I am become as sounding brass, or a tinkling cymbal."
9 "Great city, great solitude" (Latin). Erasmus, *Adagia* II.iv.54.

is in less[1] neighbourhoods. But we may go further and affirm most truly that it is a mere and miserable solitude to want true friends, without which the world is but a wilderness. And even in this sense also of solitude, whosoever in the frame of his nature and affections is unfit for friendship, he taketh it of the beast and not from humanity.

A principal fruit of friendship is the ease and discharge of the fullness and swellings of the heart, which passions of all kinds do cause and induce. We know diseases of stoppings[2] and suffocations are the most dangerous in the body, and it is not much otherwise in the mind. You may take sarza[3] to open the liver, steel to open the spleen, flower of sulphur for the lungs, castoreum[4] for the brain, but no receipt[5] openeth the heart but a true friend, to whom you may impart griefs, joys, fears, hopes, suspicions, counsels, and whatsoever lieth upon the heart to oppress it, in a kind of civil[6] shrift or confession.

It is a strange thing to observe how high a rate great kings and monarchs do set upon this fruit of friendship whereof we speak: so great as they purchase it, many times, at the hazard of their own safety and greatness. For princes, in regard of the distance of their fortune from that of their subjects and servants, cannot gather this fruit except (to make themselves capable thereof) they raise some persons to be, as it were, companions and almost equals to themselves, which many times sorteth[7] to inconvenience. The modern languages give unto such persons the name of favourites or privados, as if it were matter of grace or conversation. But the Roman name attaineth the true use and cause thereof, naming them *participes curarum*,[8] for it is that which tieth the knot. And we see plainly, that this hath been done not by weak and passionate princes only but by the wisest and most politique that ever reigned, who have oftentimes joined to themselves some of their servants, whom both themselves have called *friends* and allowed others likewise to call them in the same manner, using the word which is received between private men.

L. Sulla,[9] when he commanded Rome, raised Pompey[10] (after

---

1 Smaller.
2 Blockages, obstructions.
3 Sarsaparilla.
4 Castor oil.
5 Prescription, mixture of drugs.
6 Secular.
7 Leads.
8 "Sharers in care" (Latin).
9 Sulla (138-78 BCE), Roman dictator.
10 Pompeius Magnus (106-48 BCE), supporter of Sulla who after Sulla's death became, along with Julius Caesar and M. Licinius Crassus, a member of the first triumvirate to rule Rome.

surnamed the Great) to that height, that Pompey vaunted himself for Sulla's overmatch. For when he had carried the consulship for a friend of his against the pursuit of Sulla and that Sulla did a little resent thereat and began to speak great, Pompey turned upon him again and in effect bade him be quiet, "for that more men adored the sun rising than the sun setting."[1] With Julius Caesar,[2] Decimus Brutus[3] had obtained that interest, as he set him down in his testament[4] for heir in remainder[5] after his nephew.[6] And this was the man that had power with him to draw him forth to his death. For when Caesar would have discharged the senate in regard of some ill presages,[7] and specially a dream of Calpurnia,[8] this man lifted him gently by the arm out of his chair, telling him he hoped he would not dismiss the senate till his wife had dreamt a better dream. And it seemed his favour was so great as Antonius[9] in a letter, which is recited *verbatim*[10] in one of Cicero's *Philippics*,[11] calleth him *venefica*, witch, as if he had enchanted Caesar. Augustus[12] raised Agrippa[13] (though of mean[14] birth) to that height, as when he consulted with Maecenas[15] took the liberty to tell him "that he must either marry his daughter to Agrippa or take away his life, there was no third way, he had made him so great."[16] With

---

1 Plutarch, *Parallel Lives*, "The Life of Pompey" 14.3.
2 Julius Caesar (100-44 BCE), Roman dictator after Pompey's murder in 48 BCE and the defeat of Pompey's supporters at the battle of Thapsus in 46 BCE. He was assassinated 15 March (Ides of March) 44 BCE.
3 Decimus Junius Brutus Albinus (85 BCE-43 BCE), one of Julius Caesar's assassins.
4 Will.
5 Reversion, succession.
6 Julius Caesar Octavianus (63 BCE-14 CE), later Augustus, the first Roman emperor.
7 Omens, prophecies.
8 Julius Caesar's wife.
9 Marcus Antonius (83-30 BCE), member of the second triumvirate, which included Augustus and M. Aemilius Lepidus. He had Decimus Brutus executed in 43 BCE.
10 "Word for word" (Latin).
11 Cicero, *Philippics* XIII.xi.25.
12 Julius Caesar Octavianus (63 BCE-14 CE), later Augustus, the first Roman emperor.
13 Vipsanius Agrippa (63-12 BCE).
14 Common, low, base.
15 Cilnius Maecenas (d. 8 BCE), advisor to Augustus and patron of the poets Virgil and Horace.
16 Cassius Dio, *Roman History* liv.6.5.

Tiberius Caesar,[1] Sejanus[2] had ascended to that height as they two were termed and reckoned as a pair of friends. Tiberius in a letter to him saith, *"Haec pro amicitia nostra non occultavi,"*[3] and the whole senate dedicated an altar to friendship, as to a goddess, in respect of the great dearness of friendship between the two. The like or more was between Septimus Severus[4] and Plautianus.[5] For he forced his eldest son to marry the daughter of Plautianus and would often maintain Plautianus in doing affronts[6] to his son; and did write also in a letter to the senate, by these words: "I love the man so well as I wish he may over-live me."[7] Now if these princes had been as a Trajan[8] or a Marcus Aurelius,[9] a man might have thought that this had proceeded of an abundant goodness of nature; but being men so wise, of such strength and severity of mind, and so extreme lovers of themselves as all these were, it proveth most plainly that they found their own felicity (though as great as ever happened to mortal men) but as an half piece, except they might have a friend to make it entire. And yet, which is more, they were princes that had wives, sons, nephews, and yet all these could not supply the comfort of friendship.

3. From Richard Barnfield, "The Tears of an Affectionate Shepherd Sick for Love or The Complaint of Daphnis for the Love of Ganymede," *The Affectionate Shepherd* (1594)

[Richard Barnfield (c. 1574-1620) was a minor Elizabethan poet who published three miscellanies of verse between 1594 and 1598: *The Affectionate Shepherd* (1594), *Cynthia: with Certaine Sonnets, and the Legend of Cassandra* (1595), and *The Encomium of Lady Pecunia* (1598). Barnfield's poetry is notable for its exploration of male homo-

---

1 Tiberius Claudius Nero Caesar (42 BCE-37 CE), Roman emperor 14-37 CE.
2 Aelius Sejanus (d. 31 CE), Tiberius's friend and, after Tiberius withdrew to the island of Capreae (now Capri), *de facto* ruler of Rome. He was executed in 31 CE by the senate at the instigation of Tiberius, who had come to suspect Sejanus of imperial ambitions.
3 "Because of our friendship I have not hidden these things [from you]" (Latin). Tacitus, *Annales* IV.xl.
4 L. Septimus Severus (146-211 CE), Roman emperor 193-211 CE.
5 C. Fulvius Plautianus, whom Severus made second in command in Rome but executed in 205 CE for plotting against the imperial family.
6 Offending.
7 Cassius Dio, *Roman History* lxxvi.15.2.
8 Ulpius Trajanus (52-117 CE), Roman emperor 98-117 CE.
9 Marcus Aurelius (121-180 CE), Roman emperor 161-180 CE. Aurelius was a Stoic and the author of a work of Stoic philosophy, *Meditations*.

sexual desire. Bruce R. Smith states that *The Affectionate Shepherd* contains "the most explicitly homosexual poems of the entire English Renaissance" (99). Working within the tradition of pastoral poetry extending back to the classical poet Virgil, the poem excerpted here, "The Tears of an Affectionate Shepherd," is one of three pastoral eclogues included in *The Affectionate Shepherd*. It is modelled on Virgil's second eclogue and the eclogues of Spenser's *The Shepherd's Calendar* (1579), works that take as a central motif rejected homosexual love. Virgil's eclogue features the unrequited love of the older shepherd Corydon for the youth Alexis, and in Spenser's *The Shepherd's Calendar* the shepherd Hobbinoll is hopelessly in love with Colin Clout, who is equally desperately in love with Rosalind. "Ah foolish Hobbinal, thy gifts bene vayne: Colin them gives to Rosalind againe" (59-60), Colin proclaims in the Januarye eclogue with which *The Shepherd's Calendar* begins. Barnfield's poem similarly explores this motif, recounting Daphnis's futile pursuit of Ganymede, who in turn pursues the fair Queen Gwendolyn. It is significant that in both Spenser's and Barnfield's poems the male lover is in competition with a woman. As in *Edward the Second*, homosexual and heterosexual desire come into conflict. It is also significant that E.K., the character who supplies the glosses to the eclogues in *The Shepherd's Calendar*, feels compelled to defend Hobbinoll's love for Colin. Hobbinoll's love is not "disorderly love" (33), E.K. tells the reader. Rather, Hobbinoll's "pæderastice" is "much to be præferred before gynerastice, that is the love which enflameth men with lust toward woman kind" (34). Daphnis, the speaker in Barnfield's poem, makes a similar distinction when he pleads with Ganymede that "I love thee for thy gifts, she [Gwendolyn] for her pleasure; / I for thy virtue, she for beauty's treasure" (209-10). The pastoral world of the poems supplies the poems' various speakers with ample time to express their desire, lament the destructiveness of its non-reciprocity, and compile long catalogues of gifts they will give the object of their affection if he returns their love, all of which are argumentative strategies designed to seduce the male beloved. Marlowe's own poem, "The Passionate Shepherd to His Love," belongs to this tradition of pastoral poem, with its extensive catalogue of pastoral items that the speaker will give the beloved if he or she will "Come live with me, and be my love" (1).]

Scarce had the morning star hid from the light
Heaven's crimson canopy with stars bespangled,
But I began to rue th'unhappy sight
Of that fair boy that had my heart entangled,
    Cursing the time, the place, the sense, the sin   5
    I came, I saw, I viewed, I slipped in.

If it be sin to love a sweet-faced boy
(Whose amber locks trussed up in golden trammels[1]
Dangle adown his lovely cheeks with joy,
When pearl and flowers his fair hair enamels),   10
  If it be sin to love a lovely lad,
  O then sin I, for whom my soul is sad.

His ivory-white and alabaster skin
Is stained throughout with rare vermilion red,
Whose twinkling starry lights do never blin[2]   15
To shine on lovely Venus' (beauty's) bed.
  But as the lily and the blushing rose,
  So white and red on him in order grows.

Upon a time the nymphs bestirred themselves
To try who could his beauty soonest win,   20
But he accounted them but all as elves,
Except it were the fair Queen Gwendolyn.
  Her he embraced, of her was belovèd;
  With plaints he proved, and with tears he movèd.

[Lines 25-84 tell the story of Love and Death's angry encounter,
which leads to the two unknowingly exchanging arrows. Consequently, an old man falls in love with Gwendolyn when Death strikes
him with one of Love's arrows, while Gwendolyn's earlier love is killed
when Love shoots him with one of Death's arrows. Gwendolyn's
mourning for her earlier love seems somewhat incongruous with her
love for the fair youth of the poem.]

O would she would forsake my Ganymede,[3]   85
Whose sugared love is full of sweet delight,
Upon whose forehead you may plainly read
Love's pleasure, graved[4] in ivory tables[5] bright;
  In whose fair eyeballs you may clearly see
  Base Love still stand with foul indignity.   90

---

1 Tresses.
2 Cease.
3 Beautiful Trojan youth abducted by Jove to be his cupbearer. In the early
 modern period, the name was often used generically to denote male youths
 who were the objects of male sexual attention. Cf. note to 4.180 of the play.
4 Engraved.
5 Tablets.

O would to God he would but pity me,
That love him more than any mortal wight;[1]
Then he and I with love would soon agree,
That now cannot abide his suitor's sight.
      O would to God (so I might have my fee)   95
      My lips were honey and thy mouth a bee.

Then shouldst thou suck my sweet and my fair flower
That now is ripe and full of honey-berries;
Then would I lead thee to my pleasant bower
Filled full of grapes, of mulberries, and cherries;   100
      Then shouldst thou be my wasp or else my bee,
      I would thy hive and thou my honey be.

I would put amber bracelets on thy wrists,
Crownets[2] of pearls about thy naked arms,[3]
And when thou sit'st at swilling Bacchus'[4] feasts   105
My lips with charms should save thee from all harms,
      And when in sleep thou took'st thy chiefest pleasure,
      Mine eyes should gaze upon thine eyelids' treasure.

[Lines 109-192 present a catalogue of pastoral delights the speaker
will give the youth if he consents to be the speaker's beloved.]

All these and more I'll give thee for thy love,
If these, and more, may 'tice[5] thy love away.
I have a pigeon-house, in it a dove,   195
Which I love more than mortal tongue can say.
      And last of all, I'll give thee a little lamb
      To play withal, new weaned from her dam.[6]

But if thou wilt not pity my complaint,
My tears, nor vows, nor oaths, made to thy beauty,   200
What shall I do? But languish, die, or faint,
Since thou dost scorn my tears and my soul's duty.
      And tears contemned,[7] vows and oaths must fail,
      For where tears cannot, nothing can prevail.

---

1 Person.
2 Bracelets.
3 Cf. 1.61 of the play, "Crownets of pearl about his naked arms."
4 God of wine.
5 Entice.
6 Mother.
7 Scorned.

Compare the love of fair Queen Gwendolyn 205
With mine, and thou shalt see how she doth love thee:
I love thee for thy qualities divine,
But she doth love another swain[1] above thee;
     I love thee for thy gifts, she for her pleasure;
     I for thy virtue, she for beauty's treasure. 210

And always (I am sure) it cannot last,
But sometime nature will deny those dimples:
Instead of beauty (when thy blossom's past)
Thy face will be deformèd, full of wrinkles.
     Then she that loved thee for thy beauty's sake, 215
     When age draws on thy love will soon forsake.

But I that loved thee for thy gifts divine,
In the December of thy beauty's waning[2]
Will still admire (with joy) those lovely eyne[3]
That now behold me with their beauty's baning.[4] 220
     Though January will never come again,
     Yet April years will come in showers of rain.

When will my May come, that I may embrace thee?
When will the hour be of my soul's joying?
Why dost thou seek in mirth still to disgrace me? 225
Whose mirth's my health, whose grief's my heart's annoying.
     Thy bane[5] my bale,[6] thy bliss my blessedness,
     Thy ill my hell, thy weal my welfare is.

Thus do I honour thee that love thee so,
And love thee so that so doth honour thee, 230
Much more than any mortal man doth know
Or can discern by love or jealousy.
     But if that thou disdain'st my loving ever,
     Oh happy I if I had lovèd never.

---

1 Shepherd, man.
2 Fading.
3 Eyes.
4 Poisoning.
5 Ruin, harm.
6 Pain, woe.

Appendix E: Sodomy

1. **"An Act for the Punishment of the Vice of Buggerie,"** from *The Whole Volume of Statutes at Large Which at Any Time Heretofore Have Been Extant in Print, Since* **Magna Carta ... (1587)**

[In its 1533-34 sessions, the English parliament passed "An Act for the Punishment of the Vice of Buggerie," which made buggery or sodomy a felony, a crime punishable by death, and deprived those charged with it of "benefit of clergy," i.e., the benefit of escaping punishment if they could demonstrate their ability to read Latin. The 1533-34 parliament is one of the most important parliaments in sixteenth-century English history: it passed a series of acts, including the Act of Supremacy establishing the English monarch as the head of the English church, by which Henry VIII broke the authority of the Catholic church in England and inaugurated England's Protestant Reformation. Bruce R. Smith contends that the law criminalizing sodomy "was not an isolated piece of legislation but part of a whole battery of laws initiated by the Crown with the single purpose of undermining the political power of the Roman church" (43). Combining xenophobia and anti-clericalism, the sodomy law took aim against what was characterized as an Italianate sexual perversion especially prevalent among the clergy of the Roman Catholic church (Smith 43-44). Repealed by the Catholic Queen Mary but reinstated by Elizabeth I, the law illustrates the complex ways in which political and religious forces can shape the definition of sexual crime. As, in Smith's words, "an attempt to regulate the sex lives of a sovereign's subjects" (47), the law also illustrates the entanglement of the private and the public so prominent in *Edward the Second*.]

For as much as there is not yet sufficient and condign[1] punishment appointed and limited by the due course of the laws of this realm for the detestable and abominable vice of buggery committed with mankind or beast, it may therefore please the king's highness, with the assent of his lords spiritual[2] and temporal[3] and the commons of this

---

1 Deserved, fitting.
2 The clergy.
3 The nobility.

present parliament assembled, that it may be enacted by authority of the same that the same offence be from henceforth adjudged felony,[1] and such order and form of process therein to be used against the offenders as in cases of felony at the common law. And that the offenders, being hereof convict by verdict, confession, or as outlawry, shall suffer such pains of death and losses and penalties of their goods, chattels,[2] debts, lands, tenements, and hereditaments,[3] as felons been accustomed to do according to the order of the common laws of this realm. And that no person offending in any such offence shall be admitted to his clergy.[4] And that justices of peace shall have power and authority within the limits of their commissions and jurisdictions to hear and determine the said offence, as they use[5] to do in cases of other felonies. This act to endure till the last day of the next parliament.

2. Edward Coke, "Of Buggery, or Sodomy," *The Third Part of the Institutes of the Laws of England* (1644)

[Sir Edward Coke's (1552-1634) *Institutes of the Laws of England* continue to occupy a central role in the body of English common law, acting as a foundational text of contemporary British constitutional law. The *Institutes* was first published in 1628 as an edition of Littleton's *Tenures* (the first printed treatise on English law): known as *Coke on Littleton*, the work provided commentary on the earlier treatise. By 1641, the *Institutes* was republished with three additional books: the second book covering the *Magna Carta* and medieval statutes, and the fourth book treating on the two courts of England. The third book, and the source of the following excerpts, covers criminal law. Here sodomy is grouped amongst felonies such as treason, heresy, homocide, rape, and larceny. Coke's commentary illustrates the discursive links that could be constructed between such ostensibly different subjects as sexuality, politics, and theology: because sodomy is declared to be unnatural, it upsets God's order and good political order. Not surprisingly, sodomites were often also accused of such crimes as heresy, witchcraft, and treason. Indeed, one of the legal commentators quoted

---

1 A serious crime. A felony could be punished by death, confiscation of lands and goods, and social demotion.
2 Movable possessions.
3 Inherited lands or goods.
4 Offenders could escape secular punishment by claiming "benefit of clergy," demonstrating clerical status by reading a verse from the Latin Bible. After 1575, offenders could claim the benefit only on their first offence and only to commute their sentence from execution to branding and imprisonment.
5 Are accustomed.

by Coke asserts that sodomy *is* a form of treason. Counterbalancing the theoretically cosmic scope of the crime of sodomy, however, is the commentary's focus on sodomy as a form of anal rape.]

If any person shall commit buggery with mankind or beast, by authority of parliament this offence is adjudged felony without benefit of clergy. But it is to be known (that I may observe it once and for all) that the statute of 25 H.8[1] was repealed by the statute of 1 Mar.,[2] whereby all offences made felony or *præmunire*[3] by any Act of Parliament made since 1 H.8.[4] were generally repealed, but 25 H.8 is revived by 5 Eliz.[5]

Buggery is a detestable and abominable sin, amongst Christians not to be named, committed by carnal knowledge[6] against the ordinance of the Creator and order of nature, by mankind or with brute beast, or by womankind with brute beast.

Bugeria is an Italian word and signifies so much as is before described. *Pæderastes* or *paiderestes*[7] is a Greek word, *amator puerorum*,[8] which is but a species of buggery, and it was complained of in parliament that the Lombards[9] had brought into the realm the shameful sin of sodomy, that is not to be named, as there it is said. Our ancient authors do conclude that it deserveth death, *ultimum supplicium*,[10] though they differ in the manner of punishment. Britton[11] saith that sodomites and miscreants[12] shall be burnt, and so were the sodomites by Almighty God.[13] Fleta[14] saith, *Pecorantes & Sodomitæ in terra vivi confodiantur;*[15] and therewith agreeth the *Mirror*,[16] *pour le grand abom-*

---

1 Twenty-fifth year of the reign of Henry VIII (1534).
2 First year of the reign of Mary I (1553).
3 Denial or subversion of the monarch's legal sovereignty.
4 First year of the reign of Henry VIII (1509).
5 Fifth year of the reign of Elizabeth I (1563).
6 Sexual intercourse.
7 "Lover of boys" (Greek).
8 "Lover of boys" (Latin).
9 Lombardy is a region in Italy.
10 "The ultimate punishment" (Latin).
11 Henry of Bratton (d. 1268), author of *De legibus et consuetudinibus Anglia* (*Of the Laws and Customs of England*).
12 Heretics, unbelievers.
13 In the Old Testament, God burns the cities of Sodom and Gomorrah to punish their inhabitants for their sodomy. See Genesis 19:1-25.
14 Late thirteenth-century author of a treatise on English common law.
15 "Let buggers and sodomites be buried alive in the earth" (Latin).
16 *The Mirrour of Justices*, a fourteenth-century legal treatise by Andrew Horne.

ination,[1] and in another place he saith, *Sodomie est crime de Majestie, vers le Roi celeste*.[2] But (to say it once and for all) the judgement in all cases of felony is that the person attainted[3] be hanged by the neck until he or she be dead. But in ancient times in that case, the man was hanged and the woman was drowned, whereof we have seen examples in the reign of R.1.[4] And this is the meaning of ancient franchises granted *de furca*[5] and *fossa*[6] of the gallows, and the pit, for the hanging upon the one and drowning in the other, but *fossa* is taken away and *furca* remains.

Cum masculo non commiscearis coitu fœmineo, quia abominatio est. Cum omni pecore non coibis, nec maculaberis cum eo: Mulier non succumbet iumento, nec miscebitur ei, quia scelus est, &c.[7]

The Act of 25 H.8 hath adjudged it felony, and therefore the judgement for felony doth now belong to this offence, *viz.* to be hanged by the neck till he be dead. He that readeth the preamble of this Act shall find how necessary the reading of our ancient authors is: the statute doth take away the benefit of clergy from the delinquent. But now let us peruse the words of the said description of buggery ...

By carnal knowledge, &c.] The words of the indictment[8] be, *contra ordinationem Creatoris, et naturæ ordinem, rem habuit veneream, dictûque puerum carnaliter cognovit, &c.*[9] So as there must be *penetratio*,[10] that is, *res in re*,[11] either with mankind or with beast, but the least penetration maketh it carnal knowledge. See the indictment of Stafford,[12] which was drawn by great advice for committing buggery with a boy, for which he was attainted and hanged.

---

1 "For the great abomination" (French).

2 "Sodomy is a crime against majesty committed against the heavenly King" (French).

3 Convicted.

4 Richard I.

5 "Gallows" (Latin).

6 "Ditch" (Latin).

7 "Thou shalt not lie with mankind, as with womankind: it is abomination. Neither shalt thou lie with any beast to defile thyself therewith: neither shall any woman stand before a beast to lie down thereto: it is confusion" (Leviticus 18:22-23).

8 Formal accusation.

9 "Against the ordination of the Creator and the order of nature, he has had sex with and, as it is said, carnally known a boy, etc." (Latin).

10 "Penetration" (Latin).

11 "Thing in thing" (Latin).

12 H. Stafford, who was convicted of sodomy with a sixteen-year-old boy in 1607-08. For an account of the case and of Coke's use of it in other works, see Bruce R. Smith, *Homosexual Desire in Shakespeare's England*, 51.

The sodomites came to this abomination by four means, *viz.*, by pride, excess of diet, idleness, and contempt of the poor. *Otiosus nihil cogitat, nisi de ventre & venere.*[1] Both the agent and the consentient[2] are felons: and this is consonant to the law of God. *Qui dormierit cum masculo coitu fœmineo, uterque operatus est nefas, et morte moriatur.*[3] And this accordeth with the ancient rule of law, *Agentes & consentientes pari pœna plectentur.*[4]

Emissio seminis[5] maketh it not buggery, but is an evidence in case of buggery of penetration. And so in rape the words be also *carnaliter cognovit*,[6] and therefore there must be penetration, and *emissio seminis* without penetration maketh no rape. *Vide*[7] in the chapter of rape. If the party buggered be within the age of discretion,[8] it is no felony in him but in the agent only. When any offence is felony either by the common law or by statute, all accessories both before and after are incidentally included. So if any be present, abetting and aiding any to do the act, though the offence be personal and to be done by one only, as to commit rape, not only he that doth the act is a principal, but also they that be present, abetting and aiding the misdoer, are principals also, which is a proof of the other case of sodomy.

Or by woman.] This is within the purview of this Act of 25.H.8. For the words be, *if any person, &c.*, which extend as well to a woman as to a man, and therefore if she commit buggery with a beast, she is a person that commits buggery with a beast, to which end this word [person] was used. And the rather, for that somewhat before the making of this act, a great lady had committed buggery with a baboon and conceived by it, &c.

3. From Phillip Stubbes, *The Anatomy of Abuses* (1583)

[The anti-theatricalist pamphleteer Phillip Stubbes (c. 1555–c. 1610) published the *Anatomie of Abuses* in 1583. The pamphlet, an invective against the stage and other entertainments (including dancing, May

---

1 "The idle man knows of nothing except the stomach and sex" (Latin).
2 The passive but consenting party.
3 "If a man also lie with mankind, as he lieth with a woman, both of them have committed an abomination: they shall surely be put to death" (Leviticus 20:13).
4 "Agents and consentients are to be punished with the same punishment" (Latin).
5 "Emission of semen" (Latin).
6 "[He] has known carnally" (Latin).
7 "See" (Latin).
8 Fourteen.

games, and wakes), argues that theatre, in addition to distracting citizens from their daily work, encouraged whoring and sodomy. As the excerpt provided demonstrates, however, Stubbes is as concerned with the "vice" of costly clothing as he is with sodomy and whoredom: both are vices that lead to excessive and immoral behaviour (a connection that recalls Mortimer's descriptions in scene six of Edward's dress at the disastrous battle of Bannockburn and Gaveston's extravagant displays of fashion at court).]

(a) [Clothing.] I doubt not but it is lawful for the potestates,[1] the nobility, the gentry, yeomanry,[2] and for every private subject else to wear attire every one in his degree,[3] according as his calling[4] and condition of life requireth, yet a mean is to be kept, for *omne extremum vertitur in vitium*, every extreme is turned into vice. The nobility (though they have store of other attire) and the gentry (no doubt) may use a rich and precious kind of apparel (in the fear of God) to ennoble, garnish, and set forth their births, dignities, functions and callings, but for no other respect, they may not in any manner of wise. The magistrates also and officers in the weale publique,[5] by what title soever they be called (according to their abilities) may wear (if the prince or superintendent do godly command) costly ornaments and rich attire to dignify their callings and to demonstrate and show forth the excellency and worthiness of their offices and functions, thereby to strike a terror and fear into the hearts of the people to offend against the majesty of their callings. But yet would I wish that what so[6] is superfluous or overmuch, either in the one or in the other, should be distributed to the help of the poor members of Christ Jesus, of whom an infinite number daily do perish through want of necessary refection[7] and due sustentation[8] to their bodies. And as for the private subjects, it is not at any hand lawful that they should wear silk, velvets, satins, damasks,[9] gold, silver, and what they list[10] (though they be never so able to maintain it) except they, being in some kind of office in the common wealth, do use it for the dignifying and ennobling of the

---

1 Princes, ones in power.
2 Land-owning commoners of some social and economic standing.
3 Social rank.
4 Trade, vocation.
5 Commonwealth.
6 Whatsoever.
7 Refreshment.
8 Nourishment.
9 Embroidered silks.
10 Wish.

same. But now there is such a confuse mingle mangle of apparel in *Ailgna*,[1] and such preposterous excess thereof, as every one is permitted to flaunt it out in what apparel he list himself or can get by any kind of means. So that it is very hard to know who is noble, who is worshipful, who is a gentleman, who is not. For you shall have those which are neither of the nobility, gentility, nor yeomanry, no, nor yet any magistrate or officer in the commonwealth, go daily in silks, velvets, satins, damasks, taffetas,[2] and such like, notwithstanding that they be both base[3] by birth, mean[4] by estate, and servile[5] by calling. This is a great confusion and a general disorder, God be merciful unto us.

(b) [Plays, whoredom, and sodomy.] Then seeing that plays were first invented by the devil, practised by the heathen gentiles, and dedicate to their false idols, Gods and Goddesses: as the house,[6] stage, and apparel to Venus;[7] the music to Apollo;[8] the penning to Minerva[9] and the Muses;[10] the action and pronunciation to Mercury[11] and the rest; it is more than manifest that they are no exercises for a Christian man to follow. But if there were no evil in them save this, namely, that the arguments of tragedies is anger, wrath, immunity,[12] cruelty, injury, incest, murder, and such like; the persons or actors are Gods, Goddesses, Furies,[13] Fiends, Hags, Kings, Queens, or Potentates.[14] Of Comedies, the matter and ground is love, bawdry,[15] cozenage,[16] flattery, whoredom, adultery; the persons or agents, whores, queans,[17] bawds,[18] scullions,[19] knaves, courtesans, lecherous old men, amorous

---

1 Anglia (England).
2 Light, glossy fabrics.
3 Common.
4 Poor, of limited resources.
5 Not independent, in service, employed.
6 Playhouse.
7 Goddess of love in classical mythology.
8 God of the sun in classical mythology.
9 Goddess of wisdom and the arts in classical mythology.
10 Daughters of Zeus and Mnemosyne (Memory), the nine Muses were goddesses of learning and the arts.
11 Jupiter's messenger, Mercury was, appropriately, also the god of eloquence.
12 Lack of restraint.
13 Goddesses of vengeance in classical myth.
14 Emperors, kings, or other figures of supreme power.
15 Prostitution.
16 Deceit, fraud.
17 Prostitutes.
18 Pimps.
19 Kitchen servant.

young men, with such like of infinite variety. If I say there were nothing else but this, it were sufficient to withdraw a good Christian from the using of them. For so often as they go to those houses where players frequent, they go to Venus's palace and Satan's synagogue to worship devils and betray Christ Jesus ...

Do they not maintain bawdry, insinuate foolery, and renew the remembrance of heathen idolatry? Do they not induce whoredom and uncleanness? Nay, are they not rather plain devourers of maidenly virginity and chastity? For proof whereof but mark the flocking and running to Theatres[1] and Curtains,[2] daily and hourly, night and day, time and tide to see plays and interludes,[3] where such wanton[4] gestures, such bawdy[5] speeches, such laughing and fleering,[6] such kissing and bussing,[7] such clipping[8] and culling,[9] such winking and glancing of wanton eyes and the like is used, as is wonderful to behold. Then these goodly pageants being done, every mate sorts to his mate, every one brings another homeward of their way very friendly, and in their secret conclaves (covertly) they play the Sodomites, or worse. And these be the fruits of plays and interludes for the most part.

4. From Thomas Beard, *The Theatre of God's Judgements* (1597)

[As its subtitle tells the reader, Thomas Beard's (c. 1568-1632) *The Theatre of God's Judgements* is "a collection of histories out of sacred, ecclesiastical, and profane authors, concerning the admirable judgements of God upon the transgressors of his commandments." The work is a translation of a French work by Jean Chassanion, but Beard has supplemented it with numerous examples of God's judgement upon notable English transgressors, including Edward II and Marlowe. Beard supplies a brief summary of Edward's reign to conclude a chapter entitled "Of such princes as have made no reckoning of punishing vice, nor regarded the estate of their People." The excerpt on Marlowe below appears in a chapter on "Epicures and Atheists."

---

1 Playhouse in London's northern suburbs, erected in 1576.
2 Playhouse in London's northern suburbs, erected in 1577.
3 Short plays.
4 Sexually loose, promiscuous.
5 Lewd, ribald.
6 Grimacing, laughing.
7 Kissing.
8 Embracing.
9 Hugging.

The reader should note that Beard's account of Marlowe's death is not wholly accurate.]

As touching voluptuous epicures[1] and cursed atheists, that deny the providence of God, believe not the immortality of the soul, think there is no such thing as life to come, and consequently impugn[2] all divinity, living in this world like brute beasts and like dogs and swine, wallowing in all sensuality, they do also strike themselves against this commandment,[3] by going about to wipe out and deface the knowledge of God and, if it were possible, to extinguish his very essence; wherein they show themselves more than mad and brutish, whereas notwithstanding all the evident testimonies of the virtue, bounty, wisdom, and eternal power of God, which they daily see with their eyes and feel in themselves, do nevertheless strive to quench his light of nature, which enlighteneth and persuadeth them and all nations of this, There is a God, "by whom we live, move, and have our being"[4] ... Not inferior to any of the former[5] in atheism and impiety, and equal to all in manner of punishment, was one of our own nation, of fresh and late memory, called Marlin,[6] by profession a scholar, brought up from his youth in the University of Cambridge, but by practice a playmaker and a poet of scurrility,[7] who by giving too large a swing to his own wit and suffering his lust to have the full reins fell (not without just desert) to that outrage and extremity, that he denied God and his son Christ, and not only in word blasphemed the Trinity[8] but also (as it is credibly reported) wrote books against it, affirming our Saviour to be but a deceiver, and Moses to be but a conjuror and seducer of the

---

1 Hedonists.
2 Attack, call into question.
3 The first commandment, "Thou shalt have no other gods before me" (Exodus 20:3), which according to Beard we violate "when we ascribe not unto God the glory of his benefits to give him thanks for them, but through foolish pride extol ourselves higher than we ought, presuming above measure and reason in our own power, desire to place ourselves in a higher degree than is meet" (125).
4 Acts 17:28.
5 The many notorious atheists from ancient and modern history whose lives and deaths the work describes to demonstrate its overall point that God punishes the wicked. The work's description of Marlowe's atheism and death concludes the chapter, "Of Epicures and Atheists," bringing it up to date, as it were.
6 One of the many variant spellings of Marlowe's last name.
7 Coarse, indecent, satirical poetry.
8 The unity of God's three persons: God the Father, God the Son, and God the Holy Ghost.

people, and the Holy Bible to be but vain and idle stories, and all religion but a device[1] of policy.[2] But see what a hook the Lord put in the nostrils of this barking dog: it so fell out that in London streets as he purposed to stab one whom he ought[3] a grudge unto with his dagger, the other party perceiving so avoided the stroke, that withal catching hold of his wrist, he[4] stabbed his own dagger into his own head, in such sort that, notwithstanding all the means of surgery that could be wrought,[5] he shortly after died thereof. The manner of his death being so terrible (for he even cursed and blasphemed to his last gasp, and together with his breath an oath flew out of his mouth) that it was not only a manifest sign of God's judgement but also a horrible and fearful terror to all that beheld him. But herein did the justice of God most notably appear, in that he compelled his own hand which had written those blasphemies to be the instrument to punish him, and that in his brain, which had devised the same.

---

1 Tool, instrument.
2 Politics.
3 Owed.
4 Marlowe.
5 Performed.

Appendix F: Kings and Tyrants

1. From *An Homily against Disobedience and Wilful Rebellion* (1570)

[Alarmed by the poor quality of preaching in the new Protestant Church of England and determined to enforce doctrinal uniformity, Protestant Tudor monarchs gave their high-ranking clergy the task of writing a collection of sermons or homilies to be read in church as a regular part of church service. The homilies reflected the Protestant emphasis on the spiritual instruction of the church congregation. Written not in Latin but in plain English, they expounded on basic moral and theological principles with ample scriptural references listed in their marginal glosses. One of those basic principles was obedience to the monarch. The first *Book of Homilies*, as it came to be known, was published in 1547. In 1563 a second volume was published. In 1570, in response to a failed rebellion by northern earls in support of the Catholic Mary Queen of Scots (next in line to the English throne after the currently reigning Protestant Elizabeth I), the *Homily Against Disobedience* was published. The homily denounces any sort of rebellion as a source of chaos and urges obedience to God and to the monarch, whom God has appointed.]

[L]est all things should come into confusion and utter ruin, God forthwith[1] by laws given unto mankind[2] repaired again the rule and order of obedience thus by rebellion overthrown,[3] and besides the obedience due unto His majesty, He not only ordained that in families and households the wife should be obedient unto her husband,[4] the children unto their parents, the servants unto their masters, but also when mankind increased and spread itself more largely over the world, He by His holy word did constitute and ordain in cities and countries

---

1 Immediately.
2 The homily's marginal gloss is Genesis 3:17: "Also to Adam he said, Because thou hast obeyed the voice of thy wife, and hast eaten of the tree, (whereof I commanded thee, saying Thou shalt not eat of it), cursed is the earth for thy sake: in sorrow shalt thou eat of it all the days of thy life" (Geneva translation).
3 By the rebellion first of Lucifer then of Adam and Eve.
4 The homily's marginal gloss is Genesis 3:16: "Unto the woman he said, I will greatly increase thy sorrows, and thy conceptions. In sorrow shalt thou bring forth children, and thy desire shall be subject to thine husband, and he shall rule over thee" (Geneva translation).

several and special governors and rulers unto whom the residue[1] of His people should be obedient.

As in reading of the Holy Scriptures, we shall find in very many and almost infinite places, as well of the Old Testament as of the New, that kings and princes, as well the evil as the good, do reign by God's ordinance and that subjects are bounden to obey them, that God doth give princes wisdom, great power, and authority, that God defendeth them against their enemies and destroyeth their enemies horribly, that the anger and displeasure of the prince is as the roaring of a lion and the very messenger of death, and that the subject that provoketh him to displeasure sinneth against his own soul, with many other things concerning both the authority of princes and the duty of subjects.[2] But here let us rehearse two special places out of the New Testament, which may stand instead of all other. The first out of Saint Paul's Epistle to the Romans and the 13th chapter, where he writeth thus unto all subjects, "Let every soul be subject unto the higher powers, for there is no power but of God, and the powers that be are ordained of God. Whosoever therefore resisteth the power, resisteth the ordinance of God, and they that resist shall receive to themselves damnation. For princes are not to be feared for good works but for evil. Wilt thou then be without fear of the power? Do well, so shalt thou have praise of the same, for he is a minister of God for thy wealth; but if thou do evil, fear, for he beareth not the sword for naught, for he is the minister of God to take vengeance upon him that doth evil. Wherefore ye must be subject, not because of wrath only but also for conscience's sake. For this cause ye pay also tribute,[3] for they are God's ministers, serving for the same purpose. Give to every man therefore his duty: tribute to whom tribute belongeth; custom, to whom custom is due; fear, to whom fear belongeth; honour, to whom ye owe honour."[4] Thus far are Saint Paul's words. The second place is in Saint Peter's first Epistle, and the second chapter, whose words are these, "Submit yourselves unto all manner[5] ordinance of man for the Lord's sake, whether it be unto the king, as unto the chief head, either unto rulers, as unto them that are sent of Him for the punishment of evildoers but for the cherishing of them that do well. For so is the will of God, that

---

1 Rest, remainder.
2 As marginal references for this sentence and the latter half of the previous one, the homily provides the following: Job 34:30; Job 36:7; Ecclesiastes 8:2; Ecclesiastes 10:16, 17 and 20; Psalm 18:50; Psalm 20:6; Psalm 21:1; Psalm 144:1; Proverbs 8:15.
3 Taxes.
4 Romans 13:1-7.
5 Manner of.

with well doing ye may stop the mouths of ignorant and foolish men, as free and not as having the liberty for a cloak of maliciousness, but even as the servants of God. Honour all men, love brotherly fellowship, fear God, honour the king. Servants, obey your masters with fear, not only if they be good and courteous but also though they be froward."[1] Thus far out of Saint Peter.[2] By these two places of the Holy Scriptures, it is most evident that kings, queens, and other princes (for he speaketh of authority and power be it in men or women) are ordained of God, are to be obeyed and honoured of their subjects, that such subjects as are disobedient or rebellious against their princes disobey God and procure their own damnation, that the government of princes is a great blessing of God given for the commonwealth, specially of the good and godly, for the comfort and cherishing of whom God giveth and setteth by[3] princes, and on the contrary part, to the fear and for the punishment of the evil and wicked. Finally that if servants ought to obey their masters, not only being gentle, but such as be froward, as well and much more ought subjects to be obedient, not only to their good and courteous but also to their sharp and rigorous princes. It cometh therefore neither of chance and fortune (as they term it), nor of the ambition of mortal men and women climbing up of their own accord to dominion,[4] that there be kings, queens, princes, and other governors over men being their subjects. But all kings, queens, and other governors are specially appointed by the ordinance of God.

2. From Hugh Languet, *Vindiciae contra Tyrannos: A Defence of Liberty against Tyrants* (1648)

[*Vindiciae contra Tyrannos* presents an extended argument against unlimited sovereign power. First published in 1579 in Europe under the pseudonym Junius Brutus,[5] the work arises from the context of the French Wars of Religion and, specifically, the aftermath of the 1572 St. Bartholomew Day massacre in Paris of French Protestants or Huguenots by Catholic forces at least partially encouraged by the French monarch Charles IX. The work's attribution to Hubert Languet (1518-81), a French Huguenot, is not certain, and it is pos-

---

1 Difficult, hard to please.

2 1 Peter 2:13-18.

3 Establishes.

4 Power, rule.

5 Lucius Junius Brutus helped to found the Roman Republic by leading the rebellion that ousted Rome's last king; Marcus Junius Brutus was one of Julius Caesar's assassins.

sible that Languet may have co-authored the work with Phillippe Duplessis-Mornay, a Huguenot theologian, friend of Sir Philip Sidney, and advisor to the Huguenot leader Henri of Navarre (later Henri IV of France). Heavily grounded in the Bible, the work argues that God has invested sovereign power in the people of a kingdom, who then appoint their monarch in order to serve the good of the people. This is in direct opposition to theories articulated by the *Homily against Disobedience* or by James I in *True Law*: in these works the monarch is directly appointed by God and answerable only to God. In contrast, *Vindiciae* argues that because the monarch is appointed by the people she or he is answerable to the people. This opens up the possibility for the justification of popular resistance to tyranny. The lengthy work is divided into four sections, each of which addresses a question. The passages excerpted here are taken from the third section, by far the largest, which addresses the question of "Whether it is lawful to resist a Prince which doth oppress or ruin a public State, and how far such resistance may be extended, by whom, how, and by what right or law it is permitted." Among the signs of tyrannical government, the work includes the favouring of base men over old nobility and participating in masques and other "effeminating" entertainments akin to those Gaveston imagines providing for Edward in scene one. The work was first published in English translation in 1648, a year before the English civil war came to an end with parliament's execution of Charles I. On the title page of the Huntington Library's copy of the 1648 edition someone has scrawled "This is an abominable and unreasonable book, fit for nothing but the fire. What then is the translator worthy of? A halter."]

(a) [Kings are made by the people.] We have showed before that it is God that doth appoint kings, which chooseth them, which gives the kingdom to them. Now we say that the people establish kings, putteth the sceptre into their hands, and which with their suffrages[1] approveth the election. God would have it done in this manner, to the end that the kings should acknowledge that after God they hold their power and sovereignty from the people, and that it might the rather induce them to apply and address the utmost of their care and thoughts for the profit of the people, without being puffed with any vain imagination that they were formed of any matter more excellent than other men, for which they were raised so high above others, as if they were to command over flocks of sheep or herds of cattle. But let them remember and know that they are of the same mould[2] and condition

1 Votes.
2 Earth, clay.

as others, raised from the earth by the voice and acclamations, now as it were upon the shoulders of the people, unto their thrones, that they might afterwards bear on their own shoulders the greatest burdens of the commonwealth.

(b) [Officers of the king and officers of the kingdom.] For the officers of the king it is he which placeth and displaces them at his pleasure, yea, after his death they have no more power and are accounted as dead. On the contrary, the officers of the kingdom receive their authority from the people in the general assembly of the states[1] (or at the least were accustomed so anciently to have done) and cannot be disauthorized but by them. So then, the one depends of the king, the other of the kingdom ... [T]he charge[2] of the one hath proper relation to the care of the king's person, that of the other to look that the commonwealth receive no damage; the first ought to serve and assist the king, as all domestic servants are bound to do to their masters, the other to perceive the rights and privileges of the people and to carefully hinder the prince that he neither omit the things that may advantage the state nor commit anything that may endamage the public.[3]

(c) [Sovereignty of parliament.] In the kingdoms of England and Scotland the sovereignty seems to be in the parliament, which heretofore[4] was held almost every year. They call parliaments the assembly of the estates of the kingdom, in the which the bishops, earls, barons, deputies of towns and provinces deliver their opinions and resolve with a joint consent of the affairs of state. The authority of this assembly hath been so sacred and inviolable that the king durst[5] not abrogate or alter that which had been there once decreed. It was that which heretofore called and installed in their charges all the chief officers of the kingdom; yea, and sometimes the ordinary counsellors of that which they call the king's privy council. In sum, the other Christian kingdoms, as Hungary, Bohemia, Denmark, Sweden and the rest, they have their officers apart from the kings, and histories together with the examples we have in these our times, sufficiently demonstrate that these officers and estates have known how to make use of their own authority, even to the deposing and driving out of the tyrannors and unworthy kings.

---

1 Estates, political strata of the country (clergy, nobility, and commons).
2 Responsibility.
3 Carefully prevent the prince from omitting ... or committing ...
4 Previously.
5 Dare.

(d) [Who is a king's friend?] Without question, those are most truly the king's friends, which are most industriously careful of the welfare of his kingdom, and those his worst enemies which neglect the good of the commonwealth and seek to draw the king into the same lapse of error.

(e) [Why kings are established.] Let us then conclude, that they are established in this place to maintain by justice and to defend by force of arms, both the public state and particular persons from all damages and outrages ... Therefore, then, to govern is nothing else but to provide for. These proper ends of commanding being for the people's commodity,[1] the only duty of kings and emperors is to provide for the people's good. The kingly dignity, to speak properly, is not a title of honour but a weighty and burdensome office ... [T]he prince which applies himself to nothing but his peculiar[2] profits and pleasures, or to those ends which most readily conduce[3] thereunto, which contemns[4] and perverts all laws, which useth his subjects more cruelly than the barbarest[5] enemy would do, he may truly and really be called a tyrant, and that those which in this manner govern their kingdoms, be they never so large an extent, are more properly unjust pillagers and free-booters[6] than lawful governors.

(f) [Contrast between kings and tyrants.] A tyrant lops off those ears which grow higher than the rest of the corn, especially where virtue make them most conspicuously eminent, oppresseth by calumnies[7] and fraudulent practices the principal officers of the state, gives out reports of intended conspiracies against himself, that he might have some colourable[8] pretext to cut them off. Witness Tiberius,[9] Maximinius,[10] and others, which spared not their own kinsmen, cousins, and brothers.

---

1 Good, benefit.
2 Particular, personal.
3 Lead, conduct.
4 Scorns, despises.
5 Most barbarian.
6 The 1648 edition has "boose-haiers," a word of obscure meaning or a typographical error. I have adopted the emendation of the 1689 edition published by Richard Baldwin.
7 Slanders.
8 Seemingly reasonable or legitimate.
9 Roman emperor CE 14-37.
10 Roman emperor CE 235-38.

The king, on the contrary, doth not only acknowledge his brothers to be as it were comforts to him in the empire, but also holds in the place of brothers all the principal officers of the kingdom and is not ashamed to confess that of them (in quality as deputed from the general estates) he holds the crown.

The tyrant advanceth above and in opposition to the ancient and worthy nobility, mean and unworthy persons, to the end that these base fellows being absolutely his creatures might applaud and apply themselves to the fulfilling of all his loose and unruly desires. The king maintains every man in his rank, honours and respects the grandies[1] as the kingdom's friends, desiring their good as well as his own.

The tyrant hates and suspects discreet and wise men, and fears no opposition more than virtue, as being conscious of his own vicious courses and determining his own security to consist principally in a general corruption of all estates, introduceth multiplicity of taverns, gaming-houses, masques, stage-plays, brothel-houses, and all other licentious[2] superfluities[3] that might effeminate and bastardize noble spirits ... The king on the contrary allureth[4] from all places honest and able men and encourageth them by pensions and honours; and for seminaries of virtue erects schools and universities in all convenient places ...

A tyrant extorts unjustly from many to cast prodigally upon two or three minions, and those unworthy; he imposeth on all and exacteth from all, to furnish their superfluous and riotous expenses. He builds his own and his followers' fortunes on the ruins of the public. He draws out the people's blood by the veins of their means and gives it presently to carouse his court-leeches. But a king cuts off from his ordinary expenses to ease his people's necessities, neglecteth his private state[5] and furnisheth with all magnificence the public occasions; briefly, is prodigal of his own blood, to defend and maintain the people committed to his care ...

To speak in a word, that which the true king is, the tyrant would seem to be, and knowing that men are wonderfully attracted with and enamoured of virtue, he endeavours with much subtlety to make his vices appear yet marked with some shadow of virtue. But let him counterfeit never so cunningly, still the fox will be known by his tail, and although he fawn and flatter like a spaniel, yet his snarling and grinning will ever betray his currish[6] kind.

---

1 Great nobles.
2 Unrestrained, lawless, immoral.
3 Excesses, frivolities.
4 Draws away.
5 Estate, condition.
6 Dog-like, base, ignoble.

(g) [When a tyrant may be actively resisted.] [W]e must remember that all princes are born men, and therefore reason and passion are as hardly to be separated in them as the soul is from the body whilest the man liveth. We must not then expect princes absolute in perfection but rather repute ourselves happy if those that govern us be indifferently[1] good. And therefore although the prince observe not exact mediocrity[2] in state affairs, if sometimes passion overrule his reason, if some careless omission make him neglect the public utility, or if he do not always carefully execute justice with equality or repulse not with ready valour an invading enemy, he must not therefore be presently declared a tyrant ... [But] if the prince ... persist in his violent courses and contemn frequent admonitions, addressing his designs only to that end that he may oppress at his pleasure and effect his own desires without fear or restraint, he then doubtless makes himself liable to that detested crime of tyranny, and whatsoever either the law or lawful authority permits against a tyrant may be lawfully practised against him ... He may either be deposed by those which are lords in sovereignty over him or else justly punished according to the law Julia,[3] which condemns those which offer violence to the public. The body of the people must needs be the sovereign of those which represent it, which in some places are the electors, palatines, peers; in other, the assembly of the general estates. And if the tyranny have gotten such sure footing as there is no other means but force to remove him, then it is lawful for them to call the people to arms, to enrol and raise forces, and to employ the utmost of their power, and use against him all advantages and stratagems of war, as against the enemy of the commonwealth and the disturber of the public peace.

(h) [Who can resist a tyrant.] Jesus Christ, whose kingdom was not of this world, fled into Egypt, and so freed himself from the paws of the tyrant. Saint Paul, teaching of the duty of particular Christian men, and not of magistrates, teacheth that Nero[4] must be obeyed.[5] But if all the principal officers of state, or divers[6] of them, or but one, endeavour to suppress a manifest tyranny, or if a magistrate seek to free that province or portion of the kingdom from oppression which is com-

---

1 Moderately.
2 Moderation.
3 Roman law.
4 Roman emperor 54-68 CE, infamous for his cruelty and persecution of Christians.
5 Romans 13:5.
6 Many.

mitted to his care and custody, provided under the colour[1] of freedom he bring not in a new tyranny, then must all men with joint courage and alacrity run to arms and take part with him or them, and assist with body and goods, as if God Himself from heaven had proclaimed wars and meant to join battle against tyrants, and by all ways and means endeavour to deliver their country and commonwealth from their tyrannous oppression. For as God doth oftentimes chastise a people by the cruelty of tyrants, so also doth He many times punish tyrants by the hands of the people ... [But] let the people be advised that ... in seeking freedom from tyranny, he that was the principal instrument to dis-enthrall them become not himself a more insupportable tyrant than the former.

3. From James I of England and VI of Scotland, *The True Law of Free Monarchies or The Reciprock and Mutual Duty betwixt a Free King and His Natural Subjects* (1603)

[James I of England and VI of Scotland (1566-1625) was a poet, translator, and patron of the arts as well as king of England from 1603 to 1625. Much of his religious and political poetry is concerned with the battle between God and Satan: in the context of this battle, the king acts as God's minister. James's two major political treatises, the *True Law of Free Monarchies* (1598; first English publication 1603) and *Basilikon Doron* (1599; first English publication 1603), continue James's defence of the divine right of kings. *Basilikon Doron* was written as a book of advice for his eldest son, Prince Henry, who died in 1612. The *True Law* outlines the duties a king owes his subjects and the power a king has over his subjects. It is, as the excerpt displays, also heavily rooted in scripture. Arguing against Protestant resistance theories which claim that the king's nobles possess the right to kill their monarch if he violates his contract of just rule (the position which Hugh Languet's *Defence of Liberty* takes), James's text argues that even a tyrannical king is a better alternative to the political and social turmoil that is inevitable in a state without a monarch. Tyrants, however, will not fail to escape punishment.

Mario DiGangi's *The Homoerotics of Early Modern Drama* locates Marlowe's *Edward the Second*, and Edward and Gaveston's relationship, in the context of James's homoerotic practices and relations with his favourites (115). James's own attitude towards such practices, however, is mixed. While in the *Basilikon Doron*, James condemns sodomy, he also argues in the *True Law* that such practices are allow-

---

1 Disguise, pretext.

able so long as the monarch is able to separate public duties and private desires. DiGangi notes, however, that James's ministers, like Edward's nobles, frequently accused James of allowing his desires to intersect with court practices (102-06).]

(a) [The prince's duty.] The prince's duty to his subjects is so clearly set down in many places of the Scriptures and so openly confessed by all the good princes, according to their oath in their coronation, as not needing to be long therein, I shall as shortly as I can run through it.

Kings are called Gods[1] by the prophetical King David,[2] because they sit upon God His throne in the earth and have the count[3] of their administration to give unto Him. Their office is, "To minister justice and judgement to the people,"[4] as the same David saith; "To advance the good and punish the evil,"[5] as he likewise saith; "To establish good laws to his people and procure obedience to the same,"[6] as divers good kings of Judah did; "To procure the peace of the people,"[7] as the same David saith; "To decide all controversies that can arise among them,"[8] as Solomon[9] did; "To be the minister of God for the weal[10] of him that doth well, and as a minister of God to take vengeance upon them that do evil,"[11] as Saint Paul saith. And finally, "As a good pastor, to go out and in before his people,"[12] as is said in the first of Samuel, "That through the prince's prosperity the people's peace may be procured,"[13] as Jeremiah[14] saith.

And therefore in the coronation of our own kings, as well as of every Christian monarch, they give their oath first to maintain the religion presently professed within their country, according to their laws whereby it is established, and to punish all those that should press to alter or disturb the profession thereof.

---

1 Psalm 82:6.
2 Biblical king of Israel to whom is attributed the authorship of various parts of the Old Testament.
3 Account.
4 Psalm 101.
5 Psalm 101.
6 2 Kings 18:3, 2 Chronicles 29:2, 2 Kings 22:2 and 23:3, 2 Chronicles 34:2.
7 Psalm 72:7.
8 1 Kings 3:9.
9 King David's son.
10 Health, well-being.
11 Romans 13:4.
12 1 Samuel 8:19-20.
13 Jeremiah 29:7.
14 Old Testament prophet.

And next, to maintain all the allowable[1] and good laws made by their predecessors; to see them put in execution, and the breakers and violators thereof to be punished, according to the tenor[2] of the same. And lastly, to maintain the whole country and every state[3] therein in all their ancient privileges and liberties,[4] as well against all foreign enemies as among themselves. And shortly, to procure the weal and flourishing of his people, not only in maintaining and putting to execution the old allowable laws of the country and by establishing of new (as necessity and evil manners well require), but by all other means possible to foresee and prevent all dangers that are likely to fall upon them and to maintain concord, wealth, and civility among them, as a loving father and careful watchman, caring for them more than for himself, knowing himself to be ordained for them and they not for him, and therefore countable to that great God who placed him as His lieutenant over them, upon the peril of his soul to procure that weal of both souls and bodies, as far as in him lieth, of all them that are committed to his charge. And this oath in the coronation is the clearest, civil, and fundamental law whereby the king's office is properly defined.

(b) [A monarch may not actively be resisted.] And under the Evangel, that king whom Paul bids the Romans "Obey" and serve "for conscience's sake,"[5] was Nero,[6] that bloody tyrant, an infamy to his age and a monster to the world, being also an idolatrous persecutor, as the king of Babel[7] was. If then idolatry and defection from God, tyranny over their people, and persecution of the saints for their profession's sake, hindered not the spirit of God to command His people under all highest pain to give them all due and hearty obedience for conscience's sake, "giving to Caesar that which was Caesar's and to God that which was God's,"[8] as Christ saith, and that this practice throughout the book of God agreeth with this law, which He made in the erection of that monarchy (as is at length before deduced) what shameless presumption is it to any Christian nowadays to claim to that unlawful

---

1 Lowable in 1603 text. Subsequent occurrences have been silently emended.
2 Meaning, spirit.
3 Estate.
4 Rights.
5 Romans 13:5.
6 Roman emperor 54-68 CE, infamous for his cruelty and persecution of Christians.
7 Babylon.
8 Matthew 22:21.

liberty which God refused to His own peculiar and chosen people?[1]

Shortly then to take up in two or three sentences, grounded upon all these arguments out of the law of God, the duty and allegiance of the people to their lawful king, their obedience, I say, ought to be to him as to God's lieutenant in earth, obeying his commands in all things, except directly against God, as the commands of God's minister, acknowledging him as a judge set by God over them, having power to judge them but to be judged only by God, to whom only he must give count of his judgement; fearing him as their judge; loving him as their father; praying for him as their protector, for his continuance if he be good, for his amendment if he be wicked; following and obeying his lawful commands, eschewing[2] and flying his fury in his unlawful, without resistance but by sobs and tears to God, according to that sentence used in the primitive[3] Church in the time of persecution: *preces et lachrymae sunt arma Ecclesiae.*[4]

(c) [Refutation of the first of four principal objections to unconditional obedience: that love of country naturally inspires citizens to depose a bad monarch; that a country ruled by a bad monarch is cursed; that rebellions have succeeded in the past; that a bad monarch breaks the social contract and thus releases his or her subjects from obedience.] And in case any doubts might arise in any part of this treatise, I will (according to my promise) with the solution of four principal and most weighty doubts that the adversaries may object conclude this discourse. And first it is casten up[5] by diverse that employ their pens upon apologies for rebellions and treasons, that every man is born to carry such a natural zeal and duty to his commonwealth as to his mother; that seeing it so rent[6] and deadly wounded, as whiles[7] it will be by wicked and tyrannous kings, good citizens will be forced for the natural zeal and duty they owe to their own native country to put their hand to work for freeing their commonwealth from such a pest.[8]

Whereunto I give two answers. First, it is a sure axiom in theology that evil should not be done that good may come of it. The wickedness therefore of the king can never make them that are ordained to be judged by him to become his judges. And if it be not lawful to a private

---

1 The Israelites.
2 Avoiding.
3 Early.
4 "Prayers and tears are the weapons of the Church" (Latin).
5 Argued.
6 Torn.
7 Often.
8 Plague.

man to revenge his private injury upon his private adversary (since God hath only given the sword to the magistrate) how much less is it lawful to the people, or any part of them (who are all but private men, the authority being always with the magistrate, as I have already proved), to take upon them the use of the sword, to whom it belongs not, against the public magistrate, to whom only it belongeth.

Next, in place of relieving the commonwealth out of distress (which is their only excuse and colour[1]), they shall heap double distress and desolation upon it, and so their rebellion shall procure the contrary effects that they pretend[2] for it. For a king cannot be imagined to be so unruly and tyrannous but the commonwealth will be kept in better order, notwithstanding thereof, by him than it can be by his way-taking.[3] For first, all sudden mutations are perilous in commonwealths, hope being thereby given to all bare men to set up themselves and fly with other men's feathers, the reins being loosed to all the insolencies that disordered people can commit by hope of impunity because of the looseness of all things.

And next, it is certain that a king can never be so monstrously vicious but he will generally favour justice and maintain some order, except in the particulars wherein his inordinate lusts and passions carry him away; where, by the contrary, no king being, nothing is unlawful to be done. And so the old opinion of the philosophers proves true, that better it is to live in a commonwealth where nothing is lawful than where all things are lawful to all men, the commonwealth at that time resembling an undaunted[4] young horse that hath casten his rider. For as the divine poet Du Bartas sayeth:[5] "Better it were to suffer some disorder in the estate and some spots in the commonwealth than in pretending to reform utterly to overthrow the republic."[6]

---

1 Pretext.
2 Claim.
3 Removal.
4 Unbroken.
5 Guillaume de Salluste, seigneur du Bartas (1544–90), French Huguenot (Protestant) poet.
6 In their edition of *True Law* (1996) Fischlin and Fortier refer the reader to lines 1107–10 of du Bartas's *La Seconde Sepmaine, Les Capitaines*, which read as follows in Joshua Sylvester's translation: "'Tis better bear the youth-slips of a king / I'th'law some fault, i'th'state some blemishing, / Than to fill all with blood-floods of debate; / While, to reform, you would deform a state" (*Du Bartas His Devine Weekes and Workes Translated* [1611]).

Works Cited and Further Reading

Early Modern Editions of *Edward the Second*

Marlowe, Christopher. *The Troublesome Raigne and Lamentable Death of Edward the Second, King of England: With the Tragicall Fall of Proud Mortimer: As It Was Sundrie Times Publiquely Acted in the Honourable Citie of London, by the Right Honourable the Earle of Pembrooke His Servants. Written by Chri. Marlow Gent.* London: William Jones, 1594. STC 17437. [Q]

———. *The Troublesome Raigne and Lamentable Death of Edward the Second, King of England: With the Tragicall Fall of Proud Mortimer: And Also the Life and Death of Peirs Gaveston, the Great Earle of Cornewall, and Mighty Favorite of King Edward the Second, as It Was Publiquely Acted by the Right Honourable the Earle of Pembrooke His Servants. Written by Chri. Marlow Gent.* London: Richard Bradocke, 1598. STC 17438. [Q2]

———. *The Troublesome Raigne and Lamentable Death of Edward the Second, King of England: With the Tragicall Fall of Proud Mortimer. And Also the Life and Death of Peirs Gaveston, the Great Earle of Cornewall, and Mighty Favorite of King Edward the Second, as It Was Publiquely Acted by the Right Honourable the Earle of Pembrooke His Servants. Written by Christopher Marlow Gent.* London: Roger Barnes, 1612. STC 17439.5. [Q3]

———. *The Troublesome Raigne and Lamentable Death of Edward the Second, King of England: With the Tragicall Fall of Proud Mortimer. And Also the Life and Death of Peirs Gavestone, the Great Earle of Cornewall, and Mighty Favorite of King Edward the Second. As It Was Publikely Acted by the Right Honourable the Earle of Pembrooke His Servants. Written by Christopher Marlow Gent.* London: Henry Bell, 1622. STC 17440. [Q4a]

———. *The Troublesome Raigne and Lamentable Death of Edward the Second, King of England with the Tragicall Fall of Proud Mortimer. And Also the Life and Death of Peirs Gauestone, the Great Earle of Cornewall, and Mighty Favorite of King Edward the Second. As It Was Publikely Acted by the Late Queenes Maiesties Servants at the Red Bull in S. Johns Streete. Written by Christopher Marlow Gent.* London: Henry Bell, 1622. STC 17440a. [Q4b]

Early Modern Texts

An Homilie Agaynst Disobedience and Wylful Rebellion. London, 1570. STC 13680.6.

Bacon, Francis. *The Essayes or Counsels, Ciuill and Morall, of Francis Lo. Verulam, Viscount St. Alban.* London, 1625. STC 1148.

Baldwin, William. *The Last Part of the Mirour for Magistrates, Wherein May Be Seene by Examples Passed in this Realme, with how Greevous Plagues, Vyces Are Punished in Great Princes and Magistrats ...* London, 1578. STC 1252.

Barnfield, Richard. *The Affectionate Shepheard Containing the Complaint of Daphnis for the Loue of Ganymede.* London, 1594. STC 1480.

Beard, Thomas. *The Theatre of Gods Iudgements: or, a Collection of Histories Out of Sacred, Ecclesiasticall, and Prophane Authours Concerning the Admirable Iudgements of God Vpon the Transgressours of His Commandements. Translated Out of French and Augmented by More Than Three Hundred Examples.* London, 1597. STC 1659.

The Bible. Translated According to the Ebrew and Greeke, and Conferred with the Best Translations in Diuers Languages. With Most Profitable Annotations Vpon all the Hard Places, and Other Things of Great Importance, as May Appeare in the Epistle to the Reader: And Also a Most Profitable Concordance for the Readie Finding Out of Any Thing in the Same Conteined. London, 1599. STC 2173.

Coke, Edward. *The Third Part of the Institutes of the Laws of England Concerning High Treason, and Other Pleas of the Crown, and Criminall Causes.* London, 1644. Wing C4960.

Daniel, Samuel. *Delia. Contayning Certayne Sonnets: With the Complaint of Rosamond.* London, 1592. STC 6243.2.

Drayton, Michael. *Mortimeriados. The Lamentable Ciuell Warres of Edward the Second and the Barrons.* London, 1596. STC 7208.

Elyot, Thomas. *The Boke, Named the Gouernour Deuised by Sir Thomas Elyot Knight.* London, 1580. STC 7642.

Fabyan, Robert. *The Chronicle of Fabian Whiche He Nameth the Concordaunce of Histories, Newly Perused. And Continued from the Beginnyng of Kyng Henry the Seuenth, to Thende of Queene Mary.* London, 1559. STC 10664.

Gentillet, Innocent. *A Discourse upon the Meanes of Well Governing and Maintayning in Good Peace, a Kingdome, or Other Principalitie ... Against Nicholas Machiavell the Florentine. Translated into English by Simon Patterick.* London, 1602. STC 11743.

Golding, Arthur, trans. *The XV Books of P. Ovidius Naso, Entytled Metamorphosis, Translated oute of Latin into English Meeter.* London, 1567. STC 18956.

Holinshed, Raphael. *The Third Volume of Chronicles, Beginning at Duke William the Norman, Commonlie Called the Conqueror; and Descending by Degrees of Yeeres to all the Kings and Queenes of England in their Orderlie Successions* ... London, 1587. STC 13569.

James I of England and VI of Scotland. *The True Lawe of Free Monarchies, or, The Reciprock and Mutuall Dutie betwixt a Free King, and His Naturall Subiects.* London, 1603. STC 14410.5.

Languet, Hubert. *Vindiciae contra Tyrannos, a Defence of Liberty against Tyrants, or, Of the Lawful Power of the Prince over the People, and of the People over the Prince Being a Treatise Written in Latin and French by Junius Brutus, and Translated out of both into English.* London, 1648. Wing L415.

Newton, Thomas. *Seneca His Tenne Tragedies, Translated into Englysh.* London, 1581. STC 22221.

Puttenham, George. *The Arte of English Poesie Contriued into Three Bookes: The First of Poets and Poesie, the Second of Proportion, the Third of Ornament.* London, 1589. STC 20519.5.

Stow, John. *The Annales of England Faithfully Collected out of the Most Autenticall Authors, Records, and Other Monuments of Antiquitie, from the First Inhabitation Vntill this Present Yeere 1592.* London, 1592. STC 23334.

Stubbes, Phillip. *The Anatomie of Abuses Contayning a Discouerie, or Briefe Summarie of Such Notable Vices and Imperfections, as Now Raigne in Many Christian Countreyes of the Worlde: But (Especiallie) in a Verie Famous Ilande Called Ailgna: Together, with Most Fearefull Examples of Gods Iudgementes, Executed Vpon the Wicked for the Same, aswell in Ailgna of Late, as in Other Places, Elsewhere. Verie Godly, to Be Read of all True Christians, Euerie Where: But Most Needefull, to Be Regarded in Englande.* London, 1583. STC 23376.

Sylvester, Joshua, trans. *Du Bartas His Deuine Weekes and Workes Translated: And Dedicated to the Kings Most Excellent Maiestie by Iosuah Syluester.* London, 1611. STC 21651.

The Whole Volume of Statutes at Large which at Anie Time Heeretofore Haue Beene Extant in Print, Since Magna Gharta, Vntill the XXIX Yeere of the Reigne of Our Most Gratious Souereigne Ladie Elizabeth by the Grace of God, Queene of England, France and Ireland, Defender of the Faith, &c. With Marginall Notes, and a Table of Necessarie Vse Newlie Added Herevnto. London, 1587. STC 9305.3.

Modern Editions of Classical and Early Modern Texts

Aristotle. *Nichomachean Ethics.* Trans. H. Rackman. 2nd ed. Cambridge, MA: Harvard UP, 1934.

——. *Politics.* Trans. H. Rackham. Cambridge, MA: Harvard UP, 1932.

The Bible: Authorized King James Version With Apocrypha. Intro. Robert Carroll and Stephen Prickett. Oxford: Oxford UP, 1997.

Chaucer, Geoffrey. "General Prologue." *The Canterbury Tales. The Riverside Chaucer.* Ed. Larry D. Benson. New York: Houghton Mifflin, 1987. 23-36.

Cicero, Marcus Tullius. *De senectute, de amicitia, de divinatione.* Trans. William Armistead Falconer. Cambridge, MA: Harvard UP, 1923.

——. *De officiis.* Trans. Walter Miller. Cambridge, MA: Harvard UP, 1913.

——. *Philippics.* Trans. Walter Ker. Cambridge, MA: Harvard UP, 1926.

Cocceianus, Cassius Dio. *Roman History.* Trans. Earnest Cary. 9 Vols. Cambridge, MA: Harvard UP, 1914.

Erasmus, Desiderius. *Adages II i 1 to II vi 100.* Trans. R.A.B. Mynors. Vol. 33. *The Collected Works of Erasmus.* Toronto: U of Toronto P, 1991.

Fischlin, Daniel and Mark Fortier, eds. *The True Law of Free Monarchies and Basilikon Doron.* By James I. Toronto: Centre for Reformation and Renaissance Studies, 1996.

Forker, Charles R., ed. *Edward the Second.* By Christopher Marlowe. Manchester: Manchester UP, 1994.

Lucanus, Marcus Annaeus. *De bello civili.* Trans. J.D. Duff. Cambridge, MA: Harvard UP, 1928.

Machiavelli, Niccolò. *The Prince and The Discourses.* New York: Random House, 1940.

Marlowe, Christopher. *The Complete Plays.* Ed. Frank Romany and Robert Lindsey. London: Penguin, 2003.

——. *Lucan's First Book. The Collected Poems of Christopher Marlowe.* Ed. Patrick Cheney and Brian J. Striar. Oxford: Oxford UP, 2006. 169-92.

——. "The Passionate Shepherd to His Love." *The Collected Poems of Christopher Marlowe.* Ed. Patrick Cheney and Brian J. Striar. Oxford: Oxford UP, 2006. 157-58.

Plautus, Titus Maccius. *Truculentus.* Vol. 5. *Plautus.* Trans. Paul Nixon. 5 Vols. Cambridge, MA: Harvard UP, 1933.

Shakespeare, William. *The Tragedy of King Richard the Second. The Norton Shakespeare.* Ed. Stephen Greenblatt et al. New York: W.W. Norton, 1997. 943-1014.

——. *Twelfth Night, or What You Will. The Norton Shakespeare.* Ed. Stephen Greenblatt et al. New York: W.W. Norton, 1997. 1761-821.

Spenser, Edmund. *The Shepheardes Calender. The Shorter Poems of*

Edmund Spenser. Ed. William A. Oram, Einar Bjorvand, Ronald Bond, Thomas H. Cain, Alexander Dunlop, and Richard Schell. New Haven: Yale UP, 1989.

Tacitus, Cornelius. *Annales.* Trans. John Jackson. *The Histories and the Annals.* 4 Vols. Cambridge, MA: Harvard UP, 1925.

Wiggins, Martin and Robert Lindsey, eds. *Edward the Second.* By Christopher Marlowe. 2nd ed. London: Λ & C Black; New York: Norton, 1997.

Secondary Literature

Bailey, Amanda. *Flaunting: Style and the Subversive Male Body in Renaissance England.* Toronto: U of Toronto P, 2007.

Bevington, David and James Shapiro. "'What Are Kings When Regiment Is Gone?': The Decay of Ceremony in *Edward II.*" *"A Poet and a Filthy Play-Maker": New Essays on Christopher Marlowe.* Ed. K. Friedenreich, R. Gill, and C.B. Kuriyama. New York: AMS Press, 1988. 263-78.

Bray, Alan. *Homosexuality in Renaissance England.* 2nd ed. New York: Columbia UP, 1995.

Bredbeck, Gregory W. *Sodomy and Interpretation: Marlowe to Milton.* Ithaca: Cornell UP, 1991.

Burnett, Mark Thornton. "*Edward II* and Elizabethan Politics." *Marlowe, History, and Sexuality: New Critical Essays on Christopher Marlowe.* Ed. Paul Whitfield White. New York: AMS Press, 1998. 91-97.

Cady, Joseph. "The 'Masculine Love' of the 'Princes of Sodom' 'Practicing the Art of Ganymede' at Henri III's Court: The Homosexuality of Henri III and His *Mignons* in Pierre de L'Estoile's *Mémoires-Journaux.*" *Desire and Discipline: Sex and Sexuality in the Premodern West.* Ed. Jacqueline Murray and Konrad Eisenbichler. Toronto: U of Toronto P, 1996. 123-54.

Cornell, David. *Bannockburn: The Triumph of Robert the Bruce.* New Haven: Yale UP, 2009.

Dabbs, Thomas. *Reforming Marlowe: The Nineteenth-Century Canonization of a Renaissance Dramatist.* Lewisburg: Bucknell UP, 1991.

DiGangi, Mario. *The Homoerotics of Early Modern Drama.* Cambridge: Cambridge UP, 1997.

Gill, Roma. "Mortimer's Men." *Notes and Queries* n.s. 27.2 (1980): 159.

Griffiths, Paul. *Lost Londons: Change, Crime and Control in the Capital City 1550-1660.* Cambridge: Cambridge UP, 2008.

Gurr, Andrew. *The Shakespearean Stage 1574-1642.* 3rd ed. Cambridge: Cambridge UP, 1992.

Haines, Roy Martin. *King Edward II: Edward of Caernarfon, His Life, His Reign, and Its Aftermath, 1284-1330*. Montreal and Kingston: McGill-Queen's UP, 2003.

Harris, John Wesley. *Medieval Theatre in Context: An Introduction*. London: Routledge, 1992.

Honan, Park. *Christopher Marlowe: Poet and Spy*. Oxford: Oxford UP, 2005.

Jardine, Lisa and Alan Stewart. *Hostage to Fortune: The Troubled Life of Francis Bacon*. New York: Hill and Wang, 1998.

Kay, Dennis. "Marlowe, *Edward II*, and the Cult of Elizabeth." *Early Modern Literary Studies* 3.2 (September 1997): 1.1-30.

Keen, M.H. *England in the Later Middle Ages*. 1973. London: Routledge, 1988.

Kuriyama, Constance Brown. *Christopher Marlowe: A Renaissance Life*. Ithaca: Cornell UP, 2002.

Levin, Harry. *The Overreacher: A Study of Christopher Marlowe*. Cambridge, MA: Harvard UP, 1952.

Nicholl, Charles. *The Reckoning: The Murder of Christopher Marlowe*. London: Picador, 1992.

Normand, Lawrence. "'What Passions Call You These?': *Edward II* and James VI." *Christopher Marlowe and English Renaissance Culture*. Ed. D. Grantley and P. Roberts. Aldershot, England: Scolar Press, 1996. 172-97.

Parks, Joan. "History, Tragedy, and Truth in Christopher Marlowe's *Edward II*." *Studies in English Literature, 1500-1900* 39.2 (Spring 1999): 275-90.

Perry, Curtis. "The Politics of Access and Representations of the Sodomite King in Early Modern England." *Renaissance Quarterly* 53.4 (Winter 2000): 1054-83.

Prestwich, Michael. *The Three Edwards: War and State in England 1272-1377*. London: Routledge, 2001.

Ribner, Irving. "Marlowe's *Edward II* and the Tudor History Play." *English Literary History* 22.4 (1955): 243-53.

Riggs, David. *The World of Christopher Marlowe*. New York: Henry Holt, 2004.

Ryan, Patrick. "Marlowe's *Edward II* and the Medieval Passion Play." *Comparative Drama* 32.4 (Winter 1998-99): 465-95.

Sedgwick, Eve Kosofsky. *Between Men: English Literature and Male Homosocial Desire*. New York: Columbia UP, 1985.

Smith, Bruce R. *Homosexual Desire in Shakespeare's England: A Cultural Poetics*. Chicago: U of Chicago P, 1994.

Wickham, Glynne. *The Medieval Theatre*. 3rd ed. Cambridge: Cambridge UP, 1987.

Willis, Deborah. "Marlowe Our Contemporary: *Edward II* on Stage and Screen." *Criticism: A Quarterly for Literature and the Art.* 40.4 (October 1998). 599-622.

Further Reading

Belt, Debra. "Anti-Theatricalism and Rhetoric in Marlowe's *Edward II*." *English Literary Renaissance* 21.2 (Spring 1991): 134-60.

Callaghan, Dympna. "The Terms of Gender: 'Gay' and 'Feminist' *Edward II*." *Feminist Readings of Early Modern Culture: Emerging Subjects*. Ed. V. Traub, M. Lindsay Kaplan, and D. Callaghan. Cambridge: Cambridge UP, 1996. 275-301.

Comensoli, Viviana. "Homophobia and the Regulation of Desire: A Psychoanalytic Reading of Marlowe's *Edward II*." *Journal of the History of Sexuality* 4.2 (1993): 175-200.

Deats, Sara Munson. "Myth and Metamorphosis in Marlowe's *Edward II*." *Texas Studies in Literature and Language* 22.3 (Fall 1980): 304-21.

Forker, Charles R. "Marlowe's *Edward II* and its Shakespearean Relatives: The Emergence of a Genre." *Shakespeare's English Histories: A Quest for Form and Genre*. Ed. John W. Velz. Binghamton, NY: Medieval and Renaissance Texts and Studies, 1996. 55-90.

Fuller, David. "Love or Politics: The Man or the King? *Edward II* in Modern Performance." *Shakespeare Bulletin* 27.1 (Spring 2009): 81-115.

Haber, Judith. "Submitting to History: Marlowe's *Edward II*." *Enclosure Acts: Sexuality, Property, and Culture in Early Modern England*. Ed. R. Burt and J.M. Archer. Ithaca: Cornell UP, 1994. 170-84.

Leech, Clifford. "Marlowe's 'Edward II': Power and Suffering." *Critical Quarterly* 1 (1959): 181-96.

Martin, Mathew R. "Plays of Passion: Pain, History, and Theater in *Edward II*." *The Sacred and Profane in English Renaissance Literature*. Ed. Mary A. Papazian. Newark: U of Delaware P, 2008. 84-107.

Raber, Karen. "Gender and Property: Elizabeth Cary and the History of Edward II." *Explorations in Renaissance Culture* 26.2 (Winter 2000): 199-227.

Smith, Bruce R. "Rape, Rap, Rupture, Rapture: R-Rated Futures on the Global Market." *Textual Practice* 9.3 (1995): 421-44.

Starner-Wright, Janet and Susan M. Fitzmaurice. "Shaping a Drama out of a History: Elizabeth Cary and the Story of Edward II." *Critical Survey* 14.1 (2002): 79-92.

Stroup, Thomas B. "Ritual in Marlowe's Plays." *Drama in the Renais-*

sance: *Comparative and Critical Essays*. Ed. C. Davidson, C.J. Gianakaris, and J.H. Stroupe. New York: AMS Press, 1986. 21-44.

Stymeist, David. "Status, Sodomy, and the Theater in Marlowe's *Edward II*." *Studies in English Literature 1500-1900* 44.2 (Spring 2004): 233-53.

Sunesen, Bent. "Marlowe and the Dumb Show." *English Studies* 35 (1954): 241-53.

Thurn, David H. "Sovereignty, Disorder, and Fetishism in Marlowe's *Edward II*." *Renaissance Drama* n.s. 21 (1990): 115-41.

Waith, Eugene. "Edward II: The Shadow of Action." *Tulane Drama Review* 8.4 (1964): 59-76.

Wessman, Christopher. "Marlowe's *Edward II* as 'Actaeonesque History.'" *Connotations* 9.1 (1999-2000): 1-33.

from the publisher

A name never says it all, but the word "broadview" expresses a good deal of the philosophy behind our company. We are open to a broad range of academic approaches and political viewpoints. We pay attention to the broad impact book publishing and book printing has in the wider world; we began using recycled stock more than a decade ago, and for some years now we have used 100% recycled paper for most titles. As a Canadian-based company we naturally publish a number of titles with a Canadian emphasis, but our publishing program overall is internationally oriented and broad-ranging. Our individual titles often appeal to a broad readership too; many are of interest as much to general readers as to academics and students.

Founded in 1985, Broadview remains a fully independent company owned by its shareholders—not an imprint or subsidiary of a larger multinational.

If you would like to find out more about Broadview and about the books we publish, please visit us at **www.broadviewpress.com**. And if you'd like to place an order through the site, we'd like to show our appreciation by extending a special discount to you: by entering the code below you will receive a 20% discount on purchases made through the Broadview website.

Discount code: **broadview20%**

Thank you for choosing Broadview.